Shea Had Something
She Couldn't Resist . . .

Tracy went to the rock basin to soak. Tossing her robe over a branch, she lay down in the smoothed stone . . . Late sun filtered caressingly down on her. She shut her eyes, lulled by the constant rippling of water over rocks.

Half asleep, wholly relaxed, she didn't respond for a moment to her sensing of a denser shadow . . . Slowly, Tracy looked up.

Shea. His eyes were blue fire. He began to strip. How beautiful he was! Muscled shoulders and broad chest curved to flat belly and steel-sinewed thighs.

She closed her eyes again. He caught her shoulders, gave her a little shake. "Do you want me?"

Unable to speak, she held up her arms to him . . .

Books by Jeanne Williams

Harvest of Fury
A Mating of Hawks
The Valiant Women

Published by POCKET BOOKS

Most Pocket Books are available at special quantity discounts for bulk purchases for sales promotions, premiums or fund raising. Special books or book excerpts can also be created to fit specific needs.

For details write the office of the Vice President of Special Markets, Pocket Books, 1230 Avenue of the Americas, New York, New York 10020.

A Mating of Hawks

Jeanne Williams

PUBLISHED BY POCKET BOOKS NEW YORK

Another *Original* publication of POCKET BOOKS

 POCKET BOOKS, a Simon & Schuster division of
GULF & WESTERN CORPORATION
1230 Avenue of the Americas, New York, N.Y. 10020

ISBN: 0-671-41318-X

First Pocket Books printing May, 1983

10 9 8 7 6 5 4 3 2 1

For Julian Hayden, el viejo maderado

Always an inspiration—
Though he is not responsible for some of the
views expressed in this book!

AUTHOR'S NOTE

I would like to thank my son, Michael, who served in Viet Nam, for advising me on Shea's portrayal and the Stronghold section. Bob Morse, my husband, checked birds and natural history. As always, my daughter Kristin's comments were helpful, and Leila Madeheim did her excellent job of preparing the manuscript.

Neighboring in hawk country with raptor experts like Drs. Sally and Walter Spofford has greatly enhanced my appreciation of these birds and the part they play in a healthy natural balance.

Two fine and sensitive editors have worked on this book, Meg Blackstone and Kate Duffy. And ever and always, my gratitude to that ineffable friend and agent, Claire Smith.

There are no words for what I owe Bill Broyles for showing me the Pinacates and Cabeza Prieta.

Pia Machita's story is true. The amazing account is in "Arizona's Last Great Indian War: The Saga of Pia Machita" by Elmer Flaccus in the Spring 1981 issue of *The Journal of Arizona History*.

I

A RED-TAILED HAWK CIRCLED THE MOUNTAIN VALLEY above the creek, gliding as if in search of something. As Shea braked the pickup to the side of the road, Geronimo Sanchez gave a soft whistle.

"Reckon that's her mate up there?"

"I think so. There's a relined nest in that biggest sycamore, but no eggs." Shea glanced at the redtail loosely shrouded with burlap. She seemed a lot less nervous than Geronimo, who had a tight grip on her scaly pale-yellow legs above the wickedly curved talons. "I'll bet our gal is one of the pair that's nested in that tree for years."

"You gonna walk to the creek?" Geronimo demanded. "Must be a half-mile!"

Snorting, Shea swung his long legs out of the cab and came around to Geronimo's door. "That love grass we seeded is just starting to come up. I don't want you, me or anybody, driving over it, savvy?" He punched his friend's ample girth with his fist. "You better walk a helluva lot more, Sanchez, or you won't be the lithe, agile savage of a maiden's dream!"

"Who wants a maiden?" leered Geronimo. "I'm a lover, not a teacher." Sobering, he gave Shea a puz-

1

zled, almost worried look. "How come a scrawny rooster like you don't have a tender little pullet, or at least a tough old hen?"

Shea stiffened before he chuckled and shrugged. At thirty-two, sun lines were etched deep at the corners of his gray eyes. Thick red-gold hair waved no matter what he did to it. Since they were going to town, his worn denims were clean but his boots showed the marks of rocks and rough use. There was a faint scar above one eye, several hidden by his shirt, and his hands were ridged with scar tissue, the fingers apparently almost reconstructed.

"Now you don't think I'd clue you in to my supply?" he joshed.

Avoiding Geronimo's troubled stare, Shea grasped the redtail's legs, keeping the burlap over her head. So long as she couldn't see, that fearsome beak was no threat. Funny that a bird weighing less than three pounds could contain such energy and force, could kill a rabbit bigger than itself, though mice were the major part of the diet.

Striding across the greening field, Shea grinned at the hawk wheeling against the intense blue sky. "She's back, fella." Pausing near the towering sycamore which held the hopefully relined nest in branches sixty feet from the ground, Shea eased the hawk to a fallen giant log, let the talons grip, and then moved back, lifting the burlap.

The hawk perched there a moment, golden eyes unveiling as the nictating membrane was drawn up. Sun glinted on the proud dark head, the short, broad reddish tail before she spread her brownish wings and launched from the decaying trunk, rising into the dazzling sky.

"May be too late to populate that nest," Shea called after her. "But there's always next spring."

He watched the hawk till he could no longer make out the dark border formed on the whitish underside of the wings by the tips of the primaries and secondaries. No hint in that soaring flight that six weeks ago, in mid-January, he'd found her mangled by a shot that had disabled one wing.

Weak from hunger and exposure, she'd still flopped over on her back and showed him her talons. He'd netted them and covered her with an old gunnysack rummaged out of the pickup. For the first few days, he'd force-fed her with cut-up mice the cats brought up. After that, she'd understood they were food and managed them herself, along with pieces of rabbit he and Geronimo shot as she needed more than the cats' leavings.

There was a shrill cry from high above. The male hawk wheeled around below and above the returned one, almost touching her. And then they rose, together, dwindling against the sun.

"Hurry up!" bellowed Geronimo as Shea marveled at them, feeling as if a part of himself rose with them on invisible but mighty currents of air. "That *chica*'s going to wonder where in hell we are!"

Shea saluted the hawks and moved across the field.

Tracy Benoit bit her underlip and wondered if she should phone the ranch or simply rent a car. Vashti had said someone would meet her flight from Houston, but she'd been standing by her luggage for ten minutes, the arriving crowd had thinned away, and she was eager to get to Patrick.

Angered at her indecision, she told herself: *Wait five more minutes. Then call the ranch and say you're driving yourself. And, my girl, do it!*

Six months ago she wouldn't have needed such a pep talk. Six months ago, she wouldn't have been afraid to drive to the ranch, or anywhere. Maybe that had been her trouble. But a news photographer can't insist on escorts to trouble spots—and it hadn't been at a street fight or explosive rally or even in a dangerous part of town that it had happened. No, it was outside her own apartment house, during that short walk from carport to building.

If she could even have screamed! But those hands had gripped her throat in the same instant that the figure looming out of the dark became a solid, bruising menace, crushing her to the gravel. Choked half unconscious, her next clear memory was of car lights, returning apartment neighbors running after her attacker, wrestling him down. The doctor who examined her assured her that she hadn't actually been raped; her assailant was impotent.

That made it ludicrous—and scary. To be almost strangled by a man unable to do what he wanted! A kind of horrified pity entered her mix of feelings when she learned he was out on furlough from a veteran's hospital, supplied with downers, which, combined with a few drinks, stripped away the few controls he may have had. When he'd flipped in Viet Nam, the results had been more lethal: five squad companions slaughtered by a blast of submachine fire. She had preferred charges, not for revenge, but in the hope he'd be kept where he couldn't brutalize anyone else.

"They'll crucify you," her editor had warned. "In a rape case, the woman's on trial."

It hadn't been that bad. The judge heard the case in chambers. Her attacker's counsel had hammered at her to admit she'd been drinking or high on drugs, or had at least invited the assault, but he hadn't been able to shake the truth. The young veteran was ordered to five years' confinement with mandatory psychiatric treatment. Tracy believed he was more of a victim than she was and hoped he could get well. But she was still afraid, she'd become a fearful person, and that was intolerable.

And now she was terrified to rent a car and drive alone to the ranch! Though her palms grew clammy and she felt as if she were strangling again, she forced herself to draw a few deep, calming breaths and move toward the nearest rental booth.

Intent on exorcising this paralysis that was ruining her life, she didn't see the two young men till they stepped squarely in front of her. Startled, she retreated a pace and looked at them, something she had avoided lately with strange men.

One looked like a Mexican brigand, barrel-chested, with a luxuriant black moustache that reached to curly sideburns. His cheeks were dimpled, though, and beneath the hirsute disguise, he had a round, innocent baby face and laughing dark eyes.

The other? Hair that had been blondish-red had darkened to a vibrant auburn streaked from the sun. The lanky eighteen-year-old frame had filled out with hard muscle and use, and gray eyes that used to tease her when he'd deigned to look at her at all now regarded her with cool, critical appraisal.

"Shea! Good grief, it's been forever!"

"Miss Benoit." The austere line of his mouth relaxed in a slight grin. He returned a villainously battered gray Stetson to his head while his friend did the same with a concho-banded black one. "Did you ever know Geronimo Sanchez?"

There were a good many Sanchezes at the ranch, but she pursued a tugging memory and laughed delightedly, offering her hand. "You used to give me piñon nuts. You even cracked them for me! And you tried to teach me how to rope."

He didn't shake her hand, but pressed his warm cheek to it for a moment and kissed it. "I thought you were the cutest *chica* around." He grinned. "Now you're one damn beautiful *mujer!* Why'd you leave us for so long?"

"I went off to school six years ago while you fellows were rambling around Mexico and points south. And since I've had a job, it's been more practical for Patrick to come to see me."

Geronimo scoffed. "You mean Vashti gives you the heaves."

"If she makes Patrick happy, that's what counts," said Tracy defensively. "Especially since he went blind. How is he?"

Shea answered, but his manner was as chillingly remote as Geronimo's was flirtatiously friendly. "If you can imagine Patrick paralyzed on one side, flat in bed, that's how he is."

She flinched, not able to grasp such a disaster for the man who'd been father and grandfather to her since she came to live at the ranch when she was four, after her parents, freedom riders, had been killed in Alabama.

As nearly as Tracy could decipher the complicated Scott-O'Shea-Revier-Quintana family connections, Patrick was a sort of great-uncle. He was the only son of Santiago Scott and Christina Revier, who between them had mingled the bloods of the founders of Rancho del Socorro, Yaqui, Apache, Irish, German and assorted Anglo strains. Patrick, hence Shea, sprang from the proud, sometimes tragic legitimate side.

Tracy came from the stranger seed, a quixotic graft to the family tree added by Johnny Chance, the young labor organizer killed in the Bisbee deportation of striking miners back in 1917. Christina Revier had borne his child in the shelter of Santiago Scott's love and name, but inside the family there'd never been any mystification about it, or any shame. Johnny Chance's memory was accepted and honored. His son had died in the Spanish Civil War, leaving the daughter who died in the south.

Precariously, that line had survived, managing to reproduce itself in each generation, sustained by the rooted, stable people of the ranch. It was hard not to feel under some kind of a curse, though Tracy was determined not to be a martyr.

"My bags are over there," she said, not following up

on Shea's report of Patrick's condition because there
was nothing to say.

Shea frowned at the canvas duffel and under-seat
bag. "I hope you're planning to stay longer than that
indicates."

"I can stay as long as Patrick wants. I've learned to
travel light."

He gave her his first grudging approval. "Guess
being a big city reporter taught you that."

"I did travel quite a bit for features."

And to escape writing up weddings and engage-
ments. That was why she'd learned photography, so she
could cover more kinds of news. But even before the
mugging, she'd been wanting to get out of the city,
maybe try a children's book illustrated with her own
photos.

"Will the paper save a job for you?" Geronimo
asked.

"They'll buy any features they like."

Swinging the duffel over his shoulder and scooping
up the small bag, Shea sounded almost derisive. "It's
not exactly as if you need the money."

Though the ranch and extensive family holdings in
real estate, mining and freighting were controlled by
the main branch of the family, Tracy's inherited bar
sinister brought with it a very comfortable trust fund.
Jet-setting held no lure for her, though. Maybe it was a
legacy from Johnny Chance, but she wanted to do
something useful, something she could feel good about.
Not that she hadn't taken some glamorous vacations
and enjoyed them thoroughly. But to live that way all
the time was like a steady diet of rich desserts.

"You're not a pauper yourself," she told Shea crisp-
ly. "And maybe people who don't *have* to work need to
the most."

"Zappo!" applauded Geronimo, giving her a linger-
ing hand up into the high-floored cab of the dusty
sage-green pickup. It was scratched and dented but

sported extra-wide treads to ease through mud and deep sand that would capture most tires. "If this kissin' cousin of yours acts up, *chica,* let him have it in the chops!"

They were cousins, in a degree so elusive that she wasn't about to try to puzzle it out, but she doubted there'd be any kissing. She didn't know why, but Shea was unmistakably hostile.

Maybe he faulted her for not staying in closer touch with his stricken father? She hadn't been back since a brief visit three years ago, when Vashti had been unmistakably rude, but she had phoned Patrick every week and written him occasionally, enclosing clippings of her stories.

Shea, after three years in Viet Nam, had disappeared into Mexico and God knows where else for four years without communicating at all. With that record, it was hard to see how he could fault her. She searched her memory further. Hadn't there been a divorce while he was in Viet Nam, some kind of mess that Patrick wouldn't discuss?

She gave a mental shrug. If he was down on all women because of one, that was his problem. She wasn't going to waste energy trying to win or placate him. But a compelling tension vibrated between them, rousing a sweetly fierce awareness she hadn't experienced since the classic affair between worshiping student and married professor who regarded his seductions as necessary rites of passage for favored initiates. She just hadn't found young men very interesting, and though she had somewhat desperately had a few encounters, they had been neither physically nor emotionally fulfilling.

Shea attracted her so strongly she was sure he had to feel some of it. Damned if she'd let him see it and reinforce his apparent contempt for women. She couldn't keep from stealing a glance at his hands, though, and almost recoiled in shock.

What had happened to them? The tanned, capable hands with long sensitive fingers were ridged with white scars. She remembered, from childhood, hearing him play the grand piano that had belonged to his grandmother Christina. Patrick had loved to listen though he'd been scornful, almost frightened, when Shea had mentioned studying music in the East. At his father's insistence, there'd been one year at the state university and then Viet Nam. Since then, after that four-year Mexican hiatus, he'd gone back to the university, and had made, Tracy remembered, at least one trip to Israel. But Patrick had never mentioned this damage to Shea's hands, just that he'd been wounded in Cambodia.

There was a lot she'd like to know about this cousin of hers, distant in more ways than one, but his reserved manner didn't encourage launching into a series of "Do you remembers?" And she was tired, not so much from the flight as from the hour-and-a-half taxi ride to the Houston airport at morning rush hour.

Settling back between the two men, knees to one side of the gearshift, Tracy was amazed at how relaxed she felt—safe for the first time in months, protected. For in spite of Shea's aloof behavior, there was a rocky steadfastness about him, a certainty that exacted trust. And there was no doubting Geronimo's ebullient, admiring good will. She was tired of being on guard, tired of fending for herself, and if that was weak, she didn't care.

It wasn't only the comforting physical presence of two men she'd known in childhood, but seeing again the purple marching mountains in every direction as they proceeded down the Santa Cruz Valley on the Nogales highway. The massive Santa Catalinas rose to the north above Tucson, the Rincons were east, and to the west, against the Tucson Mountains, gleamed the white walls of San Xavier del Bac on the Papago Reservation, one of Padre Kino's missions. When

Apaches had forced Christianized Pimas to flee their mission at Tumacacori farther south, the Indians had carried their saints and sacred vessels in their burden baskets to this White Dove of the Desert.

A ribbon of green showed the track of the Santa Cruz River through the broad flat valley, defined by the Santa Ritas to the east and smaller, scattered ranges to the west.

Except for that slim fringe along the river, the country looked parched and dead in spite of its being March. "Has it been a dry year?" she asked.

"Mighty dry. We're a long way from that average eighteen inches at the ranch and of course Tucson's under its average of eleven."

Spreading beneath the highway and sprawling in all directions stretched acres of white stuccos topped with what seemed from this perspective to be overlapping red tile roofs.

"Green Valley?" gasped Tracy. "It's grown like crazy."

"Crazy is right," Shea said grimly. "And getting more so. Some big pecan growers pumped lots of precious water to get groves established, but they're selling to developers who'll root out the trees and pack in all the fake Mediterranean villas they can on the acres they've gotten zoned for building. People use less water than agribusiness, of course, but I wonder what they'll do when there isn't any."

"What this place needs is a few good Apache raids," Geronimo said. "Let me tell you, in the good old days, we were a damned efficient check on urban sprawl."

"Which part of you's bragging?" grinned Shea. "You psyched them out in the Army, Sanchez, but I happen to know you're three-quarters respectable vaquero stock. And besides, I'm everything you are," Shea reminded.

"Sure. But the proportions are a little different."

Geronimo squinted balefully at the flat-topped low ridges on their right. "Those damn mine tailings!"

"Don't bitch, Sanchez. Can't you see Duval's revegetating them?"

"I've seen more sprouts on a bald man's skull!"

"Maybe someday they'll use them to pave water catchments the way they're doing up by Black Mesa on the Navajo Reservation."

"We should live so long," grunted Geronimo.

The highway by-passed the old presidio of Tubac now, but Tracy glimpsed the adobes housing art galleries and craft shops, the steeple of the church. In Spanish, then Mexican days, the presidio's tiny garrison, sometimes less than a dozen men, had tried to ward off Apache raiders, but the valley had been depopulated from the early 1820's till the influx of American miners after the Gadsden Purchase of 1853. Tubac itself had been abandoned several times, its soldier-settlers and friendly Pimas refuging in Tucson, the region's other military outpost.

"What's happening at Rio Rico?" she asked, nodding at the roads of the old Tumacacori Mission.

"GAC Corp's still pushing its Shangri-La." Shea didn't even glance at the roads. "Calabazas had its booms between its busts. First a *visita* for Jesuits, then a sheep and goat ranch run by a couple of Germans in partnership with the governor of Sonora. After the U.S. takeover, there was a camp there on and off, and a customs collector. Big building surge in the 1880's with a classy hotel and such. Wonder how long Rio Rico will last?"

"You're just full of optimism!" Tracy charged.

He shrugged. "When you see what's brewing at the ranch, you'll know why I'm so bright and cheerful."

Turning off the Nogales highway, they followed Sonoita Creek along a bottom flanked by the Santa Ritas to the north and stretching into foothills and mountains to the south, fading into Mexico. Juniper and oak studded red earth and gray rocks ascending up the mountains. Giant black walnuts outlined white-trunked sycamores and fresh green cottonwoods. Cattle browsed among catclaw and mesquite, and there was comparatively little cactus.

Red Mountain rose behind the little town of Patagonia. "A developer wanted to put in a big subdivision here," remarked Geronimo. "But the sewage system is in such bad shape that the State Water Quality Control Board wouldn't issue a permit."

"Just wait," grunted Shea.

They were getting into country now that Tracy remembered from riding over it. Her eyes feasted on the familiar stretch of the sparkling creek, running shallow in its wide bed, but life-giving here, of boundless importance. The valley broadened, bottom lands and gentle slopes guarded by mountains, and to the east were the jagged Whetstones, dark blue against the azure of the Huachucas.

Tracy's flesh prickled and she was close to tears. It wasn't only that she knew this country. The remembering went deeper than that. "I wonder," she said softly, "how it looked to them."

"Who?" frowned Shea.

"Socorro. Patrick O'Shea. Tjúni and Santiago."

"After all they'd been through, I expect they were damned glad to find a place to stop." Tracy thought Shea must resemble the Irishman for whom he was named, who'd fought for Mexico in the San Patricio Battalion, the one Mangus Coloradas had protected for Socorro's sake and called "Hair of Flame."

"Socorro must have been some lady," said Geronimo. "There she was, brought up guarded and protected, and all of a sudden she's alone in the cinder cones and lava flows, with her escort dead. Finds water. Lives off desert plants. And then she finds her redhead, just a husk of baked rawhide, and brings him back to life."

"It's strange how all those four who started the ranch

had been the same as dead," Tracy mused. "Santiago was the only person left after scalp-hunters hit, and he'd have died if Shea and Socorro hadn't found him. Tjúni's whole village had been wiped out. So there you had an Irishman, a Spanish creole, a Mexican vaquero and a Papago, all thrown together and depending on each other." Tracy smiled at Geronimo. "And then your family came to work the cattle."

He nodded. "Don't forget Talitha Scott. She raised Socorro's and Shea's children after Socorro died so young, and she held the ranch together when Shea went off to the un-Civil War."

He'd never come back to that yellow-haired girl who'd adored him since childhood when he'd ransomed her and her half-Apache brother, James, but Talitha had at last found love and peace with Marc Revier, a young German mining engineer who'd taught her to read and waited yearningly for her to grow up.

Surprisingly, Shea joined in. "The one I've always felt for was James. He didn't fit with either Apaches or whites. When he became Fierro the raider, he must have known there was no chance for his people to shut out the whites."

"At least he and Caterina left a child," Tracy remembered.

It was Sant, a grandson of Caterina, daughter of Shea and Socorro, who had married Christina, granddaughter of Talitha and Marc, at last uniting the separated bloods in Patrick, Shea's father.

The old house was hidden by huge trees except for glimpses of mellow adobe and broad veranda, but they didn't turn in there, following instead a graded road that led back through a spine of hills, a road she didn't remember.

"Where are we going?" she demanded.

Shea slanted her a frown. "Didn't you know?"

"Know what?"

He let out an explosive breath. "Vashti never liked the old house. As Patrick got blinder, she kept yammering about how selfish he was to make her stay in a place she hated when he couldn't see it anyway. For peace's sake, he let her pick what she wanted and where, just so she'd drop nagging him to move to Tucson."

"Oh." Tracy, with a queer sense of bereavement, glanced over her shoulder at the compound with the family graveyard on the slope behind it, the corrals and barns and bunkhouses. "No one lives there?"

"My uncle does," comforted Geronimo. "He's foreman, though Judd's the overall manager."

Tracy frowned at the name, though she couldn't have said why. She scarcely knew Judd, Patrick's eldest son. Six years older than Shea, he'd been at college when she came to live at the ranch, and he'd never paid any attention to her on his visits home.

"It's so strange that Patrick never mentioned it," she murmured.

"Guess he didn't like to think about it," Geronimo offered. "Since he can't see, maybe now it's done, he doesn't mind too much."

Trying to imagine darkness, Tracy shivered and thought it would make it all the more important to be in familiar surroundings, using rooms and furniture intimately known.

"Patrick wouldn't pave the road, though," Shea chuckled. "Not that it bothers Vashti much. She's learned to fly, and her friends mostly come in their own planes."

Patrick had mentioned an airstrip and that Judd used a plane to patrol the ranch and attend to business in and out of the state. Shea swerved to avoid a snake and Tracy bumped against Geronimo.

"Sorry," she apologized.

"Anytime, *chica*."

"Watch him," Shea warned. When he smiled, it changed his whole face, making it young, warming his stern masculine beauty—and he was beautiful, though it was not a word she'd ever before applied to a man. "The main reason we don't have a phone is so his women can't track him down."

"You don't live at the main ranch?"

He shook his head. "I've moved to El Charco."

That, she knew, was the part of the ranch inherited through his mother. There was something unspoken, something mysterious, about the dead Elena, Patrick's second wife. El Charco's southern boundary was the Mexico border.

"You'll have to come see us," Geronimo invited. "I make the best Margarita you'll ever drink."

Shea frowned at him. "Sanchez, you know damn well our place isn't set up for entertaining ladies."

"Yeah?" Sanchez scowled. "Then how about—"

"Never mind," cut in Shea. "Tracy's here to see Patrick."

What's wrong with you—or is it me? Tracy wondered, hurt and a little angry. *Lord above, cousin, you act as if you were the one who'd been raped!*

The pickup cornered the side of a hill, opening up a far vista of Mexican mountains. Across a broad sandy wash, dominating a hilltop, a massive modern adobe two stories high was surrounded by adobe walls. A pool glinted in the rear courtyard. From this vantage point, Tracy saw the airstrip and hangar on a cleared expanse that covered the far end of the long flat hill beyond a tennis court.

She'd done a feature on similar airstrips in the Texas hills, and couldn't repress a nervous laugh. "What a setup for smuggling drugs!"

Shea's gray eyes flicked her with scornful rebuke. "Sensationalism may sell papers, but I hope you won't worry Patrick with your melodramas."

"Do you take scorpion juice in your coffee?" she retorted, giving him an edge of derisive smile, though inside she was smarting.

"Don't fight, kiddies," said Geronimo, getting out to open the gate. "Here comes the lady of the manor."

II

VASHTI HAD THE SLIM, DISCIPLINED, RATHER HARD BODY of a woman successfully fighting weight and years. Skin pulled snugly over her cheekbones and a slight upward tilt of carefully tweezed eyebrows suggested a skillful face lift. Her eyes were such a dark green that only sunlight kept them from looking black and her silver-blonde hair was pulled sleekly back in a French knot secured with jade pins. She wore slim black trousers and a black silk blouse that molded a high, youthful bosom.

"Tracy, love!" Taking her shoulders, Vashti bestowed a light, brushed kiss on her cheek. "You're looking marvelous, but a bit frazzled. Come see Patrick and then you must freshen up." She ran her hand over Shea's arm. "So good of you to fetch Tracy. Bring her things in, won't you, and stay for lunch? We've held it for you."

"Thanks, but we'll just say hi to Dad and get along."

He distanced himself from his stepmother so obviously that color mounted to her face, though she at once recovered, taking Tracy's arm and drawing her through an atrium where an antique Mexican fountain splashed among cool greenery, into an immense living room that seemed even larger because the furnishings were few and massive. A fireplace molded in a flow of adobe curved from the ceiling to the opposite side of

17

the wall in sculptured gradations. Tracy thought it resembled a cave but she sensuously enjoyed the smell of burning juniper.

Vashti indicated stairs on the other side of the room, polished tile, spiraling upward. "Can Patrick get up and down?" Tracy asked, ascending.

"Of course not, dear! He's paralyzed."

"Yes, but before—"

Vashti shrugged. "I had the house designed so that he wouldn't have to leave the second floor. It's simpler, and much more convenient."

For whom? Tracy wanted to ask, but swallowed her criticisms. Vashti was going out of her way to be pleasant. Sniping between family members wouldn't ease Patrick's troubles.

Hesitating at the top of the stairs, she followed Vashti's lead into a huge room that gave a breathtaking view of the Santa Ritas. Apart from that irony, Tracy saw nothing else but ran with a soft cry toward the great poster bed.

"Patrick!"

She embraced him as best she could, kissing his weathered cheek, trying not to cry. He lay like a felled oak, covered with a sheet up to where a plaid western shirt was unbuttoned down the throat. Many times she had gone to sleep against that broad chest, comforted and quieted by the steady pound of his heart.

Straightening, she looked down at him, relieved that apart from the sightless blue eyes, he didn't seem much changed. Then he tried to smile. One side of his mouth moved but the other lay slack and the eyelid drooped. That half of his face was like a dead man's. Yet there was something curiously young and vulnerable about it, too, an erasing of tensions and expressions shaped by the years.

"Tracy." The word was slightly muffled. With his good hand, he stroked her face. "You're *feelin'* mighty pretty!"

He gave a muted chuckle and she remembered from

her last visit that joking and profanity were his ways to deal with blindness. But how would he handle this?

His face changed at the sound of steps on the stairs. "That you, boy?" he demanded as Shea and Geronimo came in.

"How you doing, Dad?" Shea bent over his father. Tracy felt an oddly jealous twinge at the unmasked tenderness in his gaze.

"Hell, you can see if I can't!" snapped Patrick. "You know dang well how I'm doing!" He glared at Geronimo with one sightless eye. "Hey, Ronnie, make me a drink, will you? You're the only one puts in enough tequila."

"It's time for your lunch, dear," Vashti protested.

"It's time for a drink," Patrick grunted. "Anyone else want one?"

"There'll be wine at lunch," Vashti said with a pained frown.

"We'll drink with you, Dad," said Shea, and moved over to the bar opposite the beehive fireplace, which was faced by several heavy leather chairs and a massive couch. Christina's piano faced the window.

Patrick reached out. Quickly, Tracy took his hand. "You back for good, honey? Got enough breathing those exhaust fumes?"

"I can stay till you're up and rambunctious again. I sublet my apartment and quit the paper, though they'll buy some features."

"I never could fathom why you wanted to take such a job anyway," Vashti grimaced with a shake of her head that made jade earrings swing. "Poking into grubby places, meeting weird people—"

"Yes," agreed Tracy. "Some of those society weddings and benefit galas were pretty weird. I like doing an occasional article, but I've decided to concentrate on children's books. Mostly photos with a little text."

"I can't think what you'll find to photograph around here," said Vashti with a lift of dark eyebrows.

"Why, there's horses and cows!" roared Patrick.

"Nothing on God's earth prettier than a little foal. And vaqueros mounted up, cattle in good graze, mesquites greening after a hard winter, a full water tank after a rain—where you going to find things better than that?"

"Now, darling, don't get all worked up," soothed Vashti. "Most children live in cities, you know. I should expect them to be more interested in sports, moon flights, things like that."

"I did some market research at libraries in Houston, seeing what kids actually read, rather than what adults thought they should." Tracy laughed, squeezing Patrick's hand. "The age I'm thinking of was very big on dinosaurs."

"Then Gila monsters and chuckwallas ought to go over real big," chortled Patrick. Tracy stepped back so Geronimo could put a glass in his hand and the old rancher peered uselessly toward the young men. "You lads got your drinks?"

"You bet," said Geronimo, taking an iced beer from Shea, who held its twin.

"You, Tracy?"

"I'll just have a sip of yours, Patrick."

He lifted the amber Mexican glass, iceless since he claimed that was the only way to drink tequila. "Happy days!"

"Happy days," echoed the young men.

Tracy bent to drink from her great-uncle's glass. "Happy days," she told him.

He moved his thumb against her cheek. "I've missed you, honey. Glad you're back."

She kissed him in answer. He looked exhausted. Vashti took charge, straightening the coverlet. "I'll send up a tray, dear, after you've had a little rest. If the rest of you will come down, Henri should have lunch ready."

"No offense to Henry," muttered Patrick. "But tell Concha to rustle me up some steak and biscuits. And a bowl of chili or posole if she's got some made."

"Oh, she'll have some," predicted Vashti irritably. "The only reason we keep her is to cook for you."

"Best reason there is," Shea remarked. He clasped his father's hand. "See you later, Dad."

"Listen, boy, we need to have a talk." The old man almost clung to his son's scarred hand. "Judd tells me you're not running a single head of cattle on El Charco. Or on the grazing lease!"

"Sounds like for once Judd's got the straight of things."

Patrick dropped Shea's hand. "God a'mighty!" he rumbled weakly. "Ten thousand acres at El Charco gone to waste, and thirty thousand leased! While this has been such a tough winter we've been feeding hay! Listen, boy—"

"Dad," cut in Shea. "I'm not wasting that land. I'm trying to keep it from going desert like that Judd's overgrazing."

A vein swelled in Patrick's temple. "You'd rather see us sell cattle at a loss than run a few on ground you're not using?" His voice quavered with weakness and anger.

Shea swallowed. Muscles tautened in his lean jaws. When he spoke, his tone was under tight control. "Dad, Judd's your manager. Let us try to work this out."

"You damn well better!" Patrick seemed ready to choke and Tracy moved anxiously back to him, casting Shea a look of reproachful pleading. "I'm going to have to study hard as it is to leave part of Socorro to someone with ideas as crazy as yours."

Shea's hands clenched. Lightning seemed to flash deep in his gray eyes. He wore a stunned look, as if he couldn't believe what his father had said. Then he shrugged.

"I've tried to explain what I'm doing, Dad, but you don't want to hear it. Look, let's not talk about it. I promise you this. If Judd'll be reasonable, so will I."

"Do come along!" hissed Vashti.

Tracy cradled Patrick against her and kissed his forehead. "Finish that tequila and have a nice snooze. I'll be back later."

He didn't speak, but the frustrated grief distorting the mobile side of his face was so great that she cursed Shea for causing it, whatever the merits of his case. But Patrick rallied and patted her cheek before he reached for his glass.

"Run along, honey, and tuck in enough of Henry's food to make him feel good. It's fine if you go for kee-chays and sou-flays, but I'd rather have meat and beans and handmade tortillas." He squinted approvingly at her. "You're a mite thin but otherwise I'll bet you're just as pretty as a speckled pup!" He gestured toward the portrait above a carved chest at the far end of the room. "Always thought you were the spittin' image of my mother. Hope you'll have as good a life."

Tracy looked at her great-grandmother, painted as Santiago's bride. With child by the murdered Johnny Chance, haunted by the slaughters in Cananea and Tomochic, which had twice in her life made her hysterically blind, the young woman in the painting was indeed beginning the happy, productive years she'd have with Sant. Her dark bronze hair fell over one shoulder, rich against her creamy skin. It was a triangular face, broad at forehead and cheekbones, narrowing to a cleft chin. The deep-set amber eyes seemed even larger because of dark eyelashes and determined eyebrows that winged slightly at the ends. The mouth was fully curved, and though Christina's expression was sweetly grave, there was a hint of tough, earthy humor.

I've done nothing but survive, Tracy thought, staring almost combatively at the portrait. *But don't write me off, Christina Riordan-Scott y Revier!* She laughed, swept a kiss across Patrick's ear and used her childhood name for him.

"I don't know how good my life is going to be, Paddy, but I intend to make it interesting!"

He was chuckling as she hurried downstairs.

Rather crossly, Vashti pointed down the wing of the L-shaped house and told Tracy that her room was the first on the right. "I hope you'll find it comfortable. Patrick insisted on moving over the tacky handmade stuff you had at the old place instead of letting the decorator do something tasteful."

Tracy raced to brush her hair, a short springy crown of soft waves. A touch of lipstick, a quick stop in a bathroom that was bigger than her living room in Houston, and she started for the dining room, which Vashti had said adjoined the vast living area.

Shea and Geronimo, disreputable hats in hand, waylaid her in the hall. "We've got things to do," Shea said. "See you around."

Why that pang of disappointment? It was clear he had a hard time even being moderately civil. "Thanks," she said coldly. "I hope I haven't taken up too much of your time."

"It was our pleasure, *chica*," Geronimo assured her.

"Sorry I couldn't pick you up," drawled a resonant voice behind them. Tracy whirled and looked up into tawny eyes that flickered with sudden intrigued interest. "I'm really sorry," the tanned, broad-shouldered man repeated.

Placing his hands on Tracy's back, he drew her close and kissed her. His body was hard against her, but his mouth quested sensuously over hers for a moment, before, as she stiffened, he laughed and moved away. "Greetings, Tracy! If I'd known how pretty you'd gotten over in Texas, I'd have skipped business and picked you up in the plane."

"I got here just fine," she said, trying not to show how his kiss had shaken her. He probably guessed, though, from the way his eyes glowed.

Not quite so tall as Shea, he was heavier. Close-

fitting tan rancher's pants stretched to outline powerful-
ly muscled thighs. He reminded Tracy of a mountain
lion, brain and body perfectly coordinated, lazy of
movement till action called for speed. "You must be
Judd," she added lamely, when he only watched her
with happy anticipation and didn't seem inclined to put
anything in words.

With a touch of frost, Vashti called from the dining-
room entrance. "For heaven's sake, do come and have
lunch before it's totally ruined!"

"In a second," Judd tossed carelessly over his shoulder. "Shea, you going to let some Socorro cattle on
your place?"

"Have you thinned out that thousand head?"

Judd flushed angrily. "You know damn well I
haven't! Everyone's dumping beef now. I'd sell at a
loss."

Shea's lips tightened. He turned to go. Judd caught
his arm. "Damn you, you really mean to keep your
gates locked while my cows starve?"

"You're the one who overstocked."

Square jaw thrusting out, Judd bit off each word.
"It's got to rain sometime. When grass is decent, the
range'll carry every head I'm running."

"The grass hasn't been that decent since 1880."

Judd's hands made knotty fists. His chest swelled
heavily. "El Charco's yours, I guess. But the grazing
lease is meant for just that, running stock. I'll pay you
double the lease."

The gazes of the half-brothers clashed. No love lost,
Tracy decided. The only similarity between them was a
hint of Patrick in stubborn jaws and that indefinable
masculinity radiating from them both. For Patrick's
sake, she dreaded the battle they seemed set on wag-
ing.

"No deal, Judd." Shea turned again.

Judd took a long swinging stride to block his way. "If
you don't have the gates to the leased land open in the
morning, I'm going to call the Land Commissioner and

the Cattle Growers' Association—get that lease taken away from you!"

"Lots of luck," Shea said, stone-faced.

Judd swore. "Look, Shea, you know this kind of wrangling tears the old man up!"

"It's not been me who tells him all about it."

Veering around his half-brother, Shea didn't look back at Tracy. He clamped his hat over his fiery hair and moved through the door with his loose, easy gait. Geronimo flourished his black hat at her and grinned.

"Hasta!"

Until. As good a farewell as any. "Thanks again," Tracy called after him. Uncomfortable at Judd's smoldering presence, she walked quickly down the hall and murmured some apology to Vashti.

Vashti managed a stiff smile and took the chair at the head of the table, deferentially held for her by a slight, handsome young man in a spotless white jacket. Tracy slipped into the indicated place at her right, while Judd occupied the armed chair at the other end of the polished oak table. They began on the salads already at their plates.

"I don't care so much what Shea does with El Charco," he growled. "Piddling ten thousand acres. But that thirty thousand leased acres will carry easy the thousand head he wants me to sell!" He rubbed his broad chin. "Wonder if the old man could talk sense into him?"

"Your father threatened to disinherit him," Vashti said, covering a yawn. "In your own way, Judd dear, you're fully as tedious as Shea, though, thank God, not as sanctimonious." She appealed to Tracy. "I'm trying to make all these hardheaded Scott men see that they'd be ahead to sell the whole place for development, move to town and forget about cattle, drouths and grass."

Judd gave her a hard look. "The only way I'll move to town will be in a coffin. If the old man agrees, I don't mind getting rid of some acreage that's pretty well worn-out for grazing, putting the money into irrigating hay and alfalfa so we'll have plenty of feed. But don't get any funny notions, *madrecita*. You can move Patrick to town if he'll go. I never will."

Color burned in Vashti's cheeks. "As I've said before, you and Shea are equally tiresome!"

He shrugged and threw off his ill-humor, grinning at Tracy while the white-coated young man served slices of fragrant quiche, redolent of herbs, with a crisp golden crust. He refilled Vashti's wineglass and brought more hot, crunchy sourdough rolls.

"Too bad you had to walk into a family feud, Tracy," said Judd, tearing off a chunk of the hard bread and chewing hungrily. "No reason you should get involved, though I'd like to take you around, get you reacquainted with the ranch. You'll see for yourself that Shea's way out of line."

"Tracy scarcely qualifies as an expert on range management." Vashti's tone was acrid. "I certainly hope she'll spend a good deal of time with Patrick so I can have a chance to rest. You and Shea are no help. Whichever one of you he sees, he's upset for days."

"Maybe you ought to hire Geronimo to keep him happy on tequila," Judd suggested ironically. His golden eyes brushed negligently past his stepmother to rest on Tracy. "You can't be with Patrick all the time. I'm flying up to Phoenix tomorrow to see the land commissioner and some friends of mine, may be gone a few days. But when I'm back, let's have the tour."

She did want to go all over the ranch again, though it seemed Shea wasn't going to welcome her to his part of it. His attitude made her appreciate Judd's wish to share and so, in spite of Vashti's puzzling disapproval, Tracy nodded and smiled.

"Let's do it."

She refused more quiche but couldn't resist hot Mexican chocolate, spiced with cinnamon and whipped to a froth.

"Why don't you unpack and rest?" asked Vashti,

graciousness returning. "Then maybe you could keep Patrick company later in the day."

It seemed to Tracy that her great-uncle would have been happier, more in touch with what was going on, had he been shifted to a room downstairs, but perhaps it made him nervous to hear a lot that he couldn't see. Tracy didn't like Vashti but had no reason to doubt her devotion and concern for her stricken husband.

"I'll be glad to stay with him," Tracy promised. "After all, that's why I came."

Vashti gave a wan smile. "Very good of you, dear. But having gotten worn to a nub myself, I shan't let it happen to you! We'll have some lively people down and when it gets too boring here, you can have a few days in Tucson."

Tracy frowned slightly. Living in this splendid mansion with plenty of household help didn't seem such a martyrdom to her, though Patrick probably could be a demanding and trying patient, caged as he was in his own body and blind as well.

"Don't worry about me," she told Vashti, rising. "If I can ride and swim, that'll be recreation enough."

Vashti looked incredulous but didn't argue. Judd got to his feet, bowing slightly. "See you later. Have a nice rest."

Somehow, the innocent words managed to hint regret that he wouldn't be with her when she lay down. Muttering something, Tracy fled in confusion.

Concha would be hurt if she didn't seek her out, so before she went to her room, Tracy located the withered, tiny old woman in her room adjoining the kitchen. Keeping tight hold of Tracy's hand even after they had embraced, Concha peered at her with amazingly bright, sharp eyes.

"You belong here, Teresita. It is not good for a woman of our blood not be at the ranch." Her lip curled in scorn. "Don Patrick's señora, she likes this big house like a hotel or hospital. She has a French cook! It is not right."

"My uncle certainly prefers your cooking," Tracy said. "How are your children? Uncle Patrick told me your grandson's about to graduate from the university."

"Ay, he is," said Concha delightedly. "He will work with Shea at El Charco." Then she shook her head and snorted. "Think what they are doing! Raising plants that don't need water, or much of it. Tepary beans, jojoba, buffalo gourds. These all grow wild. My grandfather grew teparys and he couldn't write his name."

"Maybe it gets harder," Tracy suggested.

They talked a little longer. Concha gave Tracy a dish of quince and nut candies. "You're skinny," she said critically. "But we'll feed you up on good tamales and tortillas."

"You'll be sorry when I have to be trundled around in a wheelbarrow," Tracy warned. Concha's cracked, gleeful laughter followed her as she cut through the inner courtyard and entered the bedroom hall from the outside door.

She changed into a pair of the soft old jeans that filled one dresser drawer, found an outsize sweatshirt in another drawer, and quickly put away the garments she'd brought from Houston. She wouldn't need her city things much here so it was lucky she could still wear the stored shoes, boots and everyday ranch clothes. They felt wonderfully comfortable and in a strange way took her back to her teen years. Life had seemed so simple then. She was going to be an ace journalist, travel a lot, and after she'd gotten well-established, come back to live at the ranch between such fascinating assignments as she chose to take.

She was back. But far from being at the apex of her profession, she had about decided she was climbing the wrong pyramid, that she should try another direction. She'd felt that way before she was attacked, so fear wasn't at the root of her decision.

Weddings and teas might be boring, but she'd found

she didn't like covering murders, fires and break-ins.
Especially she hated asking people questions she didn't
think were her business or anybody else's, except
perhaps an investigative officer's. Television could give
close-up, full-color blood and pain, of course, which
was hard for papers to compete with.

She frowned at the camera bag she'd extracted from
the duffel, and then smiled as her gaze traveled slowly
around the room, grateful that Patrick had insisted on
salvaging the familiar furnishings vaqueros had made
from hand-hewn oak and walnut for Talitha and Caterina before the Civil War. Apart from the carved
bed, armoire, rawhide-bottomed chairs, chests and
writing table, there were shelves of books and other
treasured keepsakes.

The twin cradleboard Mangus Coloradas had given
Socorro for her sons hung with its fetishes of bone, fur
and turquoise beside the plain one in which Talitha had
carried her half-brother, James. From a corner shelf,
the doll Patrick O'Shea had given Talitha smiled mys-
teriously from the lace of her mantilla. In the window
ledge perched a little blue bird, the one Caterina's
Papago half-brother had given her, and poised above it
was the red-tailed hawk carved by James before he
became Fierro and terrorized the settlements after the
slaughter of Apache women and children at the Camp
Grant Massacre.

With a surging thrill of pride and sorrow for these
people of her blood who had loved and suffered and
not always triumphed, Tracy reverently touched the
mementoes before she sank down by the books on a
thick Saltillo rug woven in ochers, grays and blacks.

Many of the older volumes were gifts from Marc
Revier to Talitha and Socorro's children, whom he had
taught to read. Dickens' *Christmas Carol* and *Tale of
Two Cities;* Edward Lear's *Book of Nonsense,* Prescott's *The Conquest of Mexico,* Tennyson, the Brown-
ings, Longfellow and Poe. Each successive generation

left its favorites. Here was Christina Riordan-Scott's typescript account of the Bisbee deportation where Tracy's great-grandfather had been killed; next to that were Christina's family memoirs, history she'd gleaned from Talitha, who'd been at the ranch almost from the beginning, and from the first vaqueros. Tracy's mother had loved the Oz books and her whole set was there along with the *Chronicles of Narnia* and Tolkien, and Tracy's own favorite, T. H. White's *The Once and Future King*.

She picked it up at random and smiled and sighed at Merlin's advice to the Wart: *"The best thing for being sad is to learn something."*

"All right, I'll try," she said aloud. Maybe she could use this time, back at the place where her memories began, to decide where she was going, what she would be and do.

For the first time, she noticed the case atop the armoire. Rising, she climbed on a stool and discovered that it was another relic, Johnny Chance's guitar.

To her surprise, the strings didn't snap as she tuned them. Maybe Patrick had remembered that she played a little and had recently instructed someone to restring it. He always enjoyed hearing her, especially when she sang ranch songs and folk ballads. Maybe he'd like to hear her now, if he wasn't asleep. It would be less strain on him than making conversation.

Tuning till she was satisfied, Tracy gave her hair a swift brushing and left with the guitar slung over her shoulder.

III

PATRICK WAS LYING STILL, BUT THOUGH TRACY ENTERED quietly, his shaggy white head turned toward her. His half-face smiled and he spoke her name.

She came to kiss him and held his scarred brown hand. "Can you always tell who it is?"

He gave her hand a caressing squeeze. "Vashti's shoes all make a little click. Concha sort of oozes along, dragging her feet. You step too soft for a man. So I don't get real high marks for guessing."

"You had lunch?"

"I had dinner. Supper's tonight."

She stayed out of what she remembered as a running argument between him and his third wife, thanked him for seeing that her old furniture and things had been moved from the home place. His hand tightened painfully on hers.

"Sure hated to leave. But Vashti always claimed it was rundown and uncomfortable. She wanted to bulldoze it."

Tracy couldn't repress a gasp. She couldn't have been more shocked if Vashti had suggested razing the family cemetery. Patrick rumbled on forlornly, "No way I'd do that! And I sure wasn't moving to town. Seemed pretty selfish to keep Vashti in a house she hated when, hell, I couldn't see it! So here we are."

Poor Vashti! Doomed to live like a feudal queen,

31

when before she'd charmed Patrick into marriage,
she'd sold real estate for a living! Anger hummed
through Tracy, though she warned herself that she
mustn't interfere. No outsider could understand the
debits and credits of a marriage so it was presumptuous
to try to figure them. If Vashti wasn't worth the
problems she caused Patrick, he could send her to town
and hire all the housekeeper-companions he wanted.
Tracy privately considered her a calculating, cold-
hearted schemer, but there must be more to her than
that or Patrick wouldn't care about her.

Still, it seemed cruel, cruel, to force an aging blind
man from the home he'd loved all his life. Patrick
sighed gustily. "Anyhow, there's life and loving in the
old house, honey. Chuey Sanchez—he's my foreman
since Umberto died—Chuey's there with his kids and
grandkids and a couple of orphaned nieces and nephews. You'd ought to go see them. The vaqueros always
ask when their *doncellita*'s coming home."

Yes, they had called her that, little maiden, and
they'd sung "Las Mañanitas" under her window on the
dawns of her birthdays, because this had always been
done for daughters of the house. She was no maiden
anymore, though she realized with dismay that she was
the youngest of the family who had grown up at the
ranch, since neither Judd nor Shea had yet produced
children. The branches of the clan living in Phoenix and
ranching in the Verde River country east of Prescott
had gradually built up allegiance to their own locations
and didn't stay in touch.

"I'll go see Chuey and Anita tomorrow," she promised. "And now, Don Patrick, shall I play for you a
little?"

He patted her hand and his smile dragged at the lax
side of his face. "You remember some of the old family
songs?"

"If I lose the words, you help me."

Perching on a stool where she could watch him and
still gaze out where the majestic timbered rise of the

Santa Ritas faded to purple, she hummed and tuned, closing her eyes to bring back words she'd grown up with but hadn't heard in years.

The double-branding of Patrick O'Shea who endured the searing iron to ransom Talitha's baby brother from the Apaches; the valiant women, Socorro and Tjúni, who killed the ravaging scalp-hunters and earned the protection of the great Mimbreño, Mangus Coloradas; the ballad "Ay, Caterina!" told how the daughter born at the cost of Socorro's life had loved James-Fierro all her brief years and died with him along the Verde. From this tender lament, Tracy launched into the irreverent Wobbly songs Johnny Chance had played on this same guitar and wondered what genes of his, surviving in her, responded to the music.

"Long-haired preachers come out every night,
Try to tell you what's wrong and what's right;
But when asked how about something to eat
They will answer with voices so sweet:

You will eat, bye and bye,
In that glorious land above the sky;
Work and pray, live on hay,
You'll get pie in the sky when you die."

A hand closed on her shoulder. "Damned if you don't make that old 'I Won't Work' propaganda sound real good!" chuckled Judd. "But you're going to have bleeding fingers if you don't toughen them gradually. Let me play awhile."

Without waiting for her assent, he slipped the strap over her head and settled on a footstool that left his tawny head close to her knee. The warm brush of his hands had sent a slow, sensuous shock through Tracy; his proximity kept an electric awareness pulsating with every beat of her heart.

What was happening to her anyway? Was her body rebelling against her long celibacy or was it that both these distant cousins of hers aroused some deep, primitive hunger that other men didn't reach? She must be careful, very careful. She'd come here for peace, not passion. Above all, she mustn't get caught up in anything that would make it difficult to stay with Patrick as long as he needed her.

Still, she couldn't keep from watching Judd's fingers thrum the strings, caress the guitar that curved like a woman's breasts and hips with the narrow waist between. If he touched her that skillfully—

Her cheeks grew hot. She wrenched her eyes away, but not before his lion's eyes caught them and his long mouth curved into a smile.

"Do not look for me along the highway," he sang in Spanish. "Look for me along the shortcut—" He was still singing love songs when Vashti came in with that clicking Patrick had mentioned, and regarded the three of them with asperity.

"That might all be very nice if I could understand it." She took the guitar from Judd and put it on a chest. "Be a darling, Judd, and make us all a drink."

Lazily, he moved over to the bar. "Just tomato juice for me," Tracy requested.

"Don't spoil my tequila with a bunch of ice," growled Patrick.

Vashti took Judd's seat and clasped her perfectly manicured hands about her knees in a way that pulled her dark green velvet caftan tight across the curves of her high, full breasts, further defined by the heavy antique silver medallion resting between them.

"I hope all this troubadouring hasn't exhausted you, love," she said to her husband.

"It sure beats listening to recordings, or thinking about how danged useless I am!"

"Patrick! You're getting better all the time. Doctor Garth thinks you can start sitting up in a wheelchair any day you feel up to it."

"God damn a wheelchair."

Vashti flushed. When she spoke, her voice was taut

and brittle. "That's right, Patrick. Feel sorry for yourself. See how hard you can make it on those of us who're trying to take care of you."

It was clear he was no easy patient. Though Tracy's sympathies were all with him, she reluctantly had to admit that Vashti was in a trying position. Judd handed his father a drink, snapping the tension, and turned the mechanism that lifted the upper third of the bed so that Patrick was able to swallow.

Patrick took a swift draught and shifted his good leg. "Sorry, baby," he told Vashti. "I'm getting mean as a rattler in August that can't shed his skin. I can't get all worked up about straddling a wheelchair, but bring one up here tomorrow and I'll try."

Rising gracefully, she kissed his cheek, though it seemed to Tracy that she hesitated for a second, as if having to nerve herself. Well, that was natural. Something in healthy people instinctively wished to avoid sickness or disfigurement, probably out of unconscious fear that the same thing could happen to them.

"Thank you, darling," she said, and resumed her seat, accepting the martini Judd handed her. Giving Tracy her juice with a teasing smile, he fetched his own Scotch and raised it in a flourish.

"Here's to Tracy's homecoming!"

"We've already drunk to that," Vashti said with some annoyance.

Judd's mocking stare subdued her jewel-green one. "I haven't," he reminded. Bowing to Tracy, his eyes had the sheen of the rich whisky in his glass. *"Salud, cousin. Pesetas y amor y tiempo gozarlos."* Money, love, and time to enjoy them.

"The same to you," she laughed, then frowned as she discovered that he'd mixed a strong jolt of vodka into her drink.

He laughed boyishly. "Just couldn't do it, Tracy! Breaks every law of hospitality and proper welcoming of prodigal daughters."

"This once," she said, smiling, though there was an

edge to her voice. "In future, though, please give me what I ask for."

He sipped his drink, savoring it as he watched her. "But what if you don't ask for a few things I know you'd like mighty well?"

"I'd rather have what I choose than something I might like better that was foisted on me."

"The perversity of woman!"

"Free will."

He laughed caressingly. "Guess we can be thankful you haven't cut off your pretty nose to spite your face!" Patrick moved restlessly and Judd refilled his glass.

"You boys work out something on the El Charco lease?" Patrick demanded.

"Shea plays the same old record. Dump a thousand head."

Patrick's good hand clenched on his glass. "Can't figure what's got into that kid!"

"Comes from getting all scientific. Hell, he's had the nerve to map a survey of the whole ranch with recommended uses—a real fancy plan. Only trouble is, we'd go out of the cattle business."

"He talked to me about it," Patrick said slowly. The live side of his face contorted as he turned toward the window, out of which he was powerless to see. "Is the range in as bad a shape as he says, Judd?"

"It's dry," Judd admitted. "But a few good rains'll bring it back. You've pulled through enough drouths to know the answer isn't to sell at a loss every time it gets dry." He hesitated as if trying to sense his father's set of mind. "Dad, like I've told you, there's another way to go. Sell off some of that worn-out land along the highway. Use the proceeds to put in an irrigation system." Judd spread his hands expansively. "We could grow enough alfalfa to feed our herds in bad years, and in good years we could sell it."

"That'd take a lot of water."

Judd grunted impatiently. "That's why they're putting in the Central Arizona Project, running Colorado River water over this way."

Tracy frowned. "I've heard the Colorado River's already overcommitted. Anyway, don't the Papagos have first claim on CAP water since Tucson, the mines, and agribusiness have taken so much of their water?"

"If the Colorado dries up, we'll get it from someplace else," Judd said confidently.

"You sound just like the farmers I interviewed up around Lubbock in West Texas," Tracy remarked. Raised in an arid region, she knew water was life, and Judd's careless talk made her angry though she kept her tone even. "They got a water depletion allowance, just like that on oil, since everyone knew groundwater would be used up in time. Now that it's happening, they want the government to bail them out—have other taxpayers foot the cost of pumping water uphill from the Mississippi."

"Hey, now!" protested Judd. "The Ogallala aquifer underlies those high plains!"

"Sure. Fossil water from thousands of years ago. Do you know its rate of recharge?"

"What's that got to do with us?"

"The whole West is in the same position, pumping groundwater that can't be replaced." Tracy went over to stand by her great-uncle, rest her hand on his shoulder. "Patrick, the Ogallala recharges from a quarter-inch to a half-inch yearly! There's not enough surface water in all of Texas to supply West Texas growers at their present rate of use. Even if there were, the cost of delivery would be exorbitant. I'm not too familiar with Arizona's problems, but I do know agribusiness uses ninety percent of the water. It *has* to be crazy to grow high-water-volume crops where water's so scarce and costs so much."

"You've sure been to the city!" Judd snapped. "The country's got to eat."

She had done an article on that, too, and was able to

say with sweet reasonableness, "The question is, how long can we squander the grains many peoples live on in feeding up meat animals?"

Patrick's blind eyes glared at her. "Well, Tracy girl, as long as I got a tooth to chew with, I'm having my beef three times a day!" The glare switched to his son. "You're saying that land along the road's so poor we ought to get rid of it. Maybe there's something to what Shea argues."

"Those pastures closest to the old ranch house got the heaviest use for years," Judd said with bitter patience. "They're not typical of Socorro range."

"They're the heart of the home place. I want them brought back to grass."

"But that'll take years!"

"I don't care if it takes till hell freezes over!" Patrick dragged the paralyzed side of himself higher by hitching up the half that could move. "Some of our family's going to live in the old house again, and they're going to look out at good grass, not some damn beehive development!"

"But, darling—" began Vashti.

Patrick said grimly, "I've heard the last word I'm going to about selling any part of the Socorro."

Stalking to the window, Judd kept his back turned. When he spoke, his voice was strained. "You want me to quit as your manager, Dad?"

"Don't talk like a damn fool!"

"You're tying my hands. You won't let me do what it takes to keep the ranch going."

Patrick considered. At last he said wearily, "You're the manager, Judd. Sell cattle if we need to. Buy feed. Try to lease or buy more land. Sell off stocks for financing, or we'll unload some real estate. But we hold onto the land."

"Of all the pig-headed medieval ideas!" Vashti burst out. "Sacrificing valuable assets when you could get a fabulous price for used-up land with an old hovel!"

Judd swung to cross over and place a warning hand
on her shoulder, roughly, without looking to see how
she took his wordless rebuke.

"You're the boss, Dad." His tone was conciliating.
"I'll do the best I can. And I'm going to start by getting
Shea's lease revoked."

Tracy felt the old man sag against her, then say, "The
boy's got wild notions. But son, I hate to see you two
fall out."

"We're bound to have it out sometime."

Patrick sighed. "Maybe you could honey up the
medicine by giving him a free hand with the pastures
around the home place."

"You talk to him about that, Dad." Judd's face
hardened. "Reckon the less Shea and I see of each
other, the better, at least till this lease thing gets
settled."

Patrick slumped completely in his pillows. Tracy bent
to make him more comfortable. "Get me another
drink," he said. "I want to get to sleep."

Judd filled his glass. Patrick gripped Tracy's hand. "I
liked your singing, honey. Good to have you back."

"It's good to be here."

She kissed him, wishing desperately she could give
him some of her youth and strength and sight. Pitiful
that the wife and sons who should be easing his mind
seemed locked into conflicts that were bound to prey on
him. Maybe her comparative neutrality would be a
comfort.

He squeezed her hand in dismissal. She left the
guitar and started down the curving stairs.

Vashti and Judd stood near the bottom, the man
towering over the shapely woman. Vashti's gaze flew up
to Tracy. "We dress for dinner," she announced.
"Henri gets cross if we don't sit down promptly at
seven."

Tracy considered it ludicrous to gear one's life
around the timetables of those hired to make it easier,

thought with nostalgia of the days before Vashti when Concha shouted that meals were ready and the bunk-house vaqueros ate with the family.

Nodding at her hostess, she returned Judd's baffled stare of appraisal. Evidently, he belonged to the sort of man who felt persecuted and subtly betrayed when a woman knew inconvenient facts.

"I enjoyed your singing," she told him.

He laughed. Assurance restored, he said with endearing swagger, "Cousin, you ain't seen nothin' yet!"

She felt him watching her as she moved across the huge room. This consciousness injected a flowing grace into her walk though she controlled the swaying of her hips. Judd, like Shea, was supremely masculine—and *he liked women.* Yet it was Shea she thought about as she stripped for her shower.

Why was he so hostile? Still blaming all women because his wife had ditched him? That happened too much for anyone to parade around years later with his bleeding heart pinned to his sleeve. Like that mugging. She couldn't keep it from happening, but it was in her power now to fight the terror, master the experience instead of letting it dominate her. This was the ideal place to subdue that nightmare, in the protective atmosphere of her home, with Patrick's needs to respond to.

And a couple of handsome, very distant cousins? If only they didn't seem set on a collision course! Stepping out of the shower, she toweled till her skin glowed, and surveyed her clothes.

She hadn't brought anything Vashti would consider dressy, but one side of the armoire was filled with long skirts, lacy or embroidered blouses, and colorful Mexican and Guatemalan lounging gowns. Choosing a simple white drawstring blouse, she slipped on her favorite skirt, black-and-white coarse Mexican cotton, its extravagantly full hem trimmed with a wide band of scalloped black lace.

Her hair was too short for elaboration but brushing

brought soft waves to a sheen. Her married lover had
called her Rapunzel and loved to lock his fingers in her
hair. When she'd gotten rid of him, she'd had her hair
cut, too. Maybe it was time to let it grow again.

Her old jewelry chest yielded the black coral earrings
and oval pendant she'd always liked with the skirt.

Smoothing the dark eyebrows that winged up questioningly above eyes that had been called sherry or
amber, or now, by Geronimo, the shade of mesquite
honey, she glossed her lips and left her room just as the
clock struck seven.

Excellent vichyssoise, superb green salad, glorified
pot roast, coffee and glazed strawberry cake. Lit by
candles, the big table looked even larger, and the room
rather like a cave except for the gleam of gilt picture
frames. Vashti seemed abstracted but Judd took the
opportunity to quiz Tracy.

"Wasn't it a drag, busting yourself to write stuff that
went into a paper you knew would just be used to wrap
the garbage?"

"Recycled, I hope," she returned, smiling, though
he'd hit a sore spot. "I never expected anyone to frame
my articles, but I did a few that I hope made an
impression. Like the one on West Texas water."

He gave her a wary look, but Vashti set down her
crystal wine goblet with some violence. "My God,
Tracy, I hope that sanctimonious do-gooder streak in
your branch of the family isn't surfacing in you! We've
got troubles enough without a resident Ralph Nader."

That slur on her family sent a rush of anger through
Tracy. "Corny as it sounds, I prefer good to bad," she
said. "I think the only chance we have is to work for
what we believe in."

Vashti groaned. Judd's eyes glowed yellow as he
leaned forward. "Now there we agree! Tell me, cousin,
don't you think people have a right to defend themselves from thugs and gangs that rob, murder and
rape?"

Could he know what had happened to her? She hadn't told anyone but the authorities in Houston and her lawyer. His words brought back that moment of helpless dread when she'd been choked past consciousness, and her voice flamed with outrage.

"Of course I think people should defend themselves! But it'd help more to try to get at causes." Like not releasing a dangerous psychotic with his own little supply of downers. Or perpetuating poverty, hopelessness, racist injustice and a system that turned prisons into costly grad schools for crime rather than supplying job training and opportunities before people went wrong.

Judd ignored her proviso. "Then I'm doing something I think you'd be mighty interested in. It would at least give you a good feature."

"What?"

"I'd rather show you." His smile lingered on her mouth, traced the curve of her shoulders and breasts, making a sort of sweet warmth tingle through her. "There's a moon. Care for a stroll?"

She did, but a flash of Shea's mocking face cooled the magnetism surging between her and the man across the table. *Easy,* she warned herself. *Don't start something you aren't ready to finish.*

An involvement with either of her cousins was the last thing she needed, at least till she knew them better, felt herself able to handle what might follow. Not that Shea showed any sign of liking her! Still, she couldn't have mistaken that elemental attraction that had coursed between them.

"Thanks," she told Judd. "But I'm going up to Patrick for a while."

He shrugged, rose to pull out Vashti's chair before he did the same for Tracy's. His hands touched the back of her arms and as she rose he whispered in her ear, "Thank *you,* cousin, for wanting to come." Aloud, he said, "When I get back from Phoenix, I'll take you around the ranch. But you'll have to wait a couple of weeks for your big story."

"Judd," cut in Vashti, in the flattering light seeming at least as young as his thirty-eight years. "Will you come to my study a moment? I've some matters you might attend to up in Phoenix."

He looked slightly annoyed but nodded carelessly and stepped back to let the women precede him through the door. Then he followed Vashti down the sconce-lit hall while Tracy caught up her skirt and ran upstairs.

The moon spilled through the window, making a light unnecessary. Patrick lay so still that Tracy thought him asleep till half his mouth curved in that devastating way and he spoke her name.

"Can I get you anything?" she asked, placing her hand over his.

"No, honey. And I don't want to talk. But I'd sure like for you to just stay with me, quiet for a while."

Her eyes stung. How it must torment his imperious spirit to have this failure of body added to that of his sight! His sons' quarrel must weigh on him almost as much as not being able to judge for himself what was best for the ranch and take an active part, for Patrick had always worked right beside his men, been an expert rider and roper.

In the moonlight, she noticed lying beside his pillow the rawhide reata that he'd clung to long after nylon ropes replaced hand-plaited ones. It smelled of horses and sweat.

Sitting down by this man who'd lulled her childhood fears and griefs against his broad chest as tenderly as any woman could have, Tracy held his hand. At last, quietly, she let her tears fall.

Judd looked both ways before, without rapping, he entered Vashti's room. A triple mirror reflected her in a blur of multiple images, lace-covered breasts and luminous hair, as she whirled toward him. She screwed the lid on an alabaster jar with fingers that shook. He was amused at her discomfiture, caught with her face off, the way she tried to cover it with a provocative pout.

"Darling, you could knock!"

He shrugged. "You wanted to see me. I'm not going to stand around in the hall and let Concha see me come in. She'd love to take that to Patrick."

"That old witch!" Vashti shuddered, rising. "Always padding around, watching me with those damned flat black eyes! I've tried to get rid of her but Patrick won't hear of it."

"If she sees us, I'll get rid of her. Permanently."

"Judd, you sound so dangerous," Vashti teased. Her eyes deepened. Her expensive perfume floated up from between her breasts as soft arms closed around him. She filled him with the surfeited distaste he felt after a long night with her, though she knew all the tricks and, under his disgust, the familiar hot urgency was starting to build. Caressing his face and throat, she laughed softly. "You're as *macho* as any Mexican."

"It wouldn't be funny if Patrick threw you out and disowned me."

"He wouldn't, even if he guessed," she said complacently.

Judd drew away, stared at her through narrowed eyes. She seemed suddenly old. Well-preserved, but used-up beside Tracy's freshness. He'd been a fool to get mixed up with her but she'd been convenient, lushly inviting, and he'd thought her experienced enough to handle it as mutual gratification. He hadn't expected her growing possessiveness, the way she was trying to turn it into some kind of grand passion. Even less had he expected to feel compunction, a kind of shame, when she flirted with him in front of his blind father. Contemptuously, he swung away from her, thrusting his hands into his pockets.

"Blind and paralyzed, Patrick's still a hell of a lot

more man than you deserve. If he knew, he'd take care of us."

"Judd! You're in a vile mood."

"What do you want?"

She was silent. "I've got things to do," he said, turning. "If it's skipped your mind, we'll talk later."

She stepped in front of him, jaw hardening. "I'd like to know why you're taking such an interest in little cousin Tracy."

"I'm not married," he said brutally. "I can show an interest where I damn well please."

She choked. Her eyes glowed like brimstone. "If you think you can just use me and—and—"

"Yes?" he mocked, rocking back on his heels and crossing his arms.

When she swallowed and clenched her hands, strangling back whatever stupidities she wanted to hurl at him, he said in a bored tone, "I didn't seduce you, Vashti. I don't owe you a thing. If you want to finish us fast, just throw fits or threaten me."

She flinched as if he'd hit her, then smiled with obvious effort, putting her hand placatingly on his.

"Let's not quarrel, darling. I was only going to show Tracy around the place myself if you were offering out of hospitality or cousinly duty."

"Considering how you hate the place, I'd never ask you to make that sacrifice," he said sardonically. "Thanks, but I expect that little tour to be fun."

At Vashti's stricken look, his instinct not to unnecessarily make an enemy led him to say more gently, "Tracy's got influence with Patrick. It's worth some trouble to get her on my side."

The thought of Tracy touched off a wave of desire that transferred obligingly to Vashti's warm, full body. Grasping her robe, he started to husk it off.

Her eyes lifted; she understood.

Stepping back with a slight laugh, she said, "Sorry, dear. I've got a beastly headache. Maybe later."

"If you're smart, you'll take it when you can get it."
That beautiful mask-like face congealed.

"Enjoy your headache," he said with a savage grin
and let himself out. It was like escaping from the
scented lair of a treacherous, fawning animal. But there
was nothing she could do to him. He had what she
wanted, not the other way around.

IV

IT WAS LATE BEFORE TRACY KNEW BY HIS HEAVY BREATHING that he finally slept. Gently freeing her numbed hand from his, she went silently downstairs. A few electric sconces dimly lit the halls. She turned down the one leading to her room.

A cry rose in her throat as a figure loomed before her. Fingers clamped over her mouth. A steel-muscled arm dragged her against a hard, powerful body.

"Tracy!" came a startled whisper. "What the hell, honey? It's just me!"

As she quieted, Judd cautiously took his hand off her mouth. He kept his other arm around her, though it was loose now, no longer a pinion.

"I—I—" Swept back to the panic of that night six months ago, she couldn't talk.

Judd turned her about and marched her to the kitchen, a big room with all the modernities amidst dark-blue and sun-yellow Mexican tile, sculptured adobe niches and much bright copper. Installing her in Concha's rocking chair, he got a glass of milk, laced it amply with Tia Maria, and gave it to her.

"I'm sorry I scared you." He spread his big square hands appealingly. "Just thought I could show you the moon."

Restored by reality and the warming liqueur, Tracy

47

managed a laugh. "All is forgiven. But please don't lurk around in the dark."

He frowned, pulling over a low bench so that he could look directly into her eyes. "You were more than startled, you were terrified! Why, Tracy?"

She shook her head. The pulse throbbed sledgingly in her throat so that she seemed to feel again those strangling, brutal fingers. "I—I'd rather not talk about it."

She would have risen but he imprisoned her, setting a hand on either arm of the rocker. "Something's happened. I don't remember much about you, but you were no scaredy-cat."

"Please!"

The pupils of his eyes had dilated, leaving only a thin circle of gold around their blackness. "You were raped!"

She shook her head, beginning to tremble.

"Then what?"

Maybe it would help to tell. Stumblingly, eyes fixed on her tightly clasped hands, she explained. Judd was breathing heavily by the time she finished. Springing up, he gripped his hands behind him, paced the length of the room.

"So that pervert's being coddled by the shrinks till he can be turned loose!"

"I told you, he went berserk in Viet Nam—"

"That's an excuse?" Judd turned on his heel. "You wait right here."

He was back in a few minutes. "Keep this." He handed her a small gun.

She stared at the blue-black barrel, the carved ivory handle. "I don't shoot."

"Then I'll damned well teach you."

"But, Judd, I'm not in Houston!"

"You're safe enough in this house," he agreed. "But if you're out driving or walking alone, you could run into some dangerous types on the ranch. Hippies running drugs, Commies running guns, illegals—"

"Oh, come on, Judd! Illegal aliens just want work. I never heard of their hurting anyone."

"They sure have taken to robbery. Just ask anyone who lives along the border. Over around Douglas, where two ranchers were tried for defending their home, folks are ready to shoot to kill."

"Weren't those ranchers on trial for torturing an illegal?"

Judd grunted. "They just wanted to teach him a lesson he wouldn't forget. Hell, they could have just killed him and dumped the body down an old mine shaft. He'd never even have been missed."

Except by some woman, some old parents or children down in Mexico? Tracy shook her head, tried to give back the gun. "I don't know how to use it."

He let out an explosive breath. "After what happened to you? You'd by God better learn!"

When she still held out the weapon, he took a deep breath, spoke more gently. "Tracy, the night that animal jumped you, if you'd had a gun, wouldn't you have used it? Been mighty glad to?"

She shivered involuntarily. "Yes."

"Well, then?" he prodded.

She couldn't answer. Of course she'd have used any defense she could have that terrible night. But she didn't think the answer to violence was for everyone to start packing guns.

Judd said urgently, real concern in his voice. "Tracy, just keep the gun a while. Get used to it. Then let me teach you to shoot. I can't stand to think of you not being prepared if you needed to be and though I hate to say it, not even the ranch is safe anymore."

She appreciated his caring. And it couldn't hurt to learn to shoot, though she wasn't going to carry a gun. Glancing down at the small weapon, she gave Judd a teasing smile. "You were lucky I wasn't armed and dangerous when you waylaid me in the hall, Judd."

He shrugged. "You'd never have had a chance to shoot."

"Then why learn?"

He chuckled. "Because, sweet baby, not many guys know all the tricks I do." He tilted up her chin, fingers warm against the leaping pulse in her throat. "My God, have you ever grown up beautiful!"

"Is this a private party or may I have a drink?" As Vashti glided through the doorway, Judd stepped back.

"I thought you had a headache."

"I did. I do." She smiled appealingly. Her body curved voluptuously beneath a clinging dark-green panné velvet robe. "Be a love, Judd, and make me a Scotch and soda."

Disgruntled, he moved over to the refrigerator. Vashti peered at the gun Tracy now felt sheepish about holding. "Darling! What on earth have you got that dreadful thing for?"

"She's going to learn to use it," Judd interposed.

Vashti's eyebrows climbed. "Are you, Tracy? You don't seem the type. But blood will out, and from those sagas Patrick's so fond of repeating, your ancestresses thought nothing of shooting men."

"They killed scalp-hunters who were murdering Apache women and children," Tracy retorted. "In their place, I hope I could have done the same."

Vashti's jade eyes gleamed with mirth and perhaps a touch of malice. "But, dear, we don't have any scalp-hunters these days."

Handing his stepmother her drink, Judd snorted. "We've got more scum than ever, Vashti, and you ought to know it if you listen to the news."

She lifted an elegant shoulder and patted his hand. "You men! Creating terrors and alarms if there aren't any! If you think it's so bad that we should all go around with sub-machine guns and bandoliers, why not sell to the Vistas Unlimited developers and move to town?"

"My dead body may move to town, but I won't."

Vashti's laughter tinkled. "Judd, angel! You sound like John Wayne!"

He watched her moodily. "The cities are rotting. They're going to explode the way a putrid carcass blows up from trapped gases. That's when the maggots will scurry around for safety." Insolently, he looked his stepmother up and down. "On that day, Vashti, pray you can still hide here."

She made a face and yawned. "My father was a fundamentalist minister who loved to preach blood to the chariot wheels, the moon in sackcloth and the end of the world. Your notions are just as depressing, Judd dear, though they lack Biblical grandeur."

Uncomfortable at their skirmishing and something else she sensed between them, Tracy put her glass in the sink and quickly said her good-nights.

Back in her room, she stared at the gun a minute, felt a wave of revulsion. What kind of life was it if you had to go in fear and suspicion, be prepared to kill? Tomorrow, she'd give Judd back his gun. Placing it on top of the armoire, she quickly got ready for bed.

As she settled gratefully between the cool sheets, a vagrant memory of Shea crossed her mind. Now that she thought of it, his pickup had been missing the almost universal gun rack. Maybe he hid his firearms. Or maybe he didn't agree with Judd.

Whatever his views on guns, he was one standoffish character! Far from offering to take her around, as Judd had hospitably done, Shea had as good as told her he didn't want her at El Charco.

Why? And why should it sting? She stretched, feeling her stomach muscles tighten sensuously, and smiled a bit vindictively in the knowledge that though, for reasons unknown, Shea seemed to be a woman-hater, he had most certainly responded to her physically—and she hoped he was thinking about her now and repenting his surliness!

What eyes he had! Like a summer thunderstorm charged with lightning. She sighed as her thoughts moved to Patrick. Let him be sleeping, forgetful of his troubles! At least, she could lighten his dreary confinement a little bit. And it was good to be home, back in her childhood bed. Hugging a pillow to her, Tracy drifted into sleep.

When she went up to Patrick next morning, a cranky Vashti was preparing to bathe and shave him. "He should have a nurse," she complained to Tracy as if the blind man couldn't hear. "But he's run off everyone we've coaxed into coming out here."

"A bunch of ninnies," Patrick grouched. "That last old hatchet-face should've been thrilled to get a slap on the fanny!"

"Strangely enough, she wasn't," Vashti snapped. "Really, Patrick, it's not fair that all this falls on me because you shock and intimidate the people I hire!"

Patrick chortled. "And what kind of nurses are they if a blind cripple can fluster 'em? Dammit, woman, I've told you to get one of the vaqueros up here. Any man of them would be glad to do it."

Vashti's lips compressed. "It's bad enough for Chuey Sanchez to track in manure once or twice a week. Why he can't just report to Judd—"

"Chuey knows I'm still the boss." The spunk faded from Patrick's voice and he sounded very tired. "You don't have to shave me, Vashti. Judd will, or hell, I'll grow whiskers!"

"I've always wanted to be a lady barber," Tracy said, laughing as she took the razor from the older woman. "You'd look ravishing with sideburns, Patrick! Why don't we start some?"

"Why not?" he chuckled, relaxing.

Vashti, crisp in beige linen, paused in the door. "Don't spoil him too outrageously," she warned. "I have a new nurse coming and if she doesn't stay, I'm going to be extremely vexed!"

Patrick made a rude sound and grinned up at Tracy. "Thanks, honey. Try not to cut my throat."

"Keep still, then," she begged nervously.

The shave didn't take long. She bathed Patrick's face

and torso but he refused to let her do more. "I wouldn't
mind a she-nurse if she was pretty and fun," he
grumbled. "But the ones Vashti hires are skinny as
snakes or broad as hippos and talk like they broke a
thermometer in their mouth!"

"Now, Patrick, how do you know they're not gorgeous?"

"I can hear even if I can't see," he rumbled, then
grinned wickedly. "I can feel, too. And believe me,
honey, those old girls were tough as rawhide or soggy as
a wet sponge!"

"Patrick!"

He gave his good shoulder a truculent hitch. "I'm
only *half* dead, Tracy, not all the way. Now listen, you
get over to the Sanchezes' today and see them and the
vaqueros."

"Is my singing that bad?"

"You can sing when you get back." He winked his
live eye. "Get along with you now! I've got to save up
my strength for that new nurse who's supposed to show
up today."

Tracy gave her head a despairing shake and kissed
him good-bye. She could imagine that he might be a
real terror to a nurse, but surely it was better for him to
be feisty and a bit lecherous rather than lie there as if
completely paralyzed.

Downstairs, she went in search of Vashti to see if
there were horses handy or if she should drive to the
old ranchhouse. Vashti was sunning by the pool, an
almost empty glass beside her. An emerald string bikini
bared her seductively curved body and she glistened
with tanning cream.

That magnificent body needed what the crippled man
upstairs could no longer provide. Tracy felt grudging
sympathy for the woman. Even surrounded by luxury,
she was in a cruel position.

"I'm sorry, dear," she said to Tracy's question. "I
don't ride and when Judd does, he has a vaquero bring
a horse. You can do that. Call Chuey, or take anything

in the garage. The keys are labeled and hanging just inside the entry."

Tracy thanked her and was turning away when Vashti swung long legs off the lounge and looked up at her through sunglasses. "Thanks for playing valet to Patrick. He just has no consideration for the trouble it puts me to when he provokes a nurse into quitting!"

"Maybe the new one will work out."

"My God, I hope so!" Vashti drained her glass and sounded a bell that brought the young man who'd served them at table yesterday. Bowing to Tracy, he took the glass and went off without a question. Clasping her arms tightly about herself, Vashti said with drunken plaintiveness, "You know what's terrible?"

"What?"

"He—he wants me to lie down by him." Vashti shuddered. "Without my clothes!"

"You *are* his wife." Taken aback, sorry for them both, it was all Tracy could think of to say.

Vashti yanked off the sunglasses. Dark green eyes blazed and her soft mouth twisted. "That's the awful part! He's always been such a marvelous lover, even after he went blind. Now—now he's the way he is—oh, God! It's like lying down with death!"

"You must be life to him, and warmth," Tracy pointed out. "Can't you, Vashti, knowing how it is for him?"

"I—I've tried! I just can't bear it."

Grief for Patrick swept aside Tracy's pity for the woman. She said in a grim voice, "If that's how it is, then I think you should get a nurse who won't feel that way."

Vashti took a long swallow from the glass the young man had quietly placed on the table. "It's all so silly! Apart from touching, he can't *do* anything."

"Touching's mightily important." Tracy knew. She often hungered for simple physical closeness, just holding and being held.

Vashti thrust on her sunglasses and lay back, the

belly beneath her rib cage taut and flat as a girl's. Her fingers brushed nipples that pressed visibly against the bikini top. "You don't understand," she muttered.

Tracy did, too well. Patrick's wife felt only revulsion for his helplessness, his longing to be warmed by a woman's body. At the same time, Vashti missed their former sexual passion. Maybe, tormented by that, she was as incapable of the nurturing Patrick craved as he was of the prowess of which she felt cheated.

In such a miserable deadlock, reproaching Vashti would be useless. Feeling at a loss, Tracy said not to wait lunch for her and walked around the house to the long garage.

The doors were closed behind a wine-red truck fitted with rifle racks and super-wide heavy tires, a powerful camouflage-painted RV and a dark-blue Mercedes, the last probably Judd's. Tracy also dismissed a silver Cadillac, which had to be Vashti's. That left a Ford pickup, a shiny yellow Toyota truck and a sage-green Plymouth Horizon.

Stepping into the entry to the main house, she found the keys and was quickly on her way.

It was calving season. Chuey and the two married sons who lived with him had been up all night midwifing and had to get back to their work after a cup of steaming coffee and expressions of delight that the *doncellita* was back. "You will be riding," Chuey said. "Your old mare died last winter, but I've been gentling a fine young gelding for you." In spite of his weariness, his seamed face spread in a broken-toothed smile. "His mane is just the color of yours, Teresita." Puzzled by her masculine name, the vaqueros had given her one they liked.

"It was good of you to think of me, Chuey. When you're through with calving, I'd love to see the horse, but don't trouble about it now."

She'd attended school with Tivi and Roque, the sons, who introduced their pretty wives. Carla was from

Tucson, happily large with her second child by stocky, soft-spoken Tivi. Roque, wiry and tall, had married a ranch girl, Lupe, thin and quick-moving, who'd been helping with the calves. Both girls showed the utmost respect to plump, motherly Inez, who ran the establishment, in which several orphaned nieces and nephews mingled indistinguishably with grandchildren.

The family had gathered in the *sala* to welcome Tracy. Glancing from the work-stained vaqueros and the busy, happy women to the carved dark madonna that had presided over this house from its founding, Tracy relaxed. Peace flowed into her. Gazing at the blue-robed Guadalupana that had become, in ranch legend, identified inextricably with Socorro, Tracy then smiled at the dark-eyed little girl at her knee and lifted her onto her lap.

"I'm home," she told the Sanchezes.

After the men went back to work, Tracy stayed to chat awhile with Inez and Carla. "Don Patrick, how is he?" Inez asked.

Tracy gave them her impressions and added that she hoped the new nurse would suit her great-uncle. Inez sniffed. "He's fond of Lupe, who is his godchild. She and Roque would stay at the big new house and look after Don Patrick, but when Roque spoke of this to the *madama*, she was very rude."

For the sake of the Sanchez family's fierce pride, Tracy made an excuse. "I'm sure my uncle's wife thinks he needs a trained nurse."

"He needs—" began Inez strongly, and then shook her head in self-rebuke. "May our Lady bless him," she finished and inclined her head to the figure of the small madonna. "I have tamales, the way he likes them. Will you take him some?"

"Being remembered will please him as much as the tamales," Tracy said and laughed.

Within minutes she was on her way, a dozen tamales

wrapped in foil nestling on the seat beside her. Taking the road to the new house, she drove absently, worrying over Patrick's unhappy and isolated situation.

Up ahead, a pickup was parked off the road down a wash, probably by a vaquero attending to his work, Tracy thought, paying little attention. Suddenly, one of the doors swung open, and a slim, black-haired girl tumbled out, but before she could run a man threw himself on her, knocking her to the ground.

Tracy slammed on her brakes. The sound reached the struggling pair. Releasing the girl, a burly blond man jumped into the pickup, spun it around. As his victim ducked behind a mesquite, he gunned for the road, starting to swerve around Tracy.

After what had happened to her in Houston, damned if she'd let him go! She drove the car forward till it blocked his way. He honked furiously. Tracy stayed put although she was scared. He backed up, evidently meaning to cut over the bank, but as he churned up the slope, Shea's raunchy old pickup hove in sight.

Nothing had ever looked sweeter. Leaning over, Tracy opened her car door for the jeans-clad, coppery-skinned girl whose lip was bleeding from a blow that had also splotched the side of her thin, oval face.

"That son of a bitch!" she panted. "At least I broke his goddamn finger for him! Oh, hell! My duffel's in his truck!"

"He's not going anywhere," Tracy said, then gasped as the blond thug leaned out of his rolled-down window and fired a revolver at Shea.

He missed, got off a second useless shot as Shea sent the pickup crashing sideways into the other vehicle, knocking it down the bank. By the time it crunched with finality into a dead cottonwood, Shea and Geronimo were beside it, hauling the driver out, knocking the gun from his hand.

His recent passenger hurried to the wreck. Disregarding the blond punk, she swung a battered duffel out of the pickup, tossed it down and nodded approvingly at Geronimo and Shea as her direct dark eyes moved from one to the other.

"Thank you, fellas. I hope you didn't hurt your truck."

"Not like we did his," grinned Geronimo, then scowled at her cut lip and jerked his head at the glowering blond. "He do that?"

The slim girl shrugged. "Call it even." She nodded at a left forefinger that was evidently causing its owner pain.

"You guys have it all wrong," he growled sullenly. "Little bitch promised to put out if I'd give her a lift, but then she wanted money, too."

"You friggin' liar! I gave you money for gas!"

The big man whose bare chest showed beneath a denim vest glanced appealingly at Shea. "You wouldn't take a Mex whore's word over a white man's?"

A noise came from Geronimo's throat. The girl made a hissing sound. She took an Army knife out of her pocket. "I'm Apache, buster!" she said, opening the blade. "If you men'll hold the bastard, I'll make sure he doesn't try to rape anyone again!"

Shea caught his prisoner's arm. "He's got it coming, miss, but we'd better just hand him over to the sheriff. Want to come along and prefer charges on top of those we'll make?"

She sighed and knocked dust off her lean but shapely bottom. "I want Blondie to get all that's coming to him," she said with a vengeful glare. "But I'm already late for work. New job, too. What they'll think when I turn up looking like this—"

Tracy blinked. "Are you the new nurse? For Patrick Scott?"

The girl, who, close up, looked older, perhaps Tracy's age, stared, gulped and nodded. "You know him?"

"He's my great-uncle." Tracy flicked her thumb

toward Shea. "Shea's his son." She frowned slightly at
Geronimo. "And you're his godson, right?"

"You bet!" He beamed at the young woman as she
reluctantly thrust her knife into her pocket. "Hey, are
you really Apache?"

"Coyotero." She added a bit shamefacedly, "Grandpa was white."

"That's okay," said Geronimo magnanimously. "I'm
Chiricahua, but quite a lot of Mexican slipped in."

"Quite a few Mexicans," Shea remarked drily.
"Well, miss, if you're going to the house anyway, let's
take this one along and call the sheriff from there." He
kicked the crushed side of the pickup. "Exhibit A won't
be going anywhere. Let's leave the gun for the sheriff."

"Hey, man," began the captive, starting to look
scared. "I got some real good stuff under the seat. You
can have it if you'll just forget about this!"

"We'll leave that for the sheriff, too." Clamping the
blond's arm behind him, Shea marched him to the
pickup, where Geronimo shoved him inside.

"See you ladies at the house!" he called, and waved
as Shea backed off to follow them.

V

THE NEW NURSE HOPPED IN BESIDE TRACY AND STUCK OUT a slender brown hand with clean close-trimmed nails. "I'm Mary O'Rourke. Thanks for the rescue."

"I didn't do much."

Mary shook her head, bouncing the thick single plait of black hair that hung down her back. "If you hadn't stopped, I'd probably be dead by now. There was no way I was going to let the bastard get what he wanted while I could wiggle a toe. What's your name?"

Tracy told her, added that she was no heroine, but had once been assaulted herself. "So I couldn't just drive on when you were trying to get away."

Mary rummaged in her bag and came out with a bandana, which she used to clean the dried blood off her mouth and chin. "Well, Tracy, I hope you never need help again, but if you do, I want to be there." She glanced over her shoulder at the pickup behind them. "Lucky for both of us those guys came along. Guess you know them pretty well."

By the time Tracy had explained who they were and answered a few questions about Patrick, they were pulling into the garage. Shea parked in front of the house and called out to Tracy to phone the sheriff while he and Geronimo kept their prisoner outside.

As Tracy waved Mary into the entry, the newcomer

60

hung back. "Is there a bathroom? I sure need to go before I meet anyone."

There was one just off the kitchen, but before Tracy could escort Mary there, Vashti appeared at the other end of the hall, peered at them in surprise and came toward them. "You didn't tell me you were expecting a friend, Tracy dear."

Mary stepped forward. "I'm the nurse, ma'am. You know, Mary O'Rourke."

Vashti's polite smile fluttered as if loosely pinned at the corners. "The nurse?" she echoed. "You're Miss O'Rourke?"

She gave a faint laugh. "Really, you're so young! And slender. I don't see how you can take care of my husband. He's a very big man, and paralyzed."

"I'm skinny, ma'am, but real tough," Mary said with cheery dauntlessness. "We can talk all you want in a minute but I'm going to bust if I don't get to a bathroom!"

Tracy caught her arm and whisked her down the hall, gasping with laughter. "Oh, Mary! You're just what Patrick needs!"

"She doesn't think so!" Mary jerked her head in Vashti's direction.

"Don't worry about that," Tracy assured her as Mary dashed through the open door of the bath.

Suppressing her amusement, Tracy picked up the nearest phone and dialed the sheriff, to be advised that a deputy then patrolling the highway near the ranch cutoff would be sent to them immediately.

"What is all this?" demanded Vashti at her elbow as she hung up.

"Tell you in a minute." Hurrying to the front door, Tracy reported to Shea. "It'll be at least a half-hour. Why don't you tie your buddy up and come have some coffee?"

"Yeah, why don't we?" urged Geronimo.

"Oh, go on and get acquainted with the new nurse!" Shea growled. "I can watch this guy."

"I'll tie his hands and feet just to make sure," said Geronimo.

Tracy turned back to Vashti and briefly explained. "From what I've seen of Mary," she concluded, "it'll give Patrick a new lease on life just to have her around."

"But she—she's so coarse!"

You ain't heard nothin' yet, Tracy thought, and grinned. "She's certainly forthright. But she's clean, she's gutsy, and I figure she's competent. If she hitch-hiked from Tucson, I'll bet she's also hungry."

Vashti's lips slipped together. "Henri can't be expected—"

"Oh, the devil with Henry! I'll get something myself." Tracy called to Mary, who was emerging from the bathroom with a look of ineffable content. "How about a snack while you're being interviewed?"

Mary's smooth brow furrowed. "Interviewed? I thought I was already hired."

"Still, Miss O'Rourke, there are things we need to know about each other." Vashti's superior smile dripped sweet reason. Tracy longed to pinch her. "Surely, if we find areas of serious disagreement, it would be better for all concerned for you to accept a generous payment for your trouble and return to town."

Mary's puzzled gaze flicked to Tracy, who made an okay sign behind Vashti's back. This girl was just what Patrick needed; he was going to have her.

"Let's sit down in the kitchen and have some coffee," Tracy said, beckoning to Geronimo, who had just come in.

Vashti, stiff-backed, plied Mary with questions while Tracy brought coffee, crispy almond rolls and a bowl of fruit. It was fun to see Geronimo peel an orange, divide it carefully and put it on Mary's plate.

"You're a licensed practical nurse, but you're saving up to study auto mechanics?" Vashti's tone was incredulous. "Forgive me, Miss O'Rourke, but I find that astonishing."

Mary shrugged thin shoulders, licking the last trace of caramelly syrup from her fingers. "I like taking care of people. But I just love to tinker around with cars and trucks." She laughed, revealing white teeth set somewhat far apart. "Never hurts to have more than one way to make a living."

"That's another thing," said Vashti. "You must intend to get married someday. Since my husband will probably be an invalid the rest of his life, I do want someone I can rely on."

"The agreement's for a year," said Mary. "I can promise you that. From what the employment agency said, ma'am, you've had five women out here in less than three months."

"If you could call 'em women," Geronimo grimaced.

Vashti scowled murderously at him, said grudgingly to Mary, "All right, Miss O'Rourke. As soon as the deputy's taken your evidence or oath or whatever's necessary, perhaps Tracy will take you up to meet my husband, and show you your room, which is next to his." She paused, obviously displeased and baffled. "If you still think you can handle the position, you can start tomorrow."

"I'll start today," Mary said. "Just let me help get that friggin' bastard put away and—"

Vashti rose. "Miss O'Rourke! I find such language exceedingly offensive!"

"What language?" Mary asked, eyes rounding. "I only said—"

Vashti stalked out, shoes clicking, her head so high that not a hint of double chin showed. Tracy looked suspiciously at Mary, saw she was honestly puzzled and burst out laughing.

Geronimo slapped his thigh and handed Mary a slice of luscious mango. "Mary O'Rourke, you're one dynamite Apache! You'll do more for Don Patrick than all of my tequila!'' Grinning at Tracy, he added, "That took nerve, *chica,* cutting Blondie off at the pass. Shea still can't believe it."

Tracy's exultation began to ebb. Shea had come forcefully to the rescue, she couldn't fault him for that, but he hadn't said one approving word to her—not that she expected praise, but it wouldn't have hurt him to acknowledge that she'd helped Mary at some risk to herself.

Damn him anyway! If he wanted to think all women were awful because he'd married a faithless one, that was his problem. But his cold behavior rankled later, during the deputy's interrogation.

As Tracy explained why she had stopped, Shea listened with a remote smile, and as soon as the deputy had his information and prisoner, Shea reminded Geronimo that they had been on their way to pick up some fence posts that were still waiting for them.

Geronimo sighed and assured Mary that he'd see her soon. "Maybe you'd like to go riding," he suggested.

"I'd like that even better than working on a truck!" she assured him.

Geronimo nudged Shea. "Maybe you could come along. Have a picnic."

"I'm busy." Shea's tone was curt. But when his gray eyes rested on Tracy, that heady, dizzying surge of attraction ran between them like a high-voltage shock. "Next time you park in front of a hoodlum, you'd better have a plan. He might have shot you or run right over your little car."

Tracy gasped. "I couldn't just drive on!"

His gaze burned into her, making her weak, making her wish crazily that he'd take her in his arms, at the same time that she blazed with indignant hurt. "Maybe you couldn't," he said at last, slowly, as if forced to admit something he preferred to deny. "Did Judd go up to Phoenix this morning?"

She nodded. "It's hard on Patrick for you two to fight. Can't you—"

"No."

Wheeling away, Shea strode to the pickup. With a shake of his head and an apologetic show of his palms, Geronimo followed.

Shocked at Shea's rudeness, shaken by the hostile magnetism between them, Tracy turned to Mary. "Shall we?"

From the door, Mary called, "Mr. Scott?" Then she walked to him and shook his hand. "I'm Mary O'Rourke."

"Hello, Mary O'Rourke." He smiled slightly, looking up at her through his darkness. "You can't be the new nurse!"

"I hope I am," she laughed. "It's a long way back to town."

"You sound young—and pretty. Why do you want a job like this, taking care of a broke-down old critter like me?"

"I came because the pay was good. But now I've seen you, I'd work for board and room."

The movable white eyebrow bushed formidably. "And why is that?"

"You remind me of my grandfather."

"Then why aren't you home taking care of him?"

"He was breaking a colt last fall. It tossed him off and broke his neck."

Patrick was still a moment. He had heard the tremor at the end of Mary's statement. "That was a good way to go, Mary."

"Sure." She nodded and smiled, though tears glistened on her dark lashes. "I know that, Mr. Scott."

"Call me Patrick," he commanded. "Pull up a chair and tell me about yourself."

"She just got here, Patrick," Tracy objected, but Mary laughed and drew a seat close to the bed.

Tracy shrugged. They certainly seemed to be taking to each other, and she couldn't imagine that Patrick would attempt anything that might get *his* finger broken. Remembering Inez's tamales, she hurried down to get them from the car and tell Concha they were for Patrick's lunch.

Patrick insisted that Tracy and Mary share the tamales, along with refried beans and guacamole. He preferred to feed himself, though he spilled some, so Mary had made him an outsize napkin out of a quartered sheet that covered him from chin to waist.

"Has Geronimo met this one yet?" he asked Tracy. "He'll be jealous! She's three-quarters Apache."

"They've met," Tracy said. "Mary, didn't you tell him?"

"I thought maybe—" Mary began.

Patrick demanded to know. When Tracy had finished telling him, he swore. "Maybe Judd's right," he muttered. "If a woman's not safe on our ranch—"

"I *was* hitchhiking," Mary said. "I know it's dangerous but the bus would have dropped me twenty miles away."

Squinting at Tracy, Patrick's voice had an edge of wistful pride. "Shea plumb knocked that no-good down the arroyo?"

"After the man shot at him." Tracy laughed. "Considering everything, it's funny that the only real injury was the finger Mary broke for Blondie."

"Judd would have shot him, and good riddance," said Patrick.

"I don't think Shea or Geronimo had guns."

"Reckon not." Patrick's face twisted. "That damned war! When Shea came home, all he did for a year was drink, whore and raise hell. Went off to Mexico, then. When he went back to school, I was sure thankful, but damn it, the craziness he's got now is harder to put up with than the way he was before! Selling off cattle, hogging pasture he's not using, croaking about water!" He punched the mattress impotently with his good fist. "What I wouldn't give to be out of this bed again—able to see for myself!"

"You could always hire an independent range biologist to make a report on the land," Tracy suggested.

"Hell, that's what Shea is, a range biologist!"

"I'm no expert," Tracy said carefully. "And my memory may be tricky. But it looks to me as if there's a lot less grass than when I went away."

"It's a dry year," Patrick said testily.

"If it's dry now, when grass should be getting good, what'll it be by fall?"

Patrick gave the classic statement of all ranchers and farmers. "It's got to rain sometime."

The trouble was that a cow didn't clip off grass as a horse did. Cows wrapped their tongues around a tuft of grass and if it wasn't held by intertwining systems in the sod, it was pulled up by the roots. That left nothing to sprout when rains finally came.

Patrick knew that even better than Tracy. She hadn't come home to quarrel with him and felt a pang of contrition as he lay back, looking exhausted.

"I'll see you later," she said, kissed him, and went out.

Mary and Patrick got along so well that Tracy felt superfluous if she stayed with him very long, though he joined her in insisting that evening that Mary get out for a walk or a swim. After dinner, Tracy played the guitar for him, and Vashti came in briefly a few times. Though she all but ignored Mary, she must have been relieved that her recalcitrant husband had at last got a nurse he wouldn't try to run off.

Feeling rather useless and lonely as she went to bed early with a hefty novel she'd been saving, Tracy decided to take her camera out tomorrow. There was no telling when she might happen on a good picture, though she knew wildlife photography was very different from what she was used to. The outdoors editor of her paper had taken her out a few times and showed her how to use a blind and how to rig a camera for automatic exposures, but she suspected it would take more than that to get the kinds and numbers of shots she wanted.

If El Charco was closed to grazing, there should be considerable wildlife, especially around the earthen tanks that gave the sub-ranch its name. She'd try there. Photography didn't hurt grazing so Shea could scarcely object to that, even if she had the ill luck to encounter him.

Ill luck? Honesty made her laugh out loud at that. Shea drew her—and she'd bet that he felt the same attraction, though, damn him, he was apparently blaming her for all female transgressions since Eve! She wanted a chance to storm his cold reserve, have it out with him.

And for some reason she couldn't really name, she wanted to see him before Judd returned.

After breakfast and a visit with Patrick, Tracy left him swapping risqué tales with Mary. Putting nuts, fruit and cheese in a smaller cooler with a jug of lemonade, she got her camera gear, rubbed on sunscreen, got an old broad-brimmed hat out of the armoire and went to the garage.

Since she might be driving off the road, she took the little Toyota pickup. As any ranch vehicle should be, it was supplied with a jug of water, rope, and a shovel, in case it was necessary to dig out of either mud or sand.

Past the house turnoff, the road diminished to ruts. It wound back through the hills toward Mexico and, after perhaps ten jolting miles, continued beyond a heavy gate, though the pickup could not.

The gate was padlocked, and the fence running away from it was firmly stretched between posts, though Tracy was glad to see it was horse wire, not the usual barbed variety that could seriously damage an animal that ran into it.

So!

Frustrated, especially since she should have expected

this because of the disagreement between Shea and Judd, Tracy scanned the immovable object, grumbled under her breath and turned around. She had just passed a draw that had a seep at the far end, if her memory was right. She'd walk up the sandy wash and investigate. Early morning and evening were the best times to find wildlife, but a place with water could be frequented throughout the day.

She took a long draught of cold lemonade, put her camera pack over her shoulders, locked the pickup she'd parked off the road and started along the dry watercourse.

It was just warm enough for her to be glad of the spotty shade cast by the feathery leaves of greening mesquites and the occasional denser thatch of evergreen oak. The crisp clean air filled Tracy's lungs till they expanded with zestful well-being. It was a wonderful place to be, mountains rising in all directions beyond this stretch of hills and valleys, but her exuberance faltered when she remembered that Patrick couldn't see it.

That was bad enough, without being paralyzed, without his sons wrangling bitterly about what would be their inheritance.

A dozen Gambel's quail, black tassels bobbing with their quick clockwork steps, paraded across the wash, leaving tracked signatures. A pair of red-tailed hawks were soaring and swooping around each other, vanishing almost into the sun, then dropping near the big trees bordering the creek that ran through El Charco.

The cleft mark of deer hoofs followed the wash for a distance, then cut over the bank. An acorn woodpecker was busy at a dead trunk and scrub jays called raucously as they foraged on the slope amid small junipers. A javelina was rooting at the inside of a yucca, chewing out the succulent heart.

Tracy got out her camera and tripod, selected her zoom lens and got a dozen shots, including several of

the baby javelina that had come up to try to suckle its
feasting mother. The youngsters, like piglets except for
longer, darker, stiffer hair and a rangier build, were
adorable, but adults could be dangerous if crowded.
They had sharp tusks and could move with surprising
speed on their neat, small hoofs.

Moving on, Tracy saw lizards, a jackrabbit, a side-
winder's tracks. A cactus wren was singing and she
laughed at the heart-catching flash of a cardinal in a
mesquite.

A fine morning. It was good to be healthy and alive.
She didn't care anymore that Shea had locked his gate,
or care whether she got more pictures that day. It was
right and wonderful just to be here.

The wash curved around an island of rocks and trees.
Tracy heard a metallic clatter. Glancing toward the
edge of the island, she gasped in pure pleasure.

A ringtail! The impressive black-and-white-banded
tail was as long as the rest of the body and the small
fox-like head combined. Tracy had caught only
glimpses of the elusive little creatures before this day.
Then she saw why she was getting such a good look at
this one and cried out.

A trap held one tiny forefoot. The ringtail had
dragged the trap, which probably outweighed it, as far
as it could. The chain at the other end was anchored
around a big root.

Terrified of the human looming over it, the ringtail
tugged desperately to free itself, its mouth open in a
terrible soundless mewling.

What if it tore its foot off? How to get it loose?
Sickened as if the trap held her, Tracy knew she had to
immobilize the animal, keep it from biting while she
pried the trap apart. Putting down her pack, she
stripped off her shirt, doubled it, and folded it swiftly
over the ringtail.

It still fought. Dear God, how was she ever going to
get it out of the trap? Weeping with grief and outrage,

she tried to speak soothingly to the small beast. The rusted jaws were almost shut on the delicate foot. Even if Tracy had both hands free, she didn't see how she could get the trap open.

Maybe she could carry trap and ringtail to the pickup and drive to help. She couldn't think of any other course. Holding the furry little thing, which couldn't have weighed more than two pounds, Tracy leaned the trap against her knee and began to work at its fastening on the root.

"Now what?"

She jumped. Shea was scowling down at her. Before she could speak, he dropped to his knees, grabbed a stick and worked it between the jaws of the trap till he could grasp them with his hands and pull them apart.

Tracy saw a flash of bloodied foot as she drew back her shirt. Instead of being maimed as she'd feared, however, the ringtail was gone in a blur of black-banded tail.

"Will it be all right?" she asked shakily.

"Sure. Wild animals have great powers of recuperation."

Grateful for that but overwhelmed by horror, Tracy buried her face in her arms and sobbed. "H-how can they? How can people do that?"

"Pelts are money."

"He didn't have much more fur than a squirrel!"

Shea said with an angry movement of his shoulders, "For every valuable pelt taken, there are three 'trash' animals. They're supposed to be released but that's dangerous and trouble. The trapper clubs them and hopes next time he won't be so unlucky."

"I—I can't stand it!"

He said nothing to that but got out a handkerchief and wiped her face, made her blow her nose. His hands dropped to her bare shoulders. She glanced up at him, gave a soft cry at the lightnings flickering in his storm-gray eyes. His mouth burned hers. She flowed against him, trying to ease the pain in her breasts, the fiery yearning that swept away any need for words.

Pulling off his shirt and trousers, he spread them on the sparsely grassed bank and drew her down with him, unfastening her bra, stroking her nipples till she moaned and arched toward him, joying in his hard strength.

"You want this?" he whispered harshly.

"I—want this!"

He eased into her, slowly, for she was tight from having had no one. There was a moment of dread as her body remembered that futile assault six months ago. He caressed that away, filling her gently, then resting as she felt the magical wonder of his strong virility sheathed deeply, sweetly. She moved, questing. With a soft laugh, he began the rhythm that delighted and thrilled her, arousing her to a wild abandon. He restrained his pace, then, moving slowly, languorously till she gasped and implored him with her lifting thighs. Never, never had she felt anything like this, wanted a man so completely, longed so to be utterly his.

Then conscious thought ceased. He lifted her out of the world, into a spinning dizzying soft dark flame that kept exploding in deep, steady throbs of ecstasy.

Spent, she rested in his arms, loving the feel of his neck muscles beneath her hand, the sound of his heart beneath her ear. She sighed happily.

Now he'd say he loved her, explain why he'd been so horrid.

Instead, he put her from him, pulled on his underwear and stared down at Tracy so that she felt shamed.

Rising from his clothes at once, she dressed quickly, buttoning up her shirt though it was streaked with the ringtail's blood. He took the trap, thrust it on a ledge and crumbled sand over it. Picking up the camera gear, he looked at her as if they were chance-met strangers.

"Shall I walk you back to your pickup?"

"Oh," she said foolishly. "Did you see it?"

"That's why I followed you." Just the hint of a wry smile. "You seem to have a flair for getting into predicaments."

There was no denying that both yesterday and today she'd been very glad to see him. But why was he behaving like this? Baffled and hurt, Tracy searched his unreadable face.

"Shea—" She couldn't go on.

He was leading the way, tan pants showing the muscles of his thighs. "What?"

"I—I don't understand."

He stopped. Confronting her, he said flatly, "What's to understand? We wanted each other." His mouth curved down. "I think you're honest enough not to pretend I seduced you."

She blushed hotly. Certainly he hadn't coaxed or flattered or used force. But he had loved her with his hands, he'd pleased her, not just himself, and if there hadn't been tenderness and caring in his passion, then she'd give up on trying to sense any man's attitudes!

"Do you want me to say I'm sorry?" he continued in a tone of deadly soft ridicule.

"No! I just—" *Want you to say you love me.*

It was clear he wasn't going to do that. Fighting tears, Tracy reached for her pack. "I'm not ready to go home yet. And in the future, if you see my vehicle, you needn't worry about it. I'll be roaming around a lot for pictures."

He didn't relinquish the camera. "Don't roam up in this area, especially on weekends. You might meet some of Judd's Stronghold pupils."

"Stronghold?"

"He hasn't told you about his survival school?" Shea's voice was scornfully amused. "I'm sure he will. All I need to tell you is that one of the trainees probably set that trap, and even though they've got a hill behind their rifle range, it's smart to stay away when you get that many people playing sharpshooter."

Questions buzzed through her head, but Shea was so biased against Judd that she preferred not to ask him. They moved along in silence for a few minutes, Tracy still unable to believe he could so casually dismiss the kind of rapture they had shared.

She thought angrily that he would have to be an unusually skillful lover to make up for his nastiness the rest of the time!

As if guessing her thoughts, he threw her a tough, challenging smile. "Don't make a big deal of plain sex, Tracy. Leads to unnecessary problems."

"I don't make a big deal of 'plain sex,'" she thrust back at him.

Was that dismay in his eyes? If so, he covered it quickly. "Maybe you'd rather spread a romantic haze over it. Sorry. I'm fresh out of moonbeams and hogwash."

"Then you can have your simple, uncomplicated sex with somebody else!"

"With you, it was pretty fancy." He gave an unamused laugh, eyes touching her so that in spite of her furious hurt, a melting, quivering awareness of him trembled through her. "Don't worry. I won't force my crude desires on you." He put her pack in the truck and gave her a mocking smile. "Any time you'll settle for the basics, let me know."

He strode over to his own pickup, moving with controlled grace. Tracy sat at the wheel a moment, achingly bereft, feeling used and cast aside.

Damned if she was! She stiffened her spine and started the truck, clamping her teeth tight to keep from crying.

She had started to fall in love with him but she'd put a quick halt to that! Or if it was too late, as she miserably suspected it was, she'd at least keep clear of his demeaning propositions.

As she drove home, she had to admit that he'd been honest. According to his lights, he hadn't tricked her.

She had just been sure that he must care about her for their lovemaking to be so powerful.

Some of that golden, explosive warmth lingered within her, forcing her to admit, in spite of her humiliation, that the only thing she regretted about those ardent, wonderful moments was that they must not be repeated.

VI

THE REDTAILS WERE UP THERE AGAIN. MIGHT BE SOME eggs in that relined nest this spring after all. Shea left the pickup by the gate and started to walk the fence along the leased land. He wanted to be sure it was in good condition. The next thing he expected Judd to do was drive cattle into these pastures but claim innocence, say the fences must be down.

Shea's smile was grim as he thought of how riled Judd would be when he found that his half-brother had a permit designating the lease as an experimental area. The permit left to Shea the decision whether to graze this land.

Though grazing leases were public lands, such leases were attached to ranches and traditionally were sold along with the ranch. A rancher paid so much per head and this lease money went into the state fund for schools and other public facilities. There were about nine million acres of these "trust" lands in Arizona, more than the combined acreage of Connecticut and Massachusetts. Grazing leases also took up some of the over thirty-one million acres of federal land. If one added to that about nineteen million acres owned by Indians, only about seventeen percent of the state was under private ownership.

Take away Phoenix and Tucson and the state was still pretty much frontier with the accompanying mentality.

No one worried about what would happen when the water was gone. Developers, ranchers, agribusiness and mines were racing each other to the bottom of the aquifers, though the mines had started using recycled water.

Green, irrigated fields brought no joy to Shea. He got physically sick when he saw water running to waste along the roadsides. The groundwaters between Phoenix and Tucson had been pumped for alfalfa and cotton till the ground was buckling, scarred with cracks twenty feet wide, and it was the same story all over the state's arable lands. Make a bundle now and for as long as taxpayers foot the bill for bringing in water from far away. Get out when the water's gone or when it starts costing the grower what it should.

It was the same with the land. Overgrazed since the 1880's, a hundred years had turned grasslands to desert just as irrigating had sucked the rivers dry. The Socorro had been more careful than most about rotating graze and trimming herds to fit, but even before Patrick's blindness, Judd had been running more stock than the hundred thousand acres would support.

Shea looked approvingly at the way Boer and Lehman lovegrasses and plains brittlegrass were spreading over the pasture he and Geronimo had cleared laboriously of most mesquites. It took a bulldozer to knock down the trees and drag out their long taproots. But the hardy grasses were thriving despite the sparse rainfall.

A federal study Shea had cooperated with showed that if scrub and mesquite in southern Arizona was replaced with native grasses, the amount of groundwater saved over twenty years would be almost double what would come from the $2.5 billion Central Arizona Project in the same time, even if the heavily overcommitted Colorado River weren't sucked dry long before that. Revegetation would cost a fraction of that and would last as long as grazing was held to reasonable levels.

If Patrick could see, this grass would convince him.

Shea had to hope the looks of the field would eventually penetrate even Judd's more impervious blindness,
but he was braced for trouble when Judd came back
from a fruitless chat with the land commissioner.

Judd. Shea frowned. His half-brother had a way with
women; he'd give Tracy all the sweet talk and attention
she could want. That ought to console her if the hurt in
those wide-spaced dark amber eyes had been real.

Probably it had. As real as the tears she'd shed for
the trapped ringtail, as real as the fiery sweetness with
which she'd met him. A stab of desire went through
him, hummed through his blood. In spite of what he'd
said to her it hadn't been plain sex, though she was
apparently inexperienced enough to believe him. He
gave an involuntary snort. Did she think he went
through those shenanigans when all he wanted was
relief?

After Cele had ditched him, he'd left women alone
for a while. Then he'd tumbled everyone who seemed
agreeable and clean. Probably, when he was drunk,
some of them were not so clean. But once he went back
to school, he'd been less randy. He'd had arrangements
of convenience with several women, which he'd broken
off if they seemed to be forgetting their bargain. Since
returning to the ranch, he hadn't bothered to establish
a steady source of supply. Geronimo knew some oblig-
ing women in Nogales and that had sufficed.

Good, like a meal or drink when a man was hungry
or thirsty, but nothing like Tracy. Nothing ever had
been, not even with Cele.

That was small wonder. He and Cele had both been
kids when they married. After all these years, he felt an
ache like that from an old wound. She had been so
pretty and new and sweet, so soft and yielding. Too soft
and yielding to wait for him. Hadn't even had the nerve
to write. Patrick had done that. Shea hadn't contested
the divorce and he hadn't the faintest notion where she
was now.

Patrick had understood. All too well, for his second

wife, Elena, Shea's mother, had run off with a ranch foreman. Shea had been only three. One day there had been a beautiful, tender woman who hugged him. Then, suddenly, she was gone. It seemed like winter and the house went dark. The ranch women petted Shea and held him on their laps, but he had clambered down and run off to mourn.

Where was she? Why had she left him?

He knew now, of course, that the city-bred girl had detested the ranch and felt neglected by Patrick. She hadn't been evil. Nor was Cele. Both were sweet, appealing women.

Like Tracy?

Yes. Like Tracy. He could imagine both of them crying over a small trapped animal. But would they have risked themselves to help a stranger? Shea swore.

All right. Give the girl guts. It made her all the more dangerous. She had gotten to him, something he'd thought no woman could do. It was a good thing he'd made her so mad that she'd avoid him. A few more times with her and he'd be lost.

But he ached for her already, groaned under his breath as he remembered the sweetness of her flesh, the warm depths that embraced and held and urged him on, driving him crazy to have all of her, possess her as utterly as she had captured him.

If she came to him, he'd have to have her. The only hope he had was to make her believe it didn't matter, so that when she left at least she wouldn't take his soul.

Judd stalked into Patrick's room after dinner that night, while Tracy was playing and Mary was barbering Patrick's shaggy white curls.

With neither greeting nor acknowledgment, Judd burst out, "Dad! Did you know Shea's got himself a range research permit?"

"No," said Patrick slowly. "That mean you can't get his lease revoked because he's not running cattle?"

"That's what it means. I raised hell but he pulled

some pretty high-powered strings and he's got the right credentials."

Patrick sighed. "Well, boy, sounds like you better sell some cows."

"Don't you care?"

"I care," snapped Patrick. "But I can't see! You tell me one thing and Shea says another! You'll just have to work it out between the two of you."

Judd's breath sucked in heavily before he made an obvious effort at self-control. Shrugging, he said tightly, "Okay, I'll work it out."

Patrick introduced him to Mary, then. Judd gave her the careless, charming smile he seemed to have for all women. "Hope you'll like it here, Mary. You're a blessed change from the other nurses."

She thanked him with a calm, measured glance and went on with her task. Judd turned to Tracy. "Ready for the grand tour tomorrow?"

"You bet."

He dropped his hand caressingly on her shoulder. "How about a short tour tonight? There's a moon."

The vibrant shock that went through her at his touch was followed at once by a kind of shrinking, a revulsion from his bold, sensual appeal. Shea was the only man she wanted; her body felt mute loyalty to him, though he would have laughed at it. She certainly wasn't going to feel bound to him but she didn't want to take any moonlit walks with Judd.

Not yet. She begged off. Judd slanted a quizzical frown at her, talked a bit longer to Patrick, and went down for something to eat. When Tracy descended half an hour later, she heard his voice mingling with Vashti's in the dining room.

Bickering again. They seemed to have a touchy relationship. Perhaps the dozen years between them didn't give Vashti enough seniority to command Judd's deference. Tracy slipped almost stealthily into her room. Vashti was trying to be civil, but this wasn't a comfortable house to be in. Now that Mary was here, it wasn't necessary to be under the same roof with Patrick though Tracy wanted to stay close enough to see him daily.

The old ranch house was bursting with people. But there might be some prospector's cabin, some old line shack. Tomorrow she'd watch for such possibilities. She wanted to stay at Socorro, not only for Patrick's sake, but till she'd sorted out her own directions.

As she showered, she remembered Shea, felt a wave of remembered ecstasy followed by desolation. If he hadn't meant it, how could he have been so passionately tender? His urgency had bruised her slightly but she knew that, long after the soreness was gone, she would carry the painful magic of his physical memory in her, no matter how she fought it.

And she must fight. It was tempting to try to adopt his attitude, accept the marvelous sex and quell any personal attachment—or hope that in time he'd begin to love her. But that would violate what she felt. She wanted to laugh with him and talk with him, share thoughts and silences, show her love without fearing a cold glance from those storm-cloud eyes.

He didn't want that. All they could have was nothing.

Patrick was spinning yarns next morning, assuring Mary that he had a Ph.D. "Post-hole digging!" he chortled. "And let me tell you, you can sure hunt a long time for a mesquite straight enough to make a post!" He turned his face toward Judd's footfalls as his son came into the room. "Don't fly so low showing Tracy the ranch that you scare the cattle. Don't want any new calves to have wings in place of legs!"

"The aerial view will have to come later," Judd said. "Vashti took the plane. She had an appointment with the hairdresser and some other chores in Tucson."

"Oh, was that today?" asked Patrick. He winked his

good eye at the women. "Let's hope a little spending spree gets her mind off selling to that damn developer. You taking Tracy in your RV then, Judd?"

He smiled down at her. "Am I?"

"If you have time. Let me get my camera."

Shortly after, they were on their way, a lunch prepared by Concha in an ice chest, along with a jug of chablis. "I still want you to get the big picture from above," Judd said, flashing her a white grin. "But today you can see some cattle and we'll have a *pasear* over to Last Spring. Nice shady place to have lunch and relax a while."

"Last Spring?"

"That's what we've started calling it these dry years. Sometimes it's been the last spring running on the whole darn ranch. It's the Place of Skulls. You know, that mountain basin in the Santa Ritas where Great-great-great-grandmother Socorro killed that gang of scalp-hunters." He laughed, shaking his leonine head. With his strong neck resting solidly between broad shoulders, he was Tracy's idea of a gladiator. "Ranch lore makes her close to a saint but that scalp-hunter yarn makes me wonder!"

"I think it was really Tjúni who killed most of the men," Tracy said. "Socorro shot only one. Anyway, she couldn't have just let those men kill Apache women and children! What she and Tjúni did made Mangus their friend."

Judd laughed again. "Think what they could have done with an M-16!" His amusement faded. "From what Vashti tells me, you should have had a gun day before yesterday."

He wanted the whole story. When she finished, he struck the wheel in exasperation. "Why didn't Shea shoot the bastard?"

"Maybe he didn't have a gun. Anyway, what he did was effective."

"By the time you get through testifying against him,

he'll get a few years for assault, maybe a few more for assault with a deadly weapon." Judd snorted. "Then he'll be out to try his luck again. Triple-Great-grandmother had the right idea."

"She didn't have much choice."

Judd cast Tracy a somber glance. "We don't either, cousin. The law's no protection anymore. Especially here on the border, we're back in the days of the scalp-hunters."

"Oh, Judd, for goodness' sake!" She laughed, trying to tease him out of his Nostradamian prophecies. "There's always been smuggling on the border. I think you're looking for excitement!"

"Didn't you get more than you wanted the other morning?"

"Yes, but—"

His hand closed commandingly on hers. "I'm going to teach you to use that gun, Tracy. You need to defend yourself as much as Socorro did."

Incredulous laughter died in her throat. After what had happened to her in Houston, had almost happened to Mary right here, how could she argue with him?

"You'd like to pretend everything's nice and safe and civilized," he persisted. "Preparing for danger, arming against it, makes you admit it's there."

That wasn't all of it. Having a gun, making it part of her thinking, was like changing sides, giving in to the violence she feared and loathed. "Sometimes preparing for it makes it happen," she said.

"How?"

"Four times as many family members are murdered with handguns every year as are burglars—and that includes the ones police shoot. And how many children accidentally shoot each other?"

"Guns should be respected and kept where kids can't get them."

Tracy had to laugh at that, remembering some of the places she had penetrated in a search for Christmas presents. "Now where in the blue-eyed world would that be?"

He shrugged that aside. "Miami police are telling people to get guns. So, privately, do cops in D.C. and Los Angeles. The Arizona director of the Department of Public Safety has said crime is so bad that citizens who feel comfortable with guns should learn to use them and keep them."

His voice deepened sympathetically. "It's a hell of a thing, honey, and I wish it weren't so. But I'd rather you were kind of unhappy with me than running into trouble."

He changed the subject, asking about her work and life in Houston while telling her about his plans to raise enough alfalfa to keep the cows fed in spite of drouth. "We're growing some now," he said, pointing across the valley to fields where a soft hesitant green was darkening the plowed soil. "But to sustain the herds, we're going to have to produce a lot more."

Cattle, mostly dark red with white faces, were loitering near a metal water tank by a windmill. Old-fashioned corrals of mesquite poles placed horizontally between uprights were partially shaded by big mesquites and oaks. A salt block was licked to a crescent by patient tongues.

"Most of these go to market this fall," Judd said. "I'm trying to get another Santa Gertrudis bull, keep breeding to that strain. They're Hereford enough for good beef and Brahma enough to stand the heat and hustle."

That breed developed by the famed King Ranch in Texas had spread throughout the world where cattle foraged in arid country. Patrick had bought the first Santa Gertrudis bull and cows. The tough little "black" Mexican cattle and the Texas chinos that Patrick O'Shea had worked with had long ago been culled out to make room for heavier animals that yielded tenderer, fat-marbled meat.

"Not much for them to eat," she worried, looking around at the closely grazed land.

"There's plenty away from the tank." Judd grinned. "They're just like people—get the easy pickings first."

They made an irregular loop through the ranch, stopping at several camps where vaqueros were seeing to the calving. In cases where the mother had died, they tried to get a cow who'd lost her calf to accept the orphan by tying the dead calf's hide around it. The hide could be taken off in a few days after she'd adopted the little waif.

The southern extent of the ranch was the Mexican border, discernible by stone boundary markers and an ordinary fence. Heading north again, the jeep trail was often in sight of fences enclosing considerably better grass. Tracy thought it must be El Charco land, but didn't want to ask and set Judd off.

"Where do you have this Stronghold school?" she asked.

"I'll show you this weekend." Not far from the wash where she'd found the ringtail, Judd took a set of ruts that circled wide around the new ranch house, brought them barely in sight of the old one and crossed the highway.

Driving up a cañon with a sparkling stream of water gurgling over many-colored rocks and detouring boulders, they left desert growth behind them as they gradually ascended the dirt road that wound deeper and higher into the mountains amid pines and tall oaks. Rich chocolatey-red manzanita limbs were beginning to show tiny pink flowers among olive leaves. Giant alligator junipers often showed hopeful green on one part, though the rest might be charred by fire or lightning. Redolent of pine needles, the air was intoxicating.

Abruptly, the road dropped down to the stream and stopped. So did the RV. Judd got a gun and holster out of the back, buckled on the holster, thonging it snug above his knee, then loaded the chamber, grinning at Tracy.

"To commence your education, doll, this is a forty-four-caliber Smith and Wesson Magnum. It's the only handgun to bring down big game, uses a two-twenty-grain bullet. I have only four of those in here. The other two are snake shot, number eight, good up to about ten yards for snakes and small varmints."

"Do me a favor. Don't kill anything unless it jumps on us."

"Nothing's going to do that unless it's got hydrophobia," he scoffed.

"Then why kill it?"

"Hell, coyotes and wildcats kill calves!"

"They kill a lot more rabbits and rodents. Our outdoor editor told me five rabbits eat as much as a cow."

"Coyotes are no damn good." Judd spat against a rock. "If you don't care about calves, how about the fawns they put away?"

"Deer are beautiful, but our editor told me their natural enemies have been killed out till they often overrun an area and begin to starve. Then the hunters have to come in and 'mercifully' thin them out."

His golden eyes widened. "You rather they starved?"

"I'd rather people quit messing with natural balance. What happened when they killed out the predators in the Kaibab forest up by the Grand Canyon? Deer multiplied till they starved in droves. That was in 1906 and the country still bears the scars."

"I suppose you don't believe in poisoning coyotes!"

"Damn right I don't! Even if I believed in wholesale extermination of coyotes, which I don't, you can't poison them without getting a whole bunch of other animals. Anyhow, coyotes clean up carrion. I imagine a lot of the calves they get were already dead or so feeble they couldn't make it."

He stared at her as if he couldn't believe his ears, ran

his hand through his close-clipped hair. She could almost see him deciding to make allowances for her female ignorance. "You've been away too long, Tracy. Got brainwashed by city people who don't know their ass from a hole in the ground." He gave her a brief, conciliatory hug. "Come on, let's amble up to the spring and have lunch." He laughed and brushed a kiss across her ear. "I'm hungry as a—as a coyote!"

They crossed the stream on boulders rising above the flow, Judd surefooted in spite of the food cooler and blanket he carried, and were in a lovely basin perhaps a mile wide. Enclosed by pine-covered slopes and rose-gold sandstone palisades, the center of the park had better grass than the rest of the ranch, and white-trunked stands of aspens patterned themselves ethereally against somber pines.

A small log cabin stood in a broad clearing, shaded by an immense oak. The log outhouse was tucked discreetly among young aspens. A shed stood by an old corral. There was a hand-pump outside the cabin, and firewood stacked beneath the roof that extended out far enough to form an outside room. She'd forgotten the old line shack, but it struck her at once as a wonderful place to escape the troublous politics of Vashti's house. Without lying a bit, she could say it was a much better place for photographing wildlife.

"No one seems to be using this," she said.

"Not for years on a regular basis. This is just a small pocket in the National Forest, a hundred acres, home-steaded for the spring. Can't run enough cattle to make it worthwhile. Some developers have offered a bundle for it but Dad's stubborn as a mule when it comes to getting rid of any of the original holdings."

Tracy wandered over and opened the creaky door. Not so bad as she'd expected. One big room with a wood cookstove, table and chairs, and a small bed-room. The old iron bedstead was intricately scrolled and the springs were in good shape, but there was no mattress. Pegs for clothes, a chest of drawers with a tin-framed Mexican mirror above it.

All the furniture was homemade, rough and sturdy. The shelves in the main room held a few old books and magazines and a supply of canned foods, dishes and cooking utensils. A neatly lettered yellowing sign said in Spanish and English: "Eat if you are hungry, and be welcome. Please cut wood to replace what you use and leave everything in good order."

By ranch tradition, such signs were in all the line shacks. Shelter and food could save the lives of lost hikers or hunters, but Mexican workers, illegal or legal, probably benefited most.

Judd's lips thinned. He crumpled the old cardboard and stuck it in the stove. "We ought to stop encouraging drifters and bums, but Patrick won't hear of locking the shacks and keeping food out of them."

Tracy glanced around at the neat, though dusty and cobwebbed rooms. "No one seems to be abusing the policy."

"It's asking for trouble," Judd said flatly. "Let's go on up to the spring." As he steered her out of the house, his hand was warm beneath her elbow, and he laughed down at her. "Bring your bikini?"

"Darn it, no," she groaned. "And that's a terrific warm spring! I used to luxuriate in that big rock bathtub."

"Skinny-dipping?"

"What else?"

"Don't let me stop you," he challenged. "I'll even turn my head."

"Thanks, but I'll give it a miss today."

"Cowardy-cat!"

"You bet."

He put down the cooler and flipped the blanket as they reached the natural stone basin where the spring flowed from a cleft in the rocks, before overflowing and forming the stream that ran down the cañon. Dappled sun played on rocks and water, clinching Tracy's decision.

If Patrick consented, she was moving over here. She could visit him every day, but be out of range of Vashti's moods—and Judd's charm that might sweep her into an affair with him, when it was that maddening, unexplainable half-brother of his that she loved.

She had no intention of capitulating to Shea's contemptuous terms, but in spite of all he'd said she didn't want anything to block his way if he decided to move toward her.

Judd made a muffled sound and took her in his arms. Startled, she pushed vainly at his chest but he laughed and set his hand behind her head, holding her as his mouth closed on hers, hard and sure and smiling. Strength drained from her. Molten, heavy blood weighed her down. But she didn't want to feel this way, not with anyone but Shea.

If he could see them— A flash of gray eyes seared her. She wrested her lips away with a sobbing gasp.

Judd released her. "You leave some guy in Houston? Or are you still shook up over that psycho? If it's that, doll baby, you can't freeze up forever."

"I—" She searched for an explanation that wouldn't involve his pride, though she swore at doing so. Why should a woman have to apologize if she didn't care to have sex with a man? She gave a shaky laugh. "I guess it feels like incest, Judd."

He roared at that, showed the tip of his little finger. "About that much we're related! Hell, we could get a dispensation from the Pope!"

"All the same," she said firmly. In control of herself once more, she knelt and began to get out the food.

Judd sighed, poured wine into plastic glasses, and said, "That's not it, cousin. Those electric charges between us sure aren't incest. It must be what that creep in Houston did."

It was a better excuse than hers. But he had a cure. "Tracy, sweetheart, the best way to kick that is to erase it with some mighty good lovemaking."

The way an electric brush rubs off scars? When she said nothing, he handed her a glass, clicked his own to it. "I want you, Tracy. But I'm not a horny kid. I can be patient." He swallowed his wine in one draught and laughed, teeth very white in his brown face. "To a point."

VII

VASHTI'S FIRST LOOK OF RELIEF AT TRACY'S DECISION TO move was followed by a narrowing of dark-green eyes. "I can understand your needing more solitude for your work, dear, but way off like that in the wilds! We can find something closer to us. In fact, there's quite a cozy worker's cottage empty down behind the swimming-pool wall."

"Thanks, but to get the sort of wildlife shots I need, I'll have to be fairly remote." They were in Patrick's room, where she'd made the announcement, and now she turned to him, taking his hand. "No one's using the cabin, Patrick. Won't it be all right if I do?"

"I've sheltered there many a night," he remembered. "Prettiest place on the whole ranch." The left side of his mouth tugged up mischievously. "Guess you aren't scared of those scalp-hunters' ghosts?"

It was the terror by night, the terror inside, the strangling grip of a man's hands and cruel body, that still brought her nightmares and woke her with her own screams.

"Those scalpers ceased to be a problem to anyone over one hundred and thirty years ago," she said.

"But illegals—" protested Vashti. Her lips pinched thinner. "Thanks to you, Patrick, they consider our line shacks Triple-A approved motels!"

He said mildly, "The people who started this ranch

91

came up from Mexico before this area belonged to the United States, and Patrick O'Shea was a refugee from Ireland's potato famine. Marc Revier fled political tyranny in Germany, Talitha's Mormon family had been hounded out of the States. Hell, Vashti, only the Indians were here to begin with!"

"All very stirring," she gibed, "but illegals are overrunning the border from Texas to California, and something's got to be done about it."

Patrick hitched his good shoulder. Iron replaced the dogged mildness. "As long as I'm alive, there'll be shelter and food for those that come this way." He squeezed Tracy's hand. "Use the cabin and welcome, honey, but you'll come see me?"

"Every day, if I can have the use of a vehicle or horse."

"You'll have both," he said. "And any furniture you need. But there's no electricity. We'll get that put in, and a phone."

"Not just yet," she said. "Let me be sure it's going to work before anyone goes to a lot of trouble."

"Very wise," Vashti approved. "And don't stay there out of stubbornness, dear, if you find it vilely uncomfortable and lonesome."

"It sounds like a super place," Mary said.

"Well, why don't you help her get settled?" Patrick suggested. "Get the egg off my chin after breakfast in the morning and take the rest of the day off."

"But—"

Vashti looked irritated but gave a small shrug. "It's all right, Mary. Concha and I have to manage on your regular days off so one more hardly matters."

"Concha and *I* can manage when it comes to that," Patrick said with a gruffness that didn't conceal his wince at Vashti's long-suffering tone. "Go swim and sun, Vashti. Fly to town. Or go to hell!" His voice choked off before he added fiercely, with a glare of his sightless eyes, "I don't want anyone in this room who doesn't want to be here!"

"Darling!" Vashti wailed. "I didn't mean it like that! You—you've gotten so touchy and unreasonable!" She bent over him. To Tracy's astonishment, a few tears splashed on his veined hand. "I—I love you, Patrick. It just kills me to see you like this. If you're going to start thinking—"

Awkwardly, he patted her hand, "Don't, baby! I know it's a hell of a thing for you."

Exchanging incredulous glances, Tracy and Mary went quietly out. "Maybe I've been doing her wrong," Tracy said.

Mary cocked a dark eyebrow. "That one? Not a chance."

"She couldn't have expected this when she married Patrick. She's a young, vital woman and—"

"She doesn't spend a minute more than she has to with him and when she touches or kisses him—well, it's in every line of her! She'd as soon kiss a corpse."

It was almost what Vashti herself had said. "She could feel that way and still love him," Tracy argued.

Mary shook her head. "You need a keeper, lady—or a bodyguard. Don't you know why she wasn't keen on your using that cabin?"

"It was clear she wasn't but why it should matter to her is beyond me."

Mary started to burst out with something, then bit it back. "Anyhow, it sounds like a nifty place. Can I come see you on my days off?"

"I hope you will. We can go to town once in a while if you like. I'll have to get groceries and stuff."

"That'll be fun, too." A grim look crossed Mary's frank face. "I sure like your great-uncle, Tracy. He's one of that old breed like my grandpa, and we won't get more like them. But that woman drives me up the wall!"

Tracy's heart sank. "You aren't planning to quit?"

"I'm crazy about Patrick and the pay's good," said Mary cheerily. A wicked glitter lit her eyes. "When she's more than I can stomach, I start Patrick on his stories. That sends her off like a cow with a twisted tail!"

"Maybe I should feel sorry for Vashti," Tracy chuckled. "But I'm mighty glad *you're* here so I can leave!"

Lathe-thin Roque Sanchez was summoned to move a mattress, rocking chair, desk and several rugs over to the Last Spring cabin. Tracy and Mary followed in the yellow Toyota, which was loaded with food, bedding, books and other gear.

Roque hitched a chain to a big fallen cottonwood and dragged it across the stream to form a crude bridge, hacking off branches so the top was fairly smooth. The women helped him get the mattress across, swept out the cabin and carried over the Toyota's contents while he unloaded the big truck.

By noon, everything was in the little house, though most awaited permanent locations. Roque, smiling shyly, accepted their invitation to fried chicken, potato salad, minted iced tea and crusty apple pie. He offered to split more wood before leaving, but Tracy assured him that she would only be cooking a meal a day so the present supply should last a while. He showed her how to work the damper, filled the reservoir with water, pumped two steel buckets full and left somewhat reluctantly.

"He's too polite to say so, but I'm sure the Sanchezes all think I'm insane," Tracy grinned, as she poured more tea from the thermos.

"No more iced tea," Mary reminded. "And no instant hot water—or cold, for that matter."

"I will miss a shower."

"And a toilet?"

Tracy shrugged. "That little log outhouse has a lot of charm. I won't mind at all while it's warm. And if I'm still here come autumn, that'll be time to think about electricity and plumbing."

She felt silly about putting it into words, but for a

time she looked forward to living almost as her ancestresses had. Of course, she had the truck and all the
resources of a great ranch half an hour away, but in this
nearly untouched basin, it was easy to feel on her own.
Mary read her, though, and laughed delightedly.

"Playing pioneer? Tracy, you're a panic!"

Tracy grinned. "I've got one big luxury—that stone
bathtub with an unending supply of warm water. What
a place to soak! I won't use soap or shampoo in it, of
course, out of respect to the critters that drink from it
farther down."

They washed the windows inside and out and hung
the loose-woven natural cotton curtains Concha had
volunteered to sew from an Indian bedspread. The
braided rug in the main room was colored like autumn
leaves, flame, yellow and orange-brown. The rocker
had old gold cushions and a footstool to match.
Scrubbed shelves were covered with yellow vinyl adhesive, cookware and foodstuffs near the stove, books
and a few treasures on the long wall.

The red-tailed hawk carved by James-Fierro was
poised on a mesquite gnarl on the highest shelf, com-
manding the room. Tracy had placed the little blue bird
on the bedroom chest beside the old Spanish doll. The
oval hooked rug was done in shades of blue and the bed
was covered by an old blue-and-white star quilt Great-
grandmother Christina had made.

"There!" Mary placed a small hand-blown amber
vase filled with dry seed pods and bright fern in the
center of the table. "It looks like something right out of
a fairy tale—one of those huts Hansel and Gretel or
Goldilocks were always poking their noses into!"

"You grew up on *those* stories?"

Mary wrinkled her pert nose. "Sure. Think I'm
disadvantaged or something? But my Apache grandmother told me the ones I liked best. About White-
Painted Woman and her son Born-of-the-Water who
killed all the monsters." Mary laughed pridefully. "Her

mother was a friend of Lozen, Victorio's warrior sister and a great medicine woman. And Gran's uncle was one who stayed in the Mexican Sierra Madre with the Apache Kid and never was caught."

"Hey, tell Geronimo that! He's descended from the Kid."

"Haven't seen him. Or Shea, either. Patrick won't say it but I can tell he misses that hardheaded red-head."

So do I. Tracy turned to hide her face. "Want a revel in the spring before I take you home?"

"That'd be great!"

Mary got a thick towel and took herself off to the immense stone basin a few hundred yards from the cabin. Tracy filled the copper tea kettle, laid a fire ready to be set, and finished distributing her clothes between the curtained pole "closet" Roque had fixed, the chest of drawers and an old leather-bound trunk in the corner.

When Mary returned, glowing from her frolic, long black hair damp, the sun was starting down the western sky. "You sure you don't want me to stay all night?" Mary asked. "Patrick said I could."

"Thanks, but I'm sure he misses you already," Tracy said.

She drove Mary to the house, ran in quickly to tell Patrick how perfect the cabin was. "That's fine," he grunted, leveling a warning finger at her. "But you be sure you get over here every day or let me know you're not coming! Otherwise, I'll send someone to check."

With evening coming on, she wasn't inclined to object to that much mother-henning. "I'll be over," she promised, kissed him and thanked Mary again. But when she got downstairs she hesitated.

The gun Judd had given her. Should she take it?

She didn't approve of a handgun under every pillow, but remembering that terrible night in Houston and the recent encounter with Mary's attacker, she sighed unhappily, went to her old room and picked up the little automatic.

The sun was down when she parked across the stream, and twilight was beginning by the time she got the kerosene lamp lit and the fire going.

What was it about darkness that made a person want to be comforted by light? The feeling of helplessness because one couldn't see? How terrible it must be for Patrick, then. And not to be able to move half of his body! Thank goodness, Mary seemed a tonic for him.

Tracy made a cheese omelet and green salad. When the romaine and spinach in the ice chest were gone, she'd have to depend on sprouts and wild greens till she could grow some of her own, or replenish her supply daily from the ranch. That went against the self-sufficiency she wanted to enjoy. Maybe it *was* playing pioneer, but it would be fun to see how independently she could subsist.

It was cool enough to keep the fire going so she put garbanzos or chick peas on to simmer, made a pot of mint tea, and sat down at the table to go through cookbooks and make lists.

With a starter and dried milk, yogurt could be made indefinitely. She loved it with berries or honey and it made a tangy, nutritious substitute for milk in baking, soups, and casseroles. She'd always wanted to bake her own bread. This was the time to do it. She'd have to buy lots more soybeans. As well as the simple ways to use them, they could be made into a sort of curd that had a hundred uses.

She'd buy pounds of sprouting seeds: her favorite alfalfa, so crisp and succulent on grilled cheese and in salads, its vitamin count hundreds of times greater than that of the seed; tangy radish, cress and cabbage; mung, so good in Chinese dishes. And herbs! She'd have an herb garden.

Black beans, pintos and navy beans. Bulghur for

pilaf and tabouli. Brown rice, lentils, split peas, dried fruit. Nuts. It was quite a list, but at last she stretched and surveyed it with a yawn of satisfaction.

She could eat very well, without a refrigerator, frequent trips to town or dependency on the ranch. And there had to be wild foods, the ones Papago Tjúni had taught Socorro about. Hadn't they been gathering berries on a slope above this very basin when they killed the scalp-hunters who were slaughtering Apache women and children?

There was a sound outside. Tracy's spine chilled and she held her breath. There weren't any ghosts! Maybe a deer or javelina. Then she heard unmistakable footfalls on the hard earth outside the door.

The curtains were pulled but she didn't know how opaque they were. She got the automatic, flicked off the safety and reminded herself that the intruder might be a hungry but harmless illegal, hiker or hunter.

"Who is it?" she called at the same time as a soft knock, followed by Geronimo's voice.

"Open up, *chica!* I brought you a present."

Laughing in relief, she put the gun on the top shelf and unlocked the door. Geronimo stood grinning in the spill of light.

"Next time," she said breathlessly, "how about giving a few toots of your horn from the other side of the creek?" Then she saw the giant dog beside him, the size of a small calf, and gasped. "What in the world is that?"

"A Rhodesian Ridgeback," he said somewhat aggrievedly.

"A which?"

The beast made a soft sound in its throat and advanced on Tracy with squirmings of delight. It looked something like an outsized Dalmatian but had a tawny sleek coat striped with black down the back. The hopefully moving tail was black-tipped. The dog licked Tracy's hand and settled at her feet with a sigh of great content.

Geronimo beamed. "He likes you."

"What," demanded Tracy, "is this all about?"

"If you're going to stay over here alone, you need a good dog."

"One that could eat me for breakfast?"

"Le Moyne's a lamb with women. Loves 'em!" The dog thumped his tail as if in agreement. Geronimo stroked his head. "He's pretty special. The Boers needed a good farm dog that could hunt lions and protect people without being vicious, and with short hair to discourage ticks. They put together the Hottentot dog, bloodhound, greyhound and Great Dane. This is what they developed."

"Just a simple little farm dog," Tracy said, now able to identify the loose skin around the eyes as bloodhound heritage as the flipped-up ear was the greyhound's. "Lord, Geronimo, I can't keep him! I don't have any dog food and—"

"I brought a hundred-pound bag of dry stuff and a case of canned. Anyhow, he'll eat scraps. Just for the sociableness of it."

"I wonder how he'll like soybeans," Tracy muttered. "Look, Geronimo, it's kind of you, but—"

"Shea says you have to have a dog."

"Then why didn't he bring it?"

Geronimo's eyes slid away. "He—uh—he was busy."

Tracy was torn between resentment at him for not coming himself and treacherous gladness that he'd at least worried about her a little. She had always liked animals, and once she decided Le Moyne wasn't to eat her, she found his streamlined solidity as comforting as his immediate fealty was endearing.

"I don't know," she worried. "I hate to get fond of him and then have to leave him when I go away."

Geronimo scowled. "Go away? Why do you want to do that?"

"I won't as long as Patrick needs me. But I wouldn't stay here at Vashti's sufferance."

The barrel-chested, dimpled big man shrugged.

"Well, you don't have to plan it all out now. If you leave, maybe Shea'll find another lady to keep Le Moyne happy."

Improbable as that seemed, it sent a pang of jealousy through her. Yielding to what seemed to be inevitable, she helped Geronimo bring in the dog food and several big earthenware dishes. Le Moyne lapped up some water and politely crunched a few chunks of food before stretching out on the rug by Tracy's chair.

Geronimo cautiously sipped mint tea and ate half a carrot cake as he told her Le Moyne was very quiet. "He won't attack unless you order it or someone's trying to hurt you," he explained. "If you yell 'Charge!' he'll hit the target at shoulder level and bay as he springs."

When she said she was forgoing electricity and plumbing till fall but would like a shower, he promised to rig up a gravity-flow one like that at El Charco. He cleared his throat, then shyly asked how Mary was getting along. When Tracy told him Mary's great-great-uncle had been a companion of the Apache Kid's, Geronimo whooped.

"No wonder she's the first lady I thought I could stand getting married to." His dark eyes sought Tracy's anxiously. "Think she likes me?"

"She likes you," Tracy assured him. "More than that, you'll have to ask her."

With assurances that he'd get over as soon as possible to fix the shower and anything else Tracy decided would be handy, he took his leave, giving Le Moyne a farewell scratch between the ears.

As his whistling dimmed, Tracy gazed at Le Moyne. "I'm surprised your master didn't teach you to bite women on sight," she said drily.

Le Moyne opened an eye and thumped his tail. "Well, my lad," Tracy told him, as she dipped water from the reservoir into the enamel washbasin. "I confess I'll sleep easier with you here. You'd scare a

miscreant worse than that little gun, and besides it can't
wag its tail."

More than that, Shea had sent him.

She slept well that night beneath the lavender-
scented quilt and woke to sun filtering through the
heavy cotton curtains. It was nippy so she put on
slippers and her robe before she went around opening
all the curtains to let the sun spill in. She let Le Moyne
out and built a fire, both for warmth and making
breakfast.

Removing one of the round lids above the fire, she
made toast on a perforated pan lid while frying two
eggs. It all tasted delicious. Le Moyne was back and
padded after her as she made the bed and did the
dishes.

"I don't know what to do with you while I go see
Patrick," she mused to the dog. "You haven't been
here long enough to think it's home, but I hate to tie
you up or leave you inside." The best solution seemed
to be to take him along and ask one of the yard men to
keep an eye on him.

This worked well enough. Le Moyne was content to
rest in the cool damp earth behind the rosebushes in
the courtyard. Patrick chuckled at her description of
the animal but said he was glad to know she had such a
protector.

"And don't be stubborn about doing without electricity and such," he urged, patting her hand.

She had lunch with him and Mary, then collected Le
Moyne and drove off without having seen either Judd
or Vashti. Patrick wouldn't expect her next day since
she'd told him she was going to Tucson to lay in
supplies.

Le Moyne preferred to swim the creek rather than
try the log, so she ordered him to stay out and drip
while she unlocked the door and stepped inside.

The Ridgeback made a deep-throated sound as her

arm was caught and she was hiked to one side while the door slammed against Le Moyne's charge. The thud of his heavy body shook the cabin, rattling pans and dishes.

Tracy recognized Judd before she had much chance to be scared. "What's this about?"

He hefted the automatic he'd given her. "It's about what good this will do you if you leave it on a shelf! It's to show you not to put all your faith in that big mutt! I could be killing you right now and what could he do about it?"

Her anger rose. She called Le Moyne, reassuring him, and glared at Judd. "How did you break in?"

He laughed. "I have a key. Same one fits all the line shacks. That means any vaquero could get in."

"No vaquero would," she thrust.

"Tracy!" This wasn't going as he'd planned. She was accusing instead of on the defensive. Less brashly, he put the gun on the table and opened his hands placatingly. "Baby, if I didn't care about you, I wouldn't bother!" He glanced disparagingly about the room she was so proud of. "I wish I'd heard about this in time to stop it! But you'll get enough in a week or so." He grinned charmingly, tracing her cheek with his finger. "I won't even say 'I told you so!' "

She opened the door and Le Moyne came warily in, lips peeled back slightly from his teeth. He sank down on the rug at Tracy's command but he never took his eyes off Judd.

"That's one vicious monster," Judd growled. "I'm surprised Shea wished him off on you."

Tracy stood close to the Ridgeback. "He's gentle and sweet with me," she said, then smiled. "But he makes me feel quite safe."

"I showed you that was an illusion," Judd pointed out. "Even if I hadn't had a key, I could have broken in a window."

"I could doubtless stage some scary scenarios at the

big house in spite of all your guns," she retorted. "Of course, everyone's vulnerable to some degree."

"That degree lessens a lot if you know how to defend yourself." He took her hands, brought them to his face in a disarming gesture. "I don't want to scare you or make you mad, but Tracy, doll, you have to face realities."

"I think I am. I'm not sure it's worth living a longer life if you have to go armed, walk in fear, and be ready to kill any stranger before he kills you."

Judd shook his curl-clipped head. "You're looking at it wrong. After you've been to a Stronghold session, you'll see."

"Judd, I'm not sure—"

"I'll pick you up Saturday morning at seven," he said and was gone before she could argue.

VIII

STILL NOT SURE THAT LE MOYNE WOULD STAY AT THE cabin without her, Tracy took him with her to Tucson and left him in the front of the pickup with the windows partway down while she raided natural food and hardware stores.

Once home, she poured her staples into big tight-sealing plastic containers, labeled them, and ranged them on the shelf with the glow of satisfaction she thought people had experienced ever since some Neanderthal lady surveyed her hoard of nuts and seeds.

Dried milk didn't have to be boiled to kill bacteria, so it was simple to heat it to lukewarm and mix it with yogurt starter in a glass bowl, which she set in the warmest sun and covered with a dark plate that would absorb more heat.

The experiment she was most eager to try and most dubious about was a dog-food recipe she'd found in one of her books, soybeans, soy sauce, brewer's yeast, dried milk, wheat germ, eggs and chopped onion, mixed and lightly sautéed.

Le Moyne wolfed down four patties without seeming to take a breath. "Maybe you *can* survive without horsemeat," she laughed. He escorted her to the hot spring where she had a delightful soak and then briskly rubbed dry in the late sunlight.

"You'll keep the birds and wild critters away," she

told him. "So you can't always come along. But you relieve my mind, Le Moyne, and you're a very good listener."

He wriggled at that and they raced to the house, Le Moyne holding back for her.

Next morning the dog gave a softly whispered growl minutes before Tracy could hear the crunch of Judd's footsteps. "It's all right, Le Moyne." Getting her camera and tape recorder, she took him outside, and left a big bowl of water and some of his crunchies. "Stay here and guard the house."

He trotted hopefully beside her. "Stay!" she said more emphatically.

His ears drooped but he stopped obediently, nor did he run after them as they crossed the stream and got into the RV. "Pretty well trained," Judd grudgingly approved.

Tracy nodded but felt guilty as she glanced back at where the Ridgeback stood forlornly in the clearing. If she stayed very long at Last Spring, she'd probably have to get another dog to keep him company!

"Got your automatic?" Judd asked.

"It's in my camera bag. But if I'm getting a story, I won't have much time for a lesson on how to use it."

"I can teach you all you need to know in ten minutes," he said. "Not much you can do with that but shoot someone at fairly close range! What I want you to get today is an idea of the choice of weapons you have and the sort of potential they possess."

"Does the session run all weekend?"

"Yes, but it's not so tightly organized as some courses because it's a mixed group. About ten are individuals and families and the other twenty are from a church."

"A church!"

"You bet. Haven't you heard of the Posse Comitatus in Wisconsin or the Christian Patriots Defense League? They hold their own training courses."

She said slowly, "So do the KKK and the American

Nazis. The whole idea scares me, Judd. We have a mixed society with a lot of different interests. If each little segment starts arming itself and holding maneuvers, there has to be trouble sooner or later."

"The idea's to prevent trouble," he said, with an indulgent smile for her dismay. "And don't forget the Jewish Defense League and the Brown Berets!"

"It's scary that they've reason to feel they had to defend themselves!"

He shrugged. "Don't you get the picture yet, baby? Don't you know who's really threatened these days? The average white working-class American! Everything they've worked for is slipping away and they're damn sure going to fight for what they have left."

Tracy stared at him as he took a road she hadn't yet been on. "People can vote, Judd. We've got laws—"

He said brutally, "What good did that do you the night that crazy got his hands around your throat?"

She flinched but retorted sharply, "Do you think we should make fortresses of our homes and cars and wear guns as if this was a hundred years ago?"

"That's what I do think." He glanced sideways at her, golden eyes smoldering, gave a short laugh. "You'll understand after today."

A hill formed a natural backstop for the firing range where a few people were practicing on a variety of targets, some stationary, others revolving. A long prefab served as a cafeteria and lecture hall. Every imaginable sort of truck, RV or camper was parked outside. As Tracy and Judd approached, curtains opened and a projector was switched off.

Standing in front of the screen, a rosy-cheeked white-haired man with pale-blue eyes raised both hands and cried to the score of people in the folding chairs, "Godless forces are surrounding the Children of Light everywhere on this sin-cursed earth! In this America, they are trying to take away your birthright, subvert a nation founded under God. Brothers and sisters, it is your solemn duty to defend yourselves and your country!"

A round of applause and shouts of approval. "Go to your training now," exhorted the pink-cheeked leader. "Armor yourselves with righteousness and this thought: You aren't shooting to kill. You are shooting *to live!*"

Cheering him again, the people filed out. There were fourteen men and three women mostly under the age of forty, and three children aged about ten to fourteen. Tracy told Judd she'd like to interview the minister.

"All right, but watch where you're going when you come out," he said. He slipped a whistle with a chain around her neck. "If you don't see me, just whistle."

The Reverend Albert Pencker was gratified at the interview. "People need to be warned," he said. "Terrible days, young woman. But we must make ready to resist Antichrist." His church was called the Children of Light. "Based on the Gospels, young woman," he emphasized, as he might have said "young serpent." "Our doctrine is one hundred percent Jesus Christ and Him crucified."

Tracy blinked. "I thought Jesus said to love one's enemies and do good to those who offend you."

"We do pray that our enemies will see their errors and be saved," Pencker said without fluttering a silver eyelash. "But I tell you the Beast, that monster of Revelation, is already among us."

"Would you explain that, sir?"

"In the last days, the Beast will rule. No one will be able to buy or sell without having his number stamped on their forehead." The minister's voice sank to a whisper. "Young woman, how often have you wanted to pay cash and been told a credit card was preferred?"

"Credit card?" Tracy couldn't keep amazement out of her voice. "You think the card companies are the Beast or Antichrist or whatever?"

"Not exactly. But what makes their use possible, what checks your tax returns, fouls up your bank account, scrambles your health records, swathes you in printouts? What makes mistakes that no one can unravel and is utterly unreachable by reason or entreaty?"

"Computers!"

"That's it," beamed Pencker. "And when rioting and violence are so terrible that people will long for any kind of peace, the Beast will take control of the computers and rule the whole world."

Tracy asked Pencker a few more questions. As the Beast haunted his future, so Communism, crime and inflation haunted his present. Flipping off the tape recorder, she asked him to let her take a few pictures, for which he posed with a beatific smile. Then he picked up a rifle and started to join his flock.

"What sort of weapon is that?" Tracy asked.

He patted the barrel. "An AR 18. I like it because it fires faster than the Heckler & Koch 91. Manually, it can get off twenty rounds in five seconds but this one's automatic. I just squeeze the trigger and it rips off twenty rounds in one-point-eight seconds." He smiled again and went out.

Tracy reran a little of the tape to check the sound level and, satisfied with the quality, grabbed her camera and hurried out of the prefab and into—a nightmare.

The sun was dazzling, yet darkness kept filling Tracy, an enveloping horror that made her see the world around her in dizzying flashes, like speeded frames of a movie, sound coming and going in bursts. People blazing away at man-shaped targets that spun and dangled crazily. Faces hard or eager or fearful. Children shrieking: "I hit him! Look! Right in the heart!"

She almost screamed as a man loomed over her. Her own terrified face stared back at her, tiny and distorted, from reflecting glasses that turned the black face into an eerie mask with a tuft of sparse beard. Spotted camouflage clothes made the apparition seem a huge serpent.

Shrinking back, she was braced by Judd's hard arm and his deep voice. "This is Pardo. Learned his trade in

Nam. He was Infantry, extended to be a helicopter door gunner. Pardo, Tracy's just taking photos today but she'll be back for some personal coaching."

The impenetrable mirrored glasses came off. Now that she could see his eyes, she liked something about his face even before a smile warmed it. "Pleasure, Tracy. Anyone messes with you, I can sure show you how to blow 'em away."

He sounded his whistle. Everyone hurried over, all with rifles or pistols. Some had both. Children gripped .22's. An almost tangible odor of excitement filled Tracy's nostrils, a dull sickening taint like that of old blood. Again swirling darkness clouded the bright day. She lay pinned to the driveway in Houston, gasping, struggling . . .

Pardo's voice. Her brain fumbled, could not decode words. When she could see again, Pardo had vanished but the group was surging forward.

"They'll try to track him down," Judd said. His mouth seemed full and fleshy. "Come on, let's see the action."

Six times in the next hour, Pardo rose up from thickets, dropped from trees, emerged from hollows in the earth. Never was he seen till he chose to be. Frustration grew, especially among the men.

"Next time he pops up like a jackrabbit, I've a notion to crease the inside of his pants," muttered a husky, sunburned, blond young man.

Judd said pleasantly, "Mister, you stifle that kind of talk or you can turn around and leave." He added gently, though his stare made the blond man's drop, "You may be behind Pardo, but I'm behind you."

Pardo ran them back from the creek, fanning them out and telling them to hunker behind the nearest cover at one whistle, drop flat on two, and fire at three. By the time they got back to headquarters they were dusty, scratched and hot.

During the break for coffee or soft drinks, Tracy

talked to several women. One was a fragile brown-haired girl with pansy-velvet eyes. She was a nurse. Leaving a Tucson hospital one night, she'd been forced into her car by an armed man who'd made her drive out in the desert. He'd raped and beaten her, left her for dead in an arroyo. She had crawled to a house. That was over a year ago and her body had healed but her dark eyes filled with tears as she said brokenly, "I still have bad dreams. I sleep with the light on and have to use sleeping pills."

"If you'd had a gun, could you have gotten it out and used it before your attacker could have shot you?" Tracy asked.

The small woman stiffened. "I don't know. Probably not. But when I work the night shift now, I keep my gun in my hand while I'm walking to my car."

"What if a friend startled you and you shot before you recognized him?"

"Any friend of mine had better know not to come up on me suddenly," the young nurse said. She shivered, hunching her shoulders. Tracy knew exactly how she felt.

An older woman, overweight and breathless from exertion, said she was taking the course because she and her husband ran a neighborhood store that had been robbed twice that year. "It's awful," she sighed, wiping her face with a tissue. "Used to be we knew everybody who came in. Gave credit, delivered free to shut-ins. People were more than customers, they were friends. But these days—" She made a gesture of bewilderment.

The men were examining each other's weapons. Pencker's AR 18 and the similar-looking but manually fired Armalite 180 were in high favor, with the Heckler & Koch 91 heavy assault rifle also popular. The most popular handgun was the Colt Commander .45. A licensed dealer was offering to get anyone interested a deal on Remington 870 Bushmasters.

"Fires the same round as the M-16," he explained.

"There's a $200 federal tax and you've got to be checked out and given a permit by the Bureau of Alcohol, Tobacco and firearms, but I can still give you a bargain if three or more of you take one."

With a blast on the whistle, Judd announced there would now be instruction in the care of weapons and individual marksmanship coaching. Advanced students could practice with the Remington or one of the other Stronghold machine or sub-machine guns.

"Now," said Judd, steering Tracy over to face a man-shaped target twenty feet away. "Try for accuracy first, then for speed. Remember, you've got six shots. It takes just one."

Only one of the first load hit the target, and in the foot, at that. Judd blew his breath through his teeth. "Boy, do you need practice! Load up and try again."

Ten minutes later, she was hitting the target half the time, though she still had a tendency to shut her eyes and lower the barrel when she fired. When she hit the valentine pinned where a heart would be, Judd gave her a hug and a boisterous kiss.

"That's the way, doll. Told you you could learn!"

"An apt pupil," came a cold voice behind them. "I doubt if she's the hotshot I've come to see you about, though."

They whirled. Tracy flushed, for some reason feeling judged and guilty at Shea's icy stare. Judd grinned hardily. "Why did you come, little brother?"

"Someone shot a deer on my place the last day or two. Field dressed it and packed the meat over here."

"Can you prove it?"

"Someone's eating venison."

Judd said testily, "It's out of season, even if your place wasn't posted, so do you think whoever did it is going around telling people? Hell, no! He'll have it stowed away in ice chests."

"Let's have a look at those ice chests, then."

Judd's eyes blazed. "You're not a game warden and damned if you can do that to my students!"

"Why not? Call it a man practicing to defend his property." Shea started to saunter toward the parked vehicles.

"Pardo!" Judd yelled.

The tall black strode over, eyeing Shea, who had turned back. "Yeah?"

"Did you cross the fence and get a deer?" Judd's voice was tight.

Pardo shrugged. "When I start huntin', I don't pay much mind to fences. Did get me a deer yesterday. What about it?"

"You know darn well it's not deer season," Judd growled. "Part of our agreement is that you keep your nose clean! I don't want a bunch of Fish & Game people running around out here."

Ignoring him, Pardo lazily surveyed Shea. His attention sharpened. "Hey! That you, Sergeant Scott?"

He put out his hand in the brotherhood grasp and Shea responded, though his face was still grim. "What the hell are you doing here, Leopardo? Thought you were going back to Detroit and make gas guzzlers!"

Pardo's grin faded. "Lost my job, man. You know. Nerves. Got to drinkin'. Wife split, took the kids. Drifted awhile. Then I saw this ad for an instructor." He grinned. "I tell you, sarge, there's not much market for what they taught us in the war and it's tough to settle down to what you used to do. What you doin' for yourself?"

"That's a good question," put in Judd. "He's sure not ranching!"

"I've got a place right over the fence," Shea said. "If you get tired of this job, you've got one with me."

"Doin' what?"

"Trying to get the range back to what it should be. Raising dry-land food crops, stuff like that."

Pardo's jaw dropped. "You *own* that place?"

Shea nodded.

"Then how come you were just an enlisted man?

How come," Pardo asked savagely, "you were in the friggin' army at all?"

"He's got a noble soul," drawled Judd derisively. "Wouldn't take special privileges."

Shea looked past Judd to Pardo. "Come have a drink when you have a chance. And that job's open."

Pardo shrugged, a hint of puzzled suspicion in his eyes. "Sounds pretty dull, sarge. But I'll take you up on the drink." He chuckled. "Won't shoot any more of your deer, either."

He went back to his trainees. Shea gazed after him, regret and bitterness emphasizing the lines in his face. In that moment, he looked much older than Judd, who said amiably, "Anything else we can do for you?"

Slowly, Shea scanned the men, women and children who were practicing. "You could tell these people that the gun they have in their house is six times as likely to kill one of them as an intruder. You could tell them three-fourths of the crimes committed with guns are done with stolen weapons."

Judd reddened. "Sometimes," he said, "I wonder what the hell kind of a soldier you were!"

"If you'd been one," Shea returned, "you might not get so turned on by guns and all this vigilante scene."

His look included Tracy, who both wanted to explain why she was there and tell him it was none of his business. Mostly, she ached at the sight of him, a hunger deep beneath the quicksilver fire that ran through her at the flick of his eyes. Did he feel nothing of that?

He turned and moved toward his pickup. Judd got in front of him. "Shea, we need to run cattle on your lease."

"Have you culled your herd?"

"Damn it, no!"

"Then we've got nothing to talk about." Shea swung past his half-brother and climbed into his pickup. He didn't spare Tracy another glance.

Judd stared after the wake of dust, then shrugged, grinned down at Tracy and drew her back to the target. "One more round, doll, and then we'll eat."

After lunch Judd and Pardo showed films and diagrams of how to convert a room or house into a citadel. During a break Tracy heard one of the men in front of her say, "If things do blow up, I hope the people in the cities are killed. Sure don't want to have to stand off mobs of starving animals."

"We're from Tucson," growled his neighbor.

"Well, you're getting prepared," fumbled the first man. "Didn't mean you."

The pansy-eyed young nurse had joined a coalition that was working for stiffer rape sentences and publicizing judges' attitudes on the crime. No one else Tracy interviewed had tried to work for reform or to change the laws, though most were fiercely against gun control.

"If we can't have guns, how're we going to defend ourselves?" several argued.

As Judd drove Tracy home that evening, he gave her an expectant smile. "So what did you think of it?"

"There's a lot of fear."

"Stronghold replaces that with confidence."

"Is that a good thing?"

His brow furrowed. "How can it not be?"

"If people who really aren't comfortable with guns start keeping them at hand, they may feel more confident but wind up thoroughly dead."

"Shea's little speech brainwash you?" Judd asked incredulously. "After the stories you taped today?"

"If guns are the problem, and they are, then adding more guns seems like trying to put out a fire by dousing it with kerosene."

"Sounds like an interesting tactic," said Judd. Pulling off the road, he stopped the RV, pulled Tracy into his arms and closed her mouth with his.

IX

His lips were hard and eager. She pushed at him, resisting the tingling shock that coursed through her. After a moment he lifted his head, smiling, and murmured, "That didn't put out any fires for me. Tracy, sweetheart—"

"Please," she said, averting her face. "Please, Judd!"

His hands tightened on her. "Tracy, you've got to get that Houston creep out of your head!" Judd's strong warm hand fondled her throat, seeking out the pulse. "You need a lover, someone to teach you how good it can be."

I had one once. Shea.

Drawing away, she tried to laugh. "You're mightily persuasive, cousin, but I'm old-fashioned."

His eyebrows lifted and he grinned. "Tracy! Are you asking my hand in marriage?"

"No." She met his ombre gaze steadily, feeling the magnetic flow between them even as she said, "I'm not in love with you, Judd."

"My God, you are an infant!"

"All the same."

Head atilt, he studied her a moment. "Maybe I can change that. Be interesting to try."

"I'm in love with someone else."

His eyes narrowed. "That makes it all the more interesting." He started the RV and delivered her to Le Moyne's ecstatic welcome as twilight was deepening to night.

"I'll pick you up in the morning," he said as he turned to leave.

"Thanks, but I've got my story." She had also made a decision. Reaching into her bag, she got out the automatic and handed it to him. "I guess I have to put my chips where my bets are."

"Now, baby, think it over!"

She sighed. "I have. Thanks, Judd, but no thanks."

He loomed above her in the dusk. For a moment, crazily, in spite of Le Moyne's presence, she was afraid. Then Judd shrugged and dropped the gun in his pocket. "When shall we take that aerial tour of the ranch?"

"You name it."

He thought a moment. "Wednesday's good."

"Fine. I'll drive over and we can leave after I've seen Patrick."

Brushing a kiss across her forehead, he pointed at the door. "Go inside with your behemoth and lock up."

She did, grateful that he'd taken her rejection so well. She smiled as he tooted his horn in farewell and set about fixing Le Moyne's soyburgers.

That night she was grateful for the big dog's sprawling guard beside her bed. The training session and her talks with victims, especially the brown-eyed nurse, haunted her.

Had it come to that in this country, that so many felt compelled to arm themselves? Was it worth surviving a holocaust if you had to kill your neighbors? And what of the thousands of young men like Pardo who'd found no peace or homecoming in America?

Faces, voices, the sounds of firing all chased confusedly through her mind. Shea's ironic smile condemned and taunted her. If only he hadn't come while she was shooting! It was damned unfair. But so was he, drat him! He wanted to think all women were awful and he certainly wouldn't give her the benefit of any doubt.

She tossed restlessly. Maybe she was being silly. Maybe she should try to view sex as Shea did, not mix it up with love. Judd would serve very well in that case. She might even get over her useless longing for Shea.

But she moaned and her body tautened as she remembered the sweet wild way he'd loved her. It was a long time before she slept.

Geronimo appeared next morning in time to join her in a second cup of coffee. If Shea had told him about seeing her at Stronghold, he didn't bring it up. She helped carry over pipe and fittings for her shower, while Geronimo inverted a twenty-gallon tank and carried it across on his head and hands.

The tank was black-painted to absorb heat and had a black plastic cover. Tracy helped him rig the scaffolding and put up the bamboo surround for the shower, which enclosed most of a big flat rock.

"Come winter, you'll need something snugger," he said, pausing to down three glasses of tea. He added with a trace of disappointment, "I hoped Mary would be here today."

"I'll try to bring her when I go to see Patrick," Tracy promised. "But I thought I'd give you lunch first."

"Lunch? *Chica*, you go right now!"

So, laughing, Tracy changed into clean clothes and drove to the ranch. Mary, washing her hair after sleeping late, promised to be ready in an hour. Tracy went upstairs and drank coffee with Patrick, regaling him with the story of her new shower and Le Moyne's astonishing penchant for soyburgers.

He chuckled but when she stopped her bright chatter, he said in a halting voice, "Honey, those two bull-headed sons of mine! Is the grazing as bad as Shea says?"

Tracy hesitated. "I'm no expert, Patrick. But there are big stretches where there's no grass at all. None of it looks really good."

"If Shea weren't so damn stubborn!" the old cowman rumbled, knotting his good hand into a fist as brown and gnarled as a mesquite root. "His land would carry a thousand head till it rains."

"By then he might lose what gains he's made in restoring the grass." Tracy hadn't intended to get mixed up in her cousins' feud. She had defended Shea instinctively and to her considerable chagrin, but once started she went ahead. "Patrick, it's going to take more than a good rain to help. Judd knows that. Doesn't he want to irrigate to grow alfalfa? Unless you want to turn the ranch into a giant feeding lot, it might be a good idea to sell down to the land's carrying capacity."

Patrick grinned somewhat sheepishly. "You know what cow people are, girl. Give 'em a good year and ever after they want to think that was normal and calculate according. Damn it! Lyin' here like a rotten log, not being able to see for myself—"

He passed his hand violently across his sightless eyes. At a muffled sound from Tracy, he controlled himself. "You never knew my father, honey. Wish you could have heard him say grace. 'Course, once would have done it because it never changed. 'God bless the grass,' he'd say. 'God bless the grass.'"

No better thing to bless; without green plants converting air, sunlight and minerals into food, there'd be no life. Patrick sighed. "I guess I'll have to talk to Judd. If we can't lease some graze, we'll sell down to what we can carry."

Judd wouldn't take to that kindly. He was a tough opponent, even for a man in full health. Tracy felt a burst of indignation at Shea. If he were helping run the Socorro instead of withdrawing, holier-than-thou, to his own little kingdom, Patrick wouldn't have to fight these battles, at least not alone.

Mary came in to see if Patrick wanted anything before she left. Both young women kissed him good-bye and Patrick laughed. "Say, now, there are advantages to being old and helpless! Good thing for you I can't chase you around the bed, Mary *mía!*"

"I'd chase you right into it!" she teased, and hugged him with a sort of fierce protectiveness before she joined Tracy at the door.

"You're certainly good for him," said Tracy as they went out to the pickup. She had been a bit startled, though, at Mary's kissing Patrick.

Mary offered no apologies. "He's a wonderful guy. That wife of his—"

She bit the words off. Tracy turned the subject. "There's another wonderful man waiting for you. And wait till you meet Le Moyne!"

Geronimo had finished rigging the shower. He showed Tracy how to attach the fitted hose to the pump nozzle when she wanted to fill up the tank. Then he took the first shower while the women made big open-faced grilled-cheese sandwiches with spiced mustard, crisp radish sprouts and sliced dills. Tracy retrieved a bottle of chablis from the concrete cooling trough, and dessert was sesame cookies and yogurt with crushed fresh pineapple.

When Tracy said Patrick had decided to sell some cattle, Geronimo looked skeptical. "Judd'll find some way around it." He glanced shyly at Mary. "How'd you like to go to dinner in Nogales, maybe to a movie if there's anything good?"

"What's good?" asked Mary.

"A show where Apaches beat the white-eyes," he grinned.

"If you find it, I'll buy the tickets." Mary glanced at Tracy. "Sound fun to you?"

"Sounds like a date." Tracy laughed. "Have a good time. And Geronimo, thanks for putting up the shower. Pure luxury!"

She felt deserted, though, after they were gone. She did the dishes, then collected a saw and baling wire. Going to the edge of the clearing down where the spring water began to run cool, she erected a blind, a concealment of dead boughs and brush, where she could set up her camera and wait for a good shot.

Hot and dirty after she was finished, she had a lukewarm soap shower, and then, in her terry robe, went to the rock basin to soak. Tossing her robe over a branch, she lay down in the smoothed stone, resting her head against the back of the bowl.

With Le Moyne drowsing nearby, she felt completely safe, drowsy after her troubled sleep of the night before. Late sun filtered caressingly down on her. She shut her eyes, lulled by the constant rippling of water over rocks.

Half asleep, wholly relaxed, she didn't respond for a moment to her sensing of a denser shadow. When she did, fear shot piercingly through her, sent her heart pounding.

What was there? What would she see when she opened her eyes?

Shea's face. Strange and grim, his long mouth severe. But his eyes were blue fire. He began to strip. How beautiful he was! Muscled shoulders and broad chest curved to flat belly and steel-sinewed thighs. She felt weak, a thick salty taste like blood in her mouth, as she saw the proud thrusting of his desire.

She closed her eyes again. He caught her shoulders, gave her a little shake. "Do you want me?"

Unable to speak, she held up her arms to him.

He took her at once, pace going from fury to gentleness, carrying her with him, controlling her with hands and mouth and gripping legs. When she cried out in sobbing rapture, he crested like a storm, sweeping her out of time and space, laving her in a swirl of soft exploding lights and darknesses.

When that calmed, she was content to lie in his arms, face on his shoulder and chest. Content till what he'd told her so scornfully that first time came crowding into her brain. But when she stirred, he turned lazily. He was smiling as he took her lips. She trembled and was open to his hands, then to his renewed force.

He was her man. She couldn't deny that. Just as surely, she was his woman. But after a second deeper, richer, less frantic time, he got up and began to wash himself.

Tracy got up from his clothes, which had again made their bed and pulled on her robe, not at all ready to wash his scent from her. She was totally unprepared for his sardonic query.

"Well, did you learn all about how to kill people?"

His juices stung her then. She ripped off the robe and washed herself, letting him see the repudiation. Certainly, she wasn't going to admit that she'd given Judd the gun.

"What I do is none of your business!"

He nodded his red-gold head. "Right you are. But any man who found you in that basin would make it his business."

"Le Moyne would tackle anyone but you and Geronimo." She belted on the robe and thrust her feet into her sandals, keeping her face turned so he couldn't see she was close to tears.

Damn him! How could he make her feel like a cheap whore when their loving was so wonderful? She started rapidly toward the house, but he didn't have to stretch his legs to keep up with her.

"Where is Geronimo?"

"He and Mary went to Nogales. They'll be late."

"Just when I need him!" Shea frowned. "Well, we'll make do." Without being asked, he followed her inside, glanced around in reluctant approval. "Looks pretty comfortable."

"It is," she said harshly, furious in remembering the

times she'd wished him here, sitting down to a meal, reading by the stove at night, but most of all, loving each other or sleeping beneath the blue-and-white quilt.

As if he read her thought, he peered inside the bedroom, turned to her with a spreading grin and maddening confidence. Crossing to her, he set his hands at the front of her robe and opened it to his gaze.

"No," said Tracy in a voice that shook. "What do you think I am?"

"A woman." The derisive tone cut like a razor, though his smile was amiable. "That's all right, honey. If you get desperate before I do, you know where to find me."

"There are other men!" she flamed.

"Sure." From the doorway, he caressed the Ridge-back. "That's why I gave you Le Moyne."

Before she could figure that out, he was gone.

Concealed in the blind next morning, trying not to think of Shea, she got pictures of a doe with twin fawns, a dozen javelina and some coatis that came bounding along the stream and, alarmed by something, climbed trees where they perched like a cross between anteater, monkey and raccoon.

Back at the cabin, mollifying the imprisoned Le Moyne with one of her hotcakes, she breakfasted and then spaded the best soil she could find for her garden. The ground was so dry that she wetted it down with the hose in order to get the spade in. It would have to be fenced but that could wait a few days.

Though she had to keep shoving away memories that made her ache with longing, she doggedly planted carrots, tomatoes, lettuce, onions, and the garlic and marigolds that were supposed to keep off insects, took a shower and went to see Patrick.

He was amused at her excitement over the little garden. "Sounds great—if you're a rabbit." He added, in a tone of relief, that Judd had made arrangements to lease land short-term from a neighboring ranch which had switched to raising quarter horses and didn't need so much graze.

"So that's settled." He tweaked Mary's long black braid as she brought him his tequila. "This one's in love, I bet. She's hardly said a word all morning."

"I'm not in love," Mary said belligerently. "That Geronimo!" She blew out her cheeks and expressively let the air escape. "He's got the weirdest old-fashioned ideas!"

"Such as?" queried Patrick.

Mary blushed. "He wants to get married."

She sounded so annoyed that Tracy laughed and Patrick hooted. "Showing more sense than I thought he had. What's wrong with that, Mary *mía?*"

Thrusting her hands in her worn jeans pockets, Mary stared out the window at the mountains. "He doesn't want his wife to work on cars and trucks." She snorted. "He thinks I should stay in the damned house, cook his meals and have his babies. Hell's bells, Patrick! I can do that and still be a mechanic."

"Mm-hm," said Patrick mildly. "How do you feel about him?"

Mary blushed again, looking young and vulnerable. "Even if I was crazy about the big goofus, I wouldn't let him tell me what a woman should be! He can take what I am or look someplace else!"

"'Little bronco that would not be broken of dancing,'" Patrick quoted with a rueful smile. "Geronimo's a good man, honey."

"His ideas are moldier than last year's cheese," she sniffed, turning. "And now, *patrón,* it's time we got you shaved!"

Patrick drooped his movable eyelid at Tracy. "She does that when she wants to shut me up," he complained. "Sing for us, Tracy, so she can't scold while I'm at her mercy."

Though she didn't play each time she came, Tracy always brought her guitar. She played while Mary shaved Patrick and trimmed his curly white mane. By then, he was asleep.

The two young women looked at each other. Tracy was sure they were making the same wish: that Patrick would go like that, drifting into sleep lulled by music and gentle hands.

Both stiffened as they heard the click of Vashti's sandals. Barely nodding at either woman, the shapely blonde glided to Patrick and took his hand.

"Dearest," she said brightly, "that nice Mr. Fricks is here."

"That damned developer, you mean?"

Vashti winced. "Patrick, love! His company, Vistas Unlimited, does only the most tasteful, quality kind of place. He's got a wonderful idea—"

"I don't want to hear it."

The dark-green eyes glittered but she swallowed and kept control of her voice. "Patrick, even Judd thinks we should sell off that worn-out area around the old house and highway."

"Over my dead body!"

"You won't even see Mr. Fricks after he flew down from Phoenix to talk to you?"

"Especially not since he did." Patrick freed his hand from hers. "You'd better go keep him company so he won't think his trip's been a complete loss. Just be sure he knows I'm not selling."

Vashti glared speechlessly at her blind husband. Then, her back rigid with anger, she swept past Tracy and clicked down the hall and stairs.

Patrick let out a sighing breath and softly, fervently, swore. Mary, without being asked, brought him a drink. He tossed half of it down, then said reflectively, "I got thrown by a horse once up in the Santa Ritas. Had a bad concussion, lay there a couple of days. When I really came to, a couple of buzzards were sidling around. Smelled like whatever they'd been eating and had those bald red heads. Let me tell you, I sat up in a hurry!"

He glanced toward the mountains he couldn't see. "That's how I feel now," he said, and finished his drink.

Tracy was fixing supper when she heard a vehicle across the stream. Looking out the window, she saw Vashti's Cadillac and wondered what had induced her to bring the car up the narrow road with its scratching shrubs and branches. A man got out, too, and followed Vashti across the log. They walked toward the hot spring.

Fricks of Vistas Unlimited? It would seem he hadn't gotten Patrick's message. Tracy moved her egg foo yung to the table and, with Le Moyne, sauntered to the spring.

Vashti's eyes flashed a warning as she gave a tight smile and said, "Tracy, dear, this is Hal Fricks. Hal, Tracy is Patrick's adopted daughter. She's living in the line shack while she works on a wildlife picture book. Isn't that quaint?"

Hal Fricks had carefully styled blow-dry hair the same sand color as his eyes, suit and moustache. His tanned skin suggested sunlamps or a lot of time by the swimming pool. He might have been forty. His smile, as he reached for Tracy's unenthusiastic hand, radiated charm.

"Tracy, what a pleasure!" His voice was pitched to virile intimacy. "And what a marvelous spot! I'm sure Vashti has told you of Vistas' plans to share it with a select group who'll respect and appreciate it."

"Last Spring?" Tracy blinked.

Vashti smoothly interposed. "Patrick was too tired to listen, dear, but the wonderful idea Hal wanted to discuss with him would involve this area as well as the land across the highway."

"Or we'd even buy this part by itself if Mr. Scott wants to retain the old house section for sentimental

reasons." Fricks's glance was warmly confidential.
"With this spring for a spa-like attraction, we could
launch our condos here and later spread out."

Stunned, but not eager to antagonize Patrick's wife,
who so obviously still had the power to make him
unhappy though she lacked either the will or ability to
cheer him, Tracy spoke with care.

"Mr. Fricks, I don't think my great-uncle has the
slightest intention of selling any land."

Fricks's smile stayed in place though he turned
questioningly to Vashti. "Isn't Judd his manager?"

"Yes." Vashti slanted a murderous look at Tracy.
"But as I've told you, Hal, my husband is like most
strong-willed men of action who suddenly become
physically dependent. He sees plots in the most reasonable suggestions." She smiled dazzlingly, putting her
hand on Fricks's arm. "I'm sure he'll come round, but
he has to be humored."

"I can't wait too long to settle on a location," Fricks
warned. "This is superb, but we have firm commit-
ments and there are other possibilities." Gazing at
Tracy, he upped the voltage of his smile. "You must
have a lot of influence with your uncle, Tracy. I expect
we could give you a condo custom-made to your tastes
if you could convince him that it's almost criminal to let
such a beautiful place go to waste."

Outraged, Tracy spun away. "The best you can hope
for is that I won't tell him what you just said," she
threw over her shoulder. "And the only reason I won't
is because he doesn't need any more trouble! He won't
sell to you, Mr. Fricks, so you'd better look else-
where!"

She didn't look back till she was inside the house. By
then, the Cadillac was pulling away. She sank down on
the floor by Le Moyne and wept with helpless anger
against his neck. Why did Patrick have to be blind and
paralyzed? And why didn't Shea help him?

X

WEDNESDAY SHE ARRIVED AT THE RANCH IN TIME TO lunch with Patrick. Judd joined them for pecan pie and coffee. Though they'd be spending the afternoon in his plane, he wore his hand-stitched alligator boots and tailored ranch clothes that fitted like second skin to his splendidly proportioned muscular body.

"Lost many calves?" Patrick asked, stirring restlessly.

"Just a couple. And two young heifers didn't make it. Pretty good season."

"That new graze working out?"

Judd smiled. "Just fine. If you'd let me put some more land in alfalfa—"

"We don't have that kind of water."

"But Dad—"

"I can see feeding in winter," Patrick snapped. "But when the herds can't make it through the summer, it's time to thin till they can."

Square jaw clamping, Judd said, "They'll make it." He rose in one lithe motion. "Well, Tracy? Ready to see how the old homestead looks from the air?"

"You be careful with her," Patrick growled. He didn't like airplanes.

Judd grinned down at Tracy as he took her arm. "I'll be careful, Dad—as she wants me to be." Restored to good humor, Patrick chortled.

Pausing at the top of the stairs, Judd tilted her face up and gave her a quick kiss. "How careful do I have to be?" he asked with mock solemnity.

"As careful as you can, and then some." She laughed, slipping free to precede him down the stairs. Vashti appeared at the bottom, striking in soft wool-crepe jade tunic and trousers.

"How lovely that you're getting an air tour, Tracy!" she greeted. "May I come along?"

Judd's tone was bland but his tawny eyes pressed at his stepmother. "You've seen it all before, Ti. Patrick's expecting you."

She didn't protest but her mouth tucked down. Tracy uneasily felt that those green-black eyes were following them, and not with good will.

"You're not very nice to Vashti," she said as they passed the tennis court.

Judd shrugged. "She crowds."

It was something more than that, an element of dominance and submission that jarred Tracy as being out of place between a man and his father's wife. "It's dull for her here."

"Not terribly. She got in hours of swimming and tennis with Hal Fricks before he left this morning. When her stream of company slacks too much, she takes a trip."

Vashti could undeniably take care of herself. Tracy dropped that subject and asked Judd point blank if he favored selling the land called Last Spring.

"That depends on the offer."

"But Patrick doesn't want to!"

Judd patted her knee and helped strap her into the seat next to him. "Look, baby, Patrick's still the boss. I'll not buck and pitch with him in no shape to fight back. But he won't live forever."

"He's only sixty-one."

"He's blind and paralyzed." Judd's voice dropped. "Can you want him to go on like that for years?"

She couldn't, wouldn't, answer.

Judd gave her a comforting yet admonitory one-armed hug. "Don't worry about it, sweetheart. Dad'll get his way while he lives, even if it is damn nonsense. After that—well, I'll do what I think is best for the ranch. Hell, I love it just as much as he does!" He laughed as they climbed upward. "Okay, cousin! Settle back and enjoy the empire!"

The vastness astounded her. Over 200,000 acres, including that leased from the government, stretched from the jagged cañon above Last Spring to the Mexican border, broad valleys and plains marked with sandy washes and protected by hills. Apart from the forested region around Last Spring, it was a sere brown-yellow except where live oak groves sheltered cattle and horses, or along the creeks and bigger washes where cottonwoods, sycamores, walnuts and mesquites were leafing into tender green.

The velvet lushness of the irrigated fields seemed an insult to the rest of the parched land. It was all too easy to see the stark barrenness surrounding the old ranch house, but it jarred Tracy less than the sparkling pool and oasis of shrubbery and lawn at the new one.

Windmills pumped into concrete or metal tanks near line shacks. Apart from Shea's, there were two sub-ranches, each a cluster of adobes, outbuildings and corrals.

"What's going on at Stronghold?" Tracy asked as they soared over it. Below, she could see several dozen men going through what seemed to be a tightly controlled gun drill.

"Pardo's training some guys who wanted the real stuff," Judd said briefly. He pointed as they flew over several ramadas and small adobes. "The El Charco ranch house sort of melted back into the mud when Shea moved over, but he hasn't replaced it. Be damned if they're not all lazing around under that first ramada!"

Judd squinted. "There's four of them. Shea's probably sheltering some wetback though God knows what he can find for one to do."

Illegals couldn't find any water to cross at the boundary but they still bore the name bestowed on those who crossed the Rio Grande's interminable border. From what Tracy had seen of that river, darned few would get wet above the knees.

Even though they were sometimes robbed of their wages by those "coyotes" who smuggled them in and out, or by their employers; even though they sometimes had to drink water contaminated by pesticides and lived in fear of being deported by the Border Patrol, the stream of job-seekers would keep coming till Mexico offered them a way to support their families. It would take an army to police the Arizona border alone. If there was a guard at one point, it was easy to slip through the fence a mile away.

"Grubbing out mesquite and seeding grass sounds like work to me," Tracy said.

Judd only snorted. "All that graze going to waste," he brooded. The El Charco range was perceptibly better-grassed than the surrounding pastures. There were no blatantly green irrigated fields, but there were no stretches of baked caliche soil, either.

As they followed the El Charco fences toward the border, Judd began to scowl. "Should be a herd back here," he muttered. "Where in hell have they got to?"

"Cattle drift around."

"Sure, but these were just moved a few days ago." Judd banked above a white border boundary marker, circled high, then flew over into Mexico.

"Hey!" yelped Tracy. "Now we're wetbacks—or airbacks!"

"Who's to know?" grinned Judd. But he wasn't grinning when he sighted the distinctive red cattle below, scattered over the sparsely grassed hills. "By damn, there's the herd!"

"How'd they get over here?" Tracy wondered.

Judd's teeth clamped together. He spoke between them. "I don't know but I have a pretty good notion! That goddam Shea!"

"Why would he drive them across?"

Judd didn't answer. He cut back across the border.

It was hot for late March. Shea got up, making no sudden moves, and dug a beer out of the wet sand which served as their refrigerator. "Don Aniceto? Or will you have *café con pantalones?*"

The old vaquero usually liked creamed coffee but now he said, *"Cerveza, por favor."*

Even though it must have hurt his horseman's pride even more than his aged back, he'd insisted on helping to plant tepary beans and Indian corn that morning. Shea rubbed the bottle clean against his pant leg, opened it, and put it in the scarred brown hand that was missing a finger where a rope had cut it off against the saddle horn.

"Gracias, hijito," nodded the former top roper and rider of the Socorro. He had taught Shea to ride and work cattle. To him, though Shea loomed head and shoulders above him, the youngest Scott would always be "little son."

He didn't have to poll Geronimo, or Jaime, who had walked or hitchhiked the incredible distance from El Salvador and come into camp last week with bleeding feet and a nearly fatal thirst. Jaime was twenty, with wide-spaced eyes and a broad handsome face which was badly pockmarked. Fatherless, he'd come in from working in the fields to find his mother and sister shot to death by government troops firing at elusive guerrillas. As soon as he'd buried them, Jaime had taken what little food there was and started north. Sometimes, in the night, Shea heard him weeping.

Still, he grinned and thanked Shea for the beer. Geronimo accepted his with an absent nod. "Why you reckon your brother's flying over us? Your stepmother sure wouldn't be."

"Now why do you suppose?" Shea said with a grim laugh.

"Think he's found out what we did with those cows he turned in on us through those cut fences down south?"

"If he hasn't, he soon will." Shea yawned and stretched. "When he comes charging in here, just act innocent. He's got his tail in a crack. Chuey Sanchez tells me Judd got around Patrick's order to sell by letting Dad believe he'd leased more graze."

Geronimo took a long swallow. "He must think we don't ride fence just because we aren't running cattle. Wonder how long he thought he could get away with it? Damn near a thousand head!"

"Even if he can work out some deal with the Mexican authorities, he'll never collect more than a tithe of the herd," Shea predicted. "We scattered them pretty well. Any rancheros who get some of that stock will hide it out till the hunt's blown over."

Don Aniceto gave a mournful sigh. "Yet I have regret, *hijito*. Those fine red cattle—Don Patrick's herd."

"He'd told Judd to sell them," Shea reminded.

Geronimo cocked his head. "Plane's heading back."

"He can probably land by the corrals," Shea decided. "The beauty part of this is that he can't go moaning to Dad without getting caught in his little trick. I bet he doesn't try running any more cattle into El Charco."

He sat down on the army cot and sipped his beer. Judd's boldness in cutting fence had surprised him, but it had been pretty easy to cut more fence and chouse the herd into Mexico. What gnawed at Shea were Judd's other activities.

There was Pardo, mixed up in that crazy paramilitary stuff. Shea had gone back, trying to persuade his onetime comrade to come work for him. But Pardo had given that lopsided grin and shook his head.

"I'm not fighting for any more flags, man, but I'm not ready to plant nice little gardens, either."

"But—"

Pardo had raised a silencing hand. "Sarge, I'd screw up." His face twisted before he laughed. "If I ever get to where I can take all that peace and quiet, don't worry, man, I'll look you up."

Shea had to leave it there. As for Tracy— He scowled, remembering how possessively Judd's arm had encircled her as he told her to shoot. Seemed he'd been a fool to worry about her, send her Le Moyne. But she had been beautiful, naked with the sunny spring water flowing over her, that mass of auburn-tinged curls framing her face with those proud *hidalga* cheekbones and full ripe mouth.

When she'd opened her eyes, there'd been an instant of terror and then such joy, that startled welcoming. . . . But she might have looked the same if he had been Judd!

The old festering wound throbbed as Shea wondered, not for the first time, if Judd had been the one to first seduce Cele, make her so shamed that she'd gone away. Judd's combination of macho and sweet-talk seemed to make him irresistible to women. Since his teens, there'd been a parade of them. Now, less randy or more discreet, he was down to paying the rent on one woman's place in Nogales and giving an expensive jet-set strawberry blonde a free lease on a swank townhouse in Tucson's foothills. He was jaded, but not sated. And how any man could look at Tracy without wanting to try—

The plane was settling on the level area back of the corrals. Shea put down the bottle and went to meet his brother.

Shock and pure plain jealousy wrenched his guts when he saw Tracy. Tearing his gaze from her large, bewildered wild-honey eyes, he grinned at Judd, who was climbing out of the plane.

"Forced landing or would you like a beer?"

"Neither." Judd set his hands on his hips and rocked on his heels, eyes shining like an angered mountain lion's. "You wouldn't happen to know how my cows got scattered to hell over northern Sonora?"

"Did they?" Shea shook his head in condolence. "Tough luck."

"Luck?" Judd seethed. "Someone cut the fence and drove them through!"

When they'd been boys, Judd six years the eldest and always bigger and heavier, Shea had dreaded the frequent fights that left him blackeyed, bruised and bloody-nosed, but he'd never been able to truckle and avoid the clashes. Patrick had quizzically wondered how he could get so bunged up on a horse but had evidently thought his sons must come to their own understanding.

They never had. Judd was still bigger, but there was just the hint of softness in his belly. He lived soft these days, supervising from plane and RV, never doing the physical work, as Patrick always had.

Shea hadn't been afraid of him for a long time. A ferocious joy quickened every sense as he stared into those golden eyes and said softly, "Now who do you think would do a thing like that?"

"You would!" Judd blazed.

"I'll tell you what I didn't do." Shea was so wickedly pleased at Judd's rage that he found it easy to sound pleasant. "I didn't cut *your* fence. What I do to *my* fence is my own business."

Judd made a strangling sound. "You sneaking bastard! You know damn well—"

"What?" It was mean and childish, maybe, but Shea couldn't remember when he'd enjoyed anything so much—except for the puzzled fright on Tracy's face. She was still in the plane but could hear what they were saying. For her sake, though his hands were itching, Shea held back from direct challenge. "When I find someone else's cattle on my land, I figure they broke in somehow. And I let 'em out at the nearest fence."

Judd swung at him. Shea dodged. "You've got a passenger," he reminded his brother, but Judd came at him, arms outstretched.

Ducking, Shea hit him in that softening belly. Judd gasped, knocked breathless. Cautious now, he circled warily. Shea turned with him. His blood was up. This had been coming for a long time. But because of Tracy, he'd let it die if Judd would.

Suddenly, Judd's foot kicked out and up for Shea's chin, with all his weight behind it. It would have practically lifted Shea's head from his shoulders, but Shea swerved, caught the leg and brought Judd right on over with it.

Dazed, Judd sprawled groggily a moment. Rocking back and forth on his knees, he sprang up, catching Shea off balance, knocking him backward, following with sledging blows. Shea's nose felt broken. Blood trickled into his right eye. He stumbled over Judd's outstretched foot.

"You son of a bitch!" yelled Geronimo's distant voice. "Quit fouling!"

Judd's knees clamped Shea. Steely fingers bit into his throat. Shea went limp, then, as Judd laughed triumphantly, twisted sideways with all his might, broke the choking grip, and got his arm hooked around Judd's neck, twisting back an arm till it threatened to snap. Judd grunted, threw him off.

Both men climbed panting to their feet. Shea rubbed blood from his eye. When Judd charged, Shea moved to one side, caught Judd beneath the ribs and drove a fist into his jaw, putting all he had behind it.

Judd seemed to lift from the ground before he collapsed on it. "Slosh some water over him," Shea gasped to Geronimo, as Aniceto and Jaime urged him under the ramada and started washing him. He was bleeding like a stuck pig from nose and mouth, battered, wrung out. He closed his eyes and let rough, friendly hands clean him up.

Slowly, he became aware that the hands were soft. Opening his swelling eyes, he stared incredulously. Tracy was tending him. Her hands were gentle, but her eyes glistened with anger and tears.

"You'd better take care of Judd," Shea mumbled through split lips.

"Shut up!"

Too wrung out to argue, Shea let his eyes close, savored the feel of her deft, quick hands though what they were doing hurt. The pungent smell of tequila, an accompanying sting on his cuts brought him out of his sodden painful bliss. He swore and looked into Aniceto's burned-charcoal eyes.

"It is necessary, *hijito*. Now I will do the same for him."

The old vaquero bowlegged it over to Judd, who was foggily sitting up. The tequila brought him to his feet with a roar. He stood swaying for a few minutes before he made his careful, stiff-legged way to the ramada. Leaning against a pole, he spoke from the corner of a puffed mouth.

"Army taught you to fight. You're worth going a round with now, little brother. And there'll be another round." His eyes glinted as he turned his gaze on Tracy. "Let's be going, cousin, if you're through playing Florence Nightingale."

Shea felt her eyes on him in what seemed a sort of trapped pleading. What the hell? She had a tender heart, but she'd been at Stronghold and now she was flying around with Judd. Even so, remembering the blessing of her hands, watching the way her breasts lifted and fell beneath that thin cotton shirt—

Turning from the silent Shea, her pointed, cleft chin lifted, she moved proudly away. Why did he feel as if he'd failed her? Shea stood up. His head seemed to explode in blinding, throbbing pain.

He reached for Aniceto's tequila. "This time it goes inside, old friend."

"En el pobre es borrachera, en rico es alegría," grinned Geronimo. "In a poor guy, it's drunkenness, in a rich one, it's having a good time."

"Cuando no estás crudo, lo estás refinado," Shea retorted. *Crudo* was slang for "hungover," as well as the word for "crude oil." "When you're not *crudo,* you're refining it."

"Time's awasting," said Geronimo.

XI

JUDD WAS EITHER IN NO MOOD OR IN NO CONDITION TO talk. His earlier rage over the cattle seemed to have been tempered by the fight into an even more dangerous, controlled fury. It was pretty clear that instead of leasing more land, he'd had the fence at El Charco cut along the southern border. Now he had cattle spread across Lord only knew how many Mexican hills. It would be the devil to get them back. Patrick only knew what Judd told him, but a loss like that would be hard to gloss over, as well as being a substantial financial disaster.

It wasn't till he'd brought the plane to a stop on the runway that Judd faced Tracy. "I guess you know what that was all about."

She nodded.

"Wasn't smart of me to stop with you along," he said regretfully. "But I was so damn mad—"

She longed to get away from him, sort out her scrambled thoughts. If Shea had offered to get her home, she wouldn't have flown back with Judd. "Don't worry," she said tightly. "I'm not going to bother Patrick with it."

He shrugged. "I know that. But you sure ran straight past me to tidy up my brother, sweetheart."

She didn't answer. Judd took her hands, both of them, made her face him. His jaw was marked, there was a split above one eye and another on his chin. "What I'm asking, Tracy, is how do you feel about me?"

No good to fuel his grudge at Shea, but neither could she evade the direct question. "You lied to Patrick. And you kicked and tripped Shea."

"Baby doll, if a man wants to win, he can't be Sir Galahad."

"Maybe not. But I don't like cheating."

The dark pupils spread, blotting out all but thin golden circles of the irises. "You're acting like a dumb kid!"

She stared back, willing him to see her unvoiced contempt. He colored. "We're not through," he said thickly. "You need a man who can take care of you. It's damn sure not my brother!"

He got out. She scrambled down before he could help her and went ahead of him into the house.

In spite of her tormenting frustration over Shea and worry about the conflicts dividing the family, Tracy got the Stronghold article done that week. The Tucson lab had developed some good pictures. She mailed a choice of these with the text to her editor and felt she'd earned an outing when Geronimo brought Mary over early Sunday morning.

"Am I glad to see you two!" she greeted as Le Moyne whimpered his delight. "I've been wondering what plants are edible but the only ones I'm sure of are watercress, dandelions and miner's lettuce."

Mary and Geronimo eyed each other and grinned sheepishly. "What's miner's lettuce?" they asked as one.

Tracy sighed. "All right, campers. Have your coffee and then we're going for a walk."

With the help of Carolyn Niethammer's *American Indian Food and Lore*, they identified sheep sorrel and added it to the greens Tracy already knew, which had been gathered from a little side rivulet where the water ran slow enough to allow cress to grow thickly. They collected the tenderest young canaigre leaves and the similar curly dock, but the exciting find was a small marsh thick with cattails.

"We can do all kinds of things with them," Tracy said delightedly.

"My mother still makes pollen soup and muffins," Mary said. "But it's too early for that."

"According to the book, the inner stalk and root bulb and shoots are good."

Geronimo sighed. "All right, ladies. I'll liberate some." He took off his boots and socks and rolled up his jeans. Exchanging glances, Mary and Tracy did the same.

"The book says to get under the root so you can free it from the other connected ones," said Tracy, wading into the shallow water.

She slid her hand down the stalk and followed the root till it began to mesh into others. Pulling it loose, she swished the ropy-looking root till most of the mud was off. Geronimo trimmed the stalks down to where they showed green and sliced off the main roots.

"This better be good," he warned as he tugged his boots back on.

Their "wild" meal was surprisingly tasty. Salad, canaigre and dock cooked in several changes of water, and the lump at the base of the cattail stalks sliced and fried crisp. The inner stalks, chopped thin, made a crunchy addition to soybean curd flavored with green onions, garlic and soy sauce.

"That was fine," teased Geronimo. "Now where's my steak?"

"Over in Sonora, I should think," jabbed Tracy. "I'll bet you enjoyed rustling those cattle."

"Don't know what you're talking about, *chica*," he said blandly. "But how would you like to help smuggle an illegal eagle across?"

"An illegal eagle? Why?"

He frowned. "I was in Nogales last night and saw something that really got me. A guy had this eagle and was fighting him with alley cats. Tough stuff. Worst thing was the eagle was crippled, had a shot-up wing. But it fought like crazy. Killed four cats. I asked the owner if he'd sell, but he was making a pile and wanted more than I had with me."

"So," said Mary, who'd been bristling, "you spent it on some whore!"

He shrugged. "When a man wants to get married and his girl won't, what's he supposed to do?"

"Damn you, Geronimo, I never said I wouldn't—" She broke off with an embarrassed glance at Tracy. "You wind up with some awful crud and no one will marry you, ever!"

Tracy interposed at her friend's wrathful shriek. "So what do you want to do about the eagle?"

He patted his wallet pocket. "I got advance pay. But the bird won't make it if we just turn it loose and I don't know of any SPCA over there. Doubt if we could get a permit even if there was time."

"Did you ask Shea about it?"

Geronimo sobered. "No. What with Judd trying to get his lease revoked, he sure doesn't need any trouble with the law."

"I could do without it myself," Tracy said.

"If you'd seen that eagle—"

She shuddered and gave up. "Okay, eaglenapper. What's the plan?"

Crossing from Nogales, Arizona, to Nogales, Sonora, was easy. Geronimo greeted the Mexican guard by name and said they were going to shop and have a few drinks at the Caverna.

"Two beautiful ladies, no?" smiled the khaki-clad official. "Don't push your luck, though, Señor Sanchez. You brought your allowance of whiskey in last night."

Geronimo winked. "But the ladies, Don Alfredo! They haven't bought their quart."

"You are lucky!" chuckled the Indian-dark man, and waved them on.

"We'll come back through the other gate," Geronimo said. "My sister's brother-in-law's on duty. He won't look behind the seat." For the eagle was going to ride in the large space behind the seat and the cab back. Shea, though in ignorance about the "snatch," was going to have the chore of nursing the eagle back to health. Geronimo was sure he could do it if the bird was still salvageable. The eagle's captor had been feeding it dog food and the bird couldn't live long on that.

"Shea says they get their vitamins and stuff from plants in their preys' stomachs," Geronimo explained. "Then they got to have roughage—fur, bones, teeth."

They turned off the main drive and threaded through streets running beneath the hill on the left where houses in weathered lollipop colors of violet, green, pink, blue and cream clung precariously to the steep sides.

The natural stench of too many humans existing close together without plumbing competed with that of chickens as they reached the outskirts of town. A crowd had squeezed in among four parked trucks that made an informal arena, blocking off the street.

"*Ay, gatos!*" yelled one man, flailing his hat.

His exhortation was countered by encouraging shouts from other spectators. "*Viva, aguila! Mueran los gatos!*"

"My God!" breathed Tracy.

Then she saw, through floating bits of feather and dust. Inside a wire cage with a wooden lid, the eagle, a bleeding mass of brown feathers sheened with gold, clamped talons that looked like black wrought-iron hooks into the skull of what was left of a black cat. Another mewling gray-striped cat dragged itself into a corner, spilling entrails.

Tracy fought the hot scalding filling her throat, as sickened by the excitement on the faces around her as by the carnage. She caught Mary's hand, which returned a strong heartening grip as a sobbing little girl thrust her way through the people and knelt by the cage, trying to reach the dying striped cat.

"Mi gato!" she wailed. *"Mi gatito lindo!"*

The chubby brown arm was in reach of the maddened eagle. Tracy grabbed the child back, dropped on a knee to cuddle her. Sheepishly, a young man came forward to pick up the child.

"I'm sorry, little sister," he said in Spanish. "Come, I'll buy you some candy."

"I don't want candy!" she lamented. "I want my kitty! My beautiful little kitty!"

He carried her off. The onlookers drifted away, though a few lingered to see what the strangers wanted. The eagle had finished the cat's brains and was gorging on chunks torn from it.

In spite of her horror, Tracy had to admire the blazing spirit in those yellow eyes. The sheer size of the bird demanded awe. As she awkwardly flapped her torn wings to move forward, she must have measured six feet from wingtip to wingtip.

Geronimo was starting to count out bills to the fat gray-moustached impresario of cat-eagle matches. "This one's on me," Tracy said, getting out her wallet.

"It's a hundred dollars," Geronimo protested.

"Save yours for getting married," Tracy said, amazed that he'd been willing to part with what was probably half of a month's cash wages.

It was a point of pride with her not to draw from her trust fund for living expenses, but for something like this she didn't mind. After all, she gave most of her inherited income to the American Friends Service Committee and animal and environmental protection groups.

The entrepreneur looked regretful that he hadn't asked for more, since an apparently wealthy *gringa* was paying. "You like birds?" he asked in broken English. "Buy six parrots—very pretty?"

Such smuggled birds often spread diseases. "Where are they?" she asked in Spanish.

He pulled up a canvas flap over the back of one truck. Big blue-fronted birds, a few small green ones, a pair with lilac crowns moped in wire cages or pecked at the end boards. One appeared to be dead.

"How much?"

"Two hundred?"

Tracy would have consented, sick with revulsion and eager to get away, but Geronimo said toughly, "One hundred. Those birds are about to die on you."

"One-fifty?"

"One-twenty-five," Geronimo said. The man shrugged and flashed a gold-toothed smile.

"For you, a good price!"

Geronimo turned to Tracy. "What you going to do with them?"

"Have him turn them loose. Now, while we can be sure he does."

The plump bird dealer was shocked but did as he was told, taking the parrots over to the trees along an arroyo before he released them. While he was thus occupied, Geronimo got adhesive tape and sheets out of the trunk.

"Shea says an eagle can't do anything with his claws except grip," he said. "Hope he's right."

"That sounds like enough," Tracy muttered.

When the Mexican came back, he took part of a sheet, lifted off the wooden lid and dropped the cloth over the eagle. Unable to see, it offered little resistance as he lifted it up, instructing Geronimo to tape the ferocious talons together.

This done, wide bands of sheeting were used to bind the damaged wings against the body. Hissing sounds of terror came from the swaddling sheet and the dealer helpfully cut a hole.

"She breathe better," he explained. *"Buena suerte."*

They had the luck. Geronimo's sister's brother-in-law waved them by without a question and the U.S.

customs official only glanced at the heap of sheets in the back. Just to sound credible, Geronimo said they had a quart of rum and one of Scotch.

Once out of town, they uncovered the eagle except for its bindings. It didn't stir, even when its head was clear.

"Do you think it's dead?" Tracy worried.

Geronimo cautiously felt the brown breast. "Heart's beating. May be in some kind of stupor or shock."

"After all that, I hope she won't die on us," Mary said.

Geronimo shrugged. "At least she won't be torn up by a bunch of half-starved cats. Shea'll bring her around if anyone can."

Shea and Don Aniceto left the garden patch where they were working when they saw Mary and Tracy get out of the pickup. The last rays of the sun turned Shea's hair to living flame.

A subtle, internal sword seemed to turn in Tracy. His gray eyes touched her briefly before he moved to see what Geronimo was lifting out of the back.

"Hellfire, what's that?"

"You can see," grunted Geronimo. "Where you want her?"

"I don't want her," Shea retorted.

"You got her. And I know you have a nice legal permit from Fish and Game to take care of hurt wildlife."

Shea gave up. "She may not come out of this sleep. It's more of a coma, a response to stress."

"Be a good time to fix her up," urged Geronimo. "She's kind of frazzled."

They unwrapped the bird except for the disabled talons. Examining her as she lay on one of the cots under the ramada, Shea cursed savagely, sent Aniceto for medicines.

"What happened to her? Where in hell did you get her?"

Geronimo explained. "So we just went over and brought her back," he concluded with an angelic smile, looking more than ever like an outsized De Grazia cherub.

Shea's glance skidded past Mary to Tracy. "And you went along with this desperado?" he demanded incredulously. "Do you think you'd like the inside of the Nogales jail?"

"I didn't cut any border fences," she reminded him. "Do you think she'll fly again?"

"First we'll see if she lives." He spread out one of the damaged wings. "Hold this."

Fortunately, the eagle stayed in her deathlike sleep while Shea cleaned her wounds and gave antibiotics. An unused granary shaded by a mesquite and surrounded by an ocotillo stalk fence seemed the best place to put her.

"We'll just have to wait," Shea said, placing the bird on an old blanket. "Geronimo, since you're the guy that brought her, you're in charge of mice and rabbit procurement. Aniceto, we got anything to feed these smugglers?"

"Frijoles," said the old leather-skinned man with the frank, open face of a child. "Tortillas. Stewed dried beef and rice." He smiled at Tracy and Mary. "If the ladies will stay, I'll make flan."

"We'll stay," Tracy laughed. The caramel custard was a favorite of hers, but the main thing was the warm glowing delight of being near Shea.

They sipped beer in the cooling evening. When Aniceto called, they lined up in the kitchen of the small adobe and filled blue enamel plates from the various pots on the wood stove. Jaime polished off the remnants and still had room for three helpings of warm flan.

"*Muy sabrosa*, Don Aniceto," Tracy praised truthfully. After two cups of the aromatic, eggshell-settled coffee, she began to collect the dishes. Jaime barred her way to the tin dishpan.

"It's my turn for dishes, señorita."

"Don't upset our system, *chica*," drawled Geronimo. "Aniceto bosses the kitchen but the rest of us take turns cleaning up."

With a smile, she surrendered her plate to Jaime. "Could we peek at the eagle? And then I need to get home and feed Le Moyne. I don't want him eating my photographic subjects."

The eagle was already staggering drunkenly around the pen. Geronimo went to see if there were mice in any of Aniceto's traps and returned with two, which he dropped near the surprisingly long-legged bird.

"What do you think?" Tracy asked softly.

"She came out of that coma. Sometimes they don't. And she's got to be tough to have stood that cat-fighting with a bullet-shattered wing."

As if suddenly making up his mind about something, Shea loosely clasped her wrist. "Shall I take you home?"

That fire ran between them. Her body felt weighted and sweetly heavy. Despairingly, she knew she loved this man. What did he feel for her, beyond this hunger? Even if that was all of it for him, she couldn't deny this wild tremulous longing.

Unable to speak, she nodded silently.

Shea turned to Mary. "Want me to drop you off at the house?"

"I'm taking her!" Geronimo yelped.

"Only if you stay on your side of the seat," Mary told him.

He groaned. "You're one mean damn woman!"

"Shall I go with the others?"

He sighed. "No. Hell, if you want, we'll make you a chastity belt of barb-wire!"

They got in one truck, still arguing, while Shea boosted Tracy into his high-floored pickup cab. Before he put it in gear, he took her by the shoulders and kissed her. His tongue explored her mouth, thrusting, probing, sensuously teasing.

"Can you wait till we get you home?"

"I don't know."

They didn't. Stopping a few miles down the road, he spread a blanket on the soft sand of a wash. She stripped as swiftly as he, trembling, pulsating. They came together in a kind of fury, delivered each other, then lay watching the stars, so much brighter here than in the city. Tracy's heart swelled with hope.

This was the first time he hadn't turned strange and hostile after lovemaking. Was there a chance he might get over his terrible mistrust of women? He wasn't holding her in his arms but at least they lay relaxed and companionably touching.

"How come you helped spring that eagle?" he asked.

She knew he was frowning, dared to lightly stroke the furrowed lines between his straight brows. "It's hard to resist Geronimo."

"Maybe you thought you could get an article."

Hurt, she said coldly, "Maybe I did."

Sitting up, she reached for her clothes. But when they had parked beside the stream, crossed the log, and greeted Le Moyne, Shea didn't leave. When she had fed Le Moyne, he drew her into the bedroom and again there was the flame and the need that crested till the unbearable longing peaked like a fountain and diffused itself in soft ebbing flows.

I love you! almost broke from her lips. His silence forbade it. But he didn't leave or utter some brutality. Perhaps in time— With a muffled sigh, she snuggled against her pillow and enjoyed the warm peace of him near her fulfilled body until she fell asleep.

XII

SHE WOKE IN EARLY LIGHT, UNCONSCIOUSLY REACHING for him. He was gone. Dazedly, she tried to remember if he'd been there or if she'd dreamed it.

The pillow held the mark of his head. His scent was on her. Rising quickly, she found no trace of him. The green pickup was gone. A wave of desolation washed over her. If he had just stayed for breakfast! For him to leave without a word like that made her feel used as a convenience, almost like a whore.

"If this weird affair is to continue," she told Le Moyne sternly, "there have to be some ground rules."

Le Moyne thumped his tail. She rubbed the wide dome of his head and began to fix breakfast.

Thoughts of Shea haunted her, but she determined not to use the eagle for an excuse to visit El Charco, at least not for a few days. On the other hand, she did care what happened to the creature and hoped to get some good pictures as it convalesced, so she wouldn't be stopping by just to see Shea anyway.

Since she'd moved to Last Spring, she'd heard the screech of barn owls, an explosive hiss like a steam locomotive, often enough to suspect there was a nest fairly close by. Ordering Le Moyne to stay at the house, she went on a search. They liked old barns and buildings but since there were none, she concentrated on hollow trees.

Towering above the rock basin was an oak blasted by lightning, mostly dead, though branches of it showed green against the sky. There was a big hollow about ten feet above the ground but Tracy couldn't see into it. She climbed up a smaller neighboring tree and was rewarded by seeing, snugly ensconced in a leafy nest, two fluffy white little creatures with prominent heart-shaped faces. It was harder to locate the parents, who were roosting in the densest foliage.

Exultant, Tracy clambered down, then frowned as she realized she'd need some kind of platform and blind. The most interesting pictures would happen at night while the adults were feeding their young.

Carpentry wasn't her strong point, so on her way to see Patrick that day she stopped at the Sanchezes and asked if Roque or Tivi could help her.

"It might be better not to put it up all at once," she said. "I don't want to scare the adults."

Tivi made an expansive gesture. "No problem. I'll put up the legs and platform today. Two, three days from now, I can fix on the sides and top."

He promised to be as quiet as possible, even to the sacrifice of leaving his transistor radio at home.

When Tracy entered Patrick's room, Mary was regaling him with their eaglenapping. "Shea'll bring her round if anyone can," he said, and returned Tracy's kiss by shifting the better half of his face toward her. "He always had a good hand with wild things. So did his mother."

It was the first time Tracy had ever heard him speak of his second wife. "When did she die? Shea must have been pretty young. I can't remember her at all."

"Doubt if he can, either." Dry, ancient pain sounded in the old man's voice. "Elena didn't die. She left when Shea was four. Ran off with the foreman."

"Patrick! I—I didn't know! I'm sorry—"

"All blood down the creek." He hitched his shoulder. "At least she left me the boy and that shows how miserable she was, because she loved him. Guess I was too busy, and lots of the ranchwork—branding, cutting —tore her up. I was mad as hell. Wouldn't give her a divorce for a couple of years or let her see the boy." He sighed. "Looking back now, I can't blame her much."

"She never saw Shea again?"

"No. She died of cancer a year after I gave her the divorce."

Tracy was silent, trying to absorb the shock. "Have you told Shea all this?" she asked at length.

"I tried a few times. But, hell, Tracy, it's hard! And he said he didn't want to talk about it." Patrick brooded. "Of course, that made it extra bad when that flighty little Cele ran out on him."

Yes.

Tracy had to sit down. She'd derided Shea for letting a girl-child's duplicity sour him on women, but to have been deserted by his mother—one who must have been loving and playful! It made his behavior much clearer, while giving Tracy a sense of defeat.

Even if, now, Patrick convinced Shea that Elena had loved him, could the knowledge filter from brain to heart? Could Shea, even if he wanted to, really trust a woman?

Devastated for a small boy's grief, Tracy reached for a happier subject to distract Patrick. "Did Geronimo keep on his side of the seat last night?" she teased Mary.

"Yes, but there's no way to keep him from going on about how we ought to get married!"

"He's a good lad," Patrick soothed.

"With stone-age notions! His wife can't do dirty work, crawling under engines and so on." Mary snorted. "He wouldn't care if I spent the day cooking his meals and washing diapers, though!"

"You really are set on this mechanic thing, aren't you, Mary *mía?*" asked Patrick.

"I am! I like it, I'm good at it, and housework bores me stiff!"

"Well, then be a mechanic. If you give up what you want to do, you and your man'll both regret it." Patrick squeezed her hand. "We've got enough trucks and vehicles on the ranch to keep you busy. But hell, Mary *mía!* How'll I get along if you ditch me for a broken-down tractor?"

She laughed and hugged him. "I'm not leaving you, Patrick. But this summer I want to take a night class, drive in a couple of times a week."

"Good God, girl! That's a fifty-mile round trip." Patrick's right eyebrow scowled. "Don't call me Geronimo, but I don't like that much."

"Tivi Sanchez is taking the same course. I can ride with him."

"Mm," said Patrick. "What does Carla think about it?"

"She thinks it's fine," said Mary. "But that Geronimo!"

"In this case, I'm with him," Patrick grunted. "Not that I don't trust Tivi, but I don't want my nurse worn out. Give me the phone." A few minutes later, he had called a Nogales garage and arranged for their best mechanic to come over a few evenings a week and teach Mary, Tivi and any other ranch people who wanted to learn. "There," he said contentedly.

"But you're paying him a fortune!" Mary protested.

"We'll make it back on work you and Tivi can do," Patrick grinned. "Shucks, honey, I can't swing much these days! Let me manage what I can." He chuckled. "I bet Geronimo takes the class just to keep an eye on you. Which could be kind of funny, because he walked off from the Army when it was trying to make a mechanic out of him."

"Walked off?" Mary frowned.

"And never went back. He was over at Fort Huachuca and one day he just took off through those mountains. Army never caught him any more than they did old Pia Macheta."

"Pia Macheta?" prompted Tracy. "Who was he?"

"He was a Papago who never really believed the United States had taken Arizona over from Mexico," Patrick said. "This was back fairly early in World War II. Anyhow, the government got all scared about the chances of a Japanese force landing in Mexico and then coming up through Sonora and the Papago Reservation, taking Tucson, and marching on to attack California from the east. To be sure none of the Indians sided with the Japanese, the Papagos were supposed to take an oath of allegiance. Now old Pia thought Mexico was still in charge. When some local officials tried to get him and his people to take the oath, they roughed up the officials, ran up the Mexican flag, and skedaddled."

"I don't believe it!" Tracy gasped.

Patrick chortled. "You better! Pia and his band dodged around awhile till a friend who worked for the Bureau of Indian Affairs calmed him down and persuaded him to give himself up."

"What happened?"

"He was tried, and even though a bunch of profs and civil liberties people went to bat for him, he was sentenced. Eighteen months, I think it was. Then he went back to the reservation and lived in peace and quiet."

"It's about the wildest tale I ever heard," said Tracy skeptically.

"All true," Patrick vowed. "What's wilder, he and his fellow prisoners really liked the Pima County jail! Said it was very comfortable and they loved the food."

Mary grimaced. "Bet they're the first and last to say anything good about that dump!"

Patrick was in a reminiscing mood that day. "You've heard of Santa Teresa, who cured my mother's blindness?" he asked. "Well, Teresita, as they called her, lived right near the customs house in Nogales after Díaz drove her out of Mexico. Later, she and her father lived for a time pretty close to Calabazas where Rio Rico is now. That's where my mother saw her, at a place called Bosque."

He went on to tell how his parents had developed a grudging respect for Emilio Kosterlitzky, the Russian officer who had made General Díaz's *rurales* into a notorious but effective body of mounted police. According to his lights, the colonel had been just and had once compelled a *rico* to marry the peon girl he had raped, with the warning that he had better not hear of any mistreatment of the unwanted bride.

Tracy had lunch with Patrick and Mary before she left. She hadn't seen Judd since the disastrous plane tour, nor Vashti in almost as long. It was not a happy house, though Mary had made a tremendous difference. Strangely, it was the paralyzed blind man who seemed most at peace in the family.

His revelations about Shea's mother dismayed Tracy more the longer she thought about them. It was no wonder he was guarded. Maybe it was more than that, maybe he really meant all he said about not making a big thing of sex. He might be willing to oblige her several times a week, but that wasn't what she wanted, damn it! She loved him.

In stages, Tivi got the blind mounted where Tracy could set up her camera and he made holes through which she could observe or take pictures. Following remembered advice from her outdoor editor, she placed reflectors on the outside. The owls seemed to accept the box-like thing on stilts that had suddenly appeared in the vicinity, so Tracy went up the ladder at twilight and settled to wait. She would have liked Le Moyne's company in the dark but had shut him in the house for fear he might alarm the owls.

Suddenly, a white, valentine-shaped face appeared in the big knothole. Though Tracy didn't want to take pictures that night lest she frighten the birds, she watched excitedly as the owl waited for a few minutes, then spread wide wings, and dissolved into the deeper night.

A moment later, the ghostly white body of its mate filled the hole before it, too, launched forth. There was not the slightest whisper of sound. Tracy remembered Chuey's telling her that the forward edges of an owl's main flight feathers were lined with soft fluff that made its flight inaudible as falling snow. Its prey heard nothing till the talons closed.

The terror by night. Tracy shivered and turned up the collar of her jacket. Somewhere in the darkness, in order to live and feed their young, the owls must kill. Their large ear openings would detect the slightest mouse rustle or movement. They hunted by night what hawks and eagles took by day.

This swift, impersonal doom in the night brought back to Tracy the attack outside her apartment. She told herself, as she had so often, *It happened to me but it wasn't me. It was the leap of a rabid beast, a bolt of lightning hitting the nearest grounding. Nothing personal. Think of it that way, a senseless accident.*

A screech sounded from the distance. The owlets began a "shh" that mounted in intensity as more screeches announced the return of a parent. Tracy could see only a blur of white as it lit. It was barely gone when the other owl flew in.

During the next hour, the owls made five returns but the clamor of their nestlings seemed no less demanding. Shaking her head at the rigors of being an owl parent, Tracy climbed quietly down and was soon in bed with Le Moyne's comforting bulk stretched out nearby. She touched the pillow where Shea's head had rested and hoped vengefully that he thought of her even half as often as she thought of him.

Flashbulbs startled the owls but they went on with their hunting and feeding. She got shots of them bringing in field mice, a small snake, a gopher. The adults' big dark eyes in the valentine faces must have been temporarily blinded by the flashes, but their brood's hungry slurping sounds soon had them scavenging again.

Tracy's photos were accumulating gradually, and their subjects ranged from the slapstick of a javelina making off with a bag of Fritos, to the tender one of a doe and a fawn touching noses. She had rigged a sugarwater container on a raised log and put out scraps each evening. A beautiful fox, its bushy tail as long as it was, loved the sugarwater and drank daintily each night though it vacated the log when a raccoon approached. Skunks fed with the slow deliberation of gourmets from the "salad" Tracy put out, elegant little animals who could fluff their tails in a manner reminiscent of a peacock's display.

The elusive fox thrilled Tracy, but her favorite was a ringtail, with its miniature fox face and luxuriant banded tail. It so enjoyed some hardened fig bars she put out that she began to toss a couple on top of the roof for it and attach from the edge its own special jar of sugarwater. The greedy racoons caught on to that, hanging over the ledge to grip the jar in their clever dextrous "hands," so she abandoned that idea and kept more sugarwater down low.

Patrick enjoyed hearing about her creatures and told her of some of his encounters with wild creatures. "I killed a bear one time," he said. "I never killed another. It cried just like a woman—cried for a long time. But that's not what stopped me hunting."

"What did?"

"When it hit me that man's a killer at a distance—the only predator that can kill without touching his prey." Patrick thought back as if picturing the scene in his darkness. "I was riding one day and came out of some trees to spot three deer. One took off. One kept feeding. The third made a couple of bounds, then turned to wait. It watched me as if it thought the space between made it safe." He shook his head. "Nothing showy. It just made me sorry—kind of ashamed—that

animals don't know what they're up against." He went
on after a moment. "Later, I thought man's long reach
isn't only with guns. It's a time thing, too. Animals fight
over territory or mates but they don't hold grudges the
way humans do. People kill years after the first trouble.
It's this awful knack we have for distance killing."

"Have you ever talked to Shea about the war?"

"No. Have you seen him lately?"

"Not since we left that eagle with him." Tracy turned
to Mary, who was coming in with Patrick's shaving
things. "Do you know how the eagle's making it?"

"Alive and meaner by the day, Geronimo says."

"And how's Geronimo?"

Mary grinned. "He's studying mechanics along with
Tivi and me. We're both a lot quicker than he is."

"Wouldn't blame him if he kidnapped you down into
the Sierra Madre the way the Apache Kid would have,"
chided Patrick.

"I'd bend a wrench over his head," said Mary
succinctly.

Tracy laughed and kissed Patrick good-bye. She still
got her mail at the ranch and the bundle of Houston
papers made her wonder if the Stronghold article was
in them.

It was, in the Sunday magazine section. The photos
of Pardo and his trainees had reproduced well, and very
little of the story had been cut. Judd's voice behind her
made her jump.

"God job!" He flourished a clip of the feature. "Just
got it from a friend in Houston. And that's not all,
baby! AP's picked it up. I've been asked to be on one of
those big morning talk shows! How about that?"

Stunned, Tracy said, "I didn't think you'd like the
story."

He laughed. "It's clear enough that you don't approve, but your interviews with trainees show they've
got a right to be scared and getting prepared. Hell,
some Houston businessmen were so impressed that

they're asking me to tailor a special program they can fly over and take on a long weekend."

Confounded, for the last thing she'd intended was to get Stronghold more clients, Tracy turned speechlessly away. Judd caught her arm. "I'm flying up to New York next week, cousin. Come along and we'll do the town!"

"Thanks, but I'm busy."

His exultant smile faded. Tawny eyes probed hers. "Hey, you aren't still huffy about that deal I tried to pull on Shea? I'm the one who got hurt! Bushels of red tape, plenty of bribes and arm-twisting, and with it all, I got back only two-thirds of the cattle. Must be a couple hundred trucked off to the butcher or stashed out in the boonies."

"Your hassles with Shea are one thing. Lying to Patrick is another."

"Lying? Goddam! Man in his condition can't be told a lot of things." Pausing, Judd reined in his anger and a broad persuasive grin showed his strong white teeth. "Tracy, you must know I have to be careful with Dad," he said earnestly. "A real upset could kill him. Maybe I was wrong to tell him I had a new lease, but damned if I was going to sell the cows!"

"Well, what are you going to do with them?"

"Right now I'm buying hay and you can bet I'm cussing my brother with every bale!" Judd's face tightened. "It'll take time, but I'll get his lease revoked."

"Patrick won't be very happy about that."

"He doesn't need to know. I'll give Shea one thing, he doesn't run to Dad."

"If you two could just compromise—"

"We could, if he'd let cattle on the lease."

"He said he would if you'd reduce the number."

"He can go to hell." Judd's teeth showed again, but this time he wasn't smiling. "Come with me, Tracy. You won't be sorry." His broad hands dropped on her shoulders.

"Well!" cut in Vashti's bright voice. She held a plum robe around her with one hand and a drink with the other. "I haven't seen you in ages, Tracy, though I know you're here almost daily. You must stay for dinner one evening or at least have a cocktail."

"You could drop into your husband's room," Tracy said. Stepping clear of Judd's hands, she turned and left the house.

XIII

XIII

SHE WAS SITTING ON A LOG NEXT MORNING, BRUSHING LeMoyne, who responded with soft rumbles of pleasure, when she heard the crunch of hoofs.

"Geronimo!" she called, rising. "I didn't know you ever rode anything but a pickup!"

"Try not to." He grimaced as he shifted in the saddle. "We don't have a horse trailer, though, so Shea asked me to bring you this filly. Like her?"

Tracy gazed in delight and wonder at the golden mare he was leading. "She's for me? That's my old saddle and bridle on her."

"Chuey rustled them up," Geronimo explained. Getting down from a rangy bay gelding, he trailed the reins and patted the palomino's gleaming neck. "Shea was breaking Güera for himself but decided she was just right for you."

"Why didn't he bring her?"

Geronimo flushed. "Now, *chica,* he was busy and anyhow you know how he is."

"I know how he is. And I don't like it!"

Geronimo sighed. "He's not as cantankerous as Mary! How about some coffee, *chica?* She bumped a wrench into my head last night and it's still aching."

"I wonder what you were doing," Tracy commented unsympathetically. "Coffee should still be hot." She went to bring him a cup.

160

When she returned, he was unsaddling the horses. "I'm leaving Sangre with Güera. They're special friends, the way horses get to be, and she wouldn't be very happy by herself."

"Who's going to ride him?"

"Mary might like to when she's visiting." He flashed a smile. "Or Shea or I will often enough to keep him from going bronco." He drained the cup. "Will you give me a lift to the Sanchezes, *chica?*"

"Sure." *And as soon as I get back here, I'm riding that gift horse over to see why His Mightiness won't deliver his own presents.*

"One thing you better watch with Güera," warned Geronimo as they got in the pickup. "She's scared of snakes. If she hears a rattler, she skitters, and sometimes she thinks she hears one when she doesn't."

"In other words, she's spooky. Is this Shea's way of getting my neck broken?"

"*Chica!* He wouldn't do that! Güera's sweet-tempered. She's got speed and endurance." He shrugged broadly. "Horses are like people. They all have their little problems."

"Some more than others."

"Yeah. Mary and her crazy fix on being a hotshot mechanic!"

"I wasn't talking about Mary. Say, have you heard anything about Blondie? The guy Shea rammed into the wash?"

Geronimo's black eyes widened. "Didn't you know? He broke jail a couple of weeks ago. It was on the radio."

Muscles tightened in Tracy's stomach. "Does Mary know?"

"Sure. I thought she'd told you."

"Maybe she thought it'd make me nervous—and it would! It does!"

"No need. He's deep in Mexico by now. Doubt if he's in any hurry to come back."

That was probably true. Tracy decided not to worry about it, but she was glad of Le Moyne.

She had coffee with the Sanchez women when she dropped Geronimo off. They were astonished that she'd want or dare to photograph owls.

"Very bad luck," said plump Inez firmly. "When they hoot, someone dies."

"But they hoot every night," Tracy protested.

"Not where a certain person can hear," asserted the older woman. "One night there were many in a tree outside the house. Chuey and the boys shot at them. Two fell, but the others kept calling." She paused. "And that very hour, in Los Angeles, my brother died suddenly! He hadn't been sick at all. The owls knew."

Tracy smothered the impulse to ask if the warning was adjusted to Pacific Standard Time, and turned the subject to Carla's baby. "It will be a boy," predicted Lupe.

Carla pulled a face at her sister-in-law. "Have your own boys! I want a little girl." She was scarcely more than a girl herself, coltishly thin except for her burden. Her large brown eyes fixed appealingly on Tracy.

"Will you be the child's *madrina,* the godmother?" she asked shyly. "Tivi and I want this very much."

Patrick must have been godfather to half the children on the ranch, but Vashti had probably not inspired or encouraged such relationships. With a certain shock, Tracy realized that for a long time the Socorro ranch had lacked a mistress the people could feel close to. She was a poor excuse, but at least she was of the family.

"I'd be honored," she said truthfully. "But do you want a long-distance *madrina?* I won't be staying here after—"

She broke off, but Inez finished for her. "After Don Patrick dies? But why not, *doncellita?*"

"I will have no place," Tracy explained. "I'm only his foster-daughter, you know. The ranch will go to his wife and sons."

Inez sighed and shook her graying head. "If Don Shea were in charge—" She didn't continue, but Carla smiled at Tracy.

"All the same, I want you for *madrina*."

"Then I will be," Tracy promised.

Strange, but accepting the responsibility, in this house beneath the dark madonna's serene gaze, gave her a sense of linking with this place where she had been nurtured, of taking up the obligations other women of her blood had long fulfilled. But the ranch was not her inheritance. And, it seemed, neither was Shea.

Tracy dropped in to see Patrick and then drove back to Last Spring. It was about a three-hour ride to El Charco. She'd have to leave right away if she wanted to be home by dark—and she did, more than ever now that she knew the blond thug had broken out of jail. Geronimo was almost certainly right about the fugitive staying safe in Mexico, but it was still unsettling.

Geronimo had put both horses in the old corral and pumped water into the tank for them. Tracy got an apple which she divvied between Sangre and the mare, talking gently to them both. Getting the riding gear out of the little shed, Tracy bridled and saddled Güera.

"Behave yourself," she told Sangre as he watched gloomily. "Mary's coming Sunday and we'll all go riding."

He whickered disconsolately as they moved off. Horses were among the most sociable of creatures and hated to be alone. To keep one in solitary confinement without at least a dog or goat or some companion was actually cruel. Tracy talked to Güera, getting her used to her voice, and noted with pleasure that the mare tilted one ear and eye forward and one back, attentive both to the rider and the road ahead.

Tracy had ridden a lot as a girl. It was good to be on a beautiful smooth-gaited horse again, though she expected to ache that night. Güera shied once at a rustle in the brush, but Tracy kept a firm rein and soothed her.

"I think you like to get scared," she chided. "If we met a big *cascabel*, do you suppose he'd want to lose his rattles under your hoofs?"

Steller jays screeched and made blue flashes among the big trees, but as they descended to the level, throngs of white-crowned sparrows and titmice hopped in the leafing bushes and mesquites. Gambel's quail clockworked across a sandy draw. Farther along, a roadrunner was devouring a lizard. Even without rain, grass was trying to green, but Tracy rode the length of the western part of the Socorro without seeing any good graze. At one tank, vaqueros were unloading hay, an almost unheard-of thing at this time of year.

She made a wide swing around the Stronghold site and entered El Charco through a plain gate once used for cattle. Her heart thudded at a dizzying rate.

Was she a fool to come here? Knowing about Shea's mother might embolden her to risk her pride as she otherwise wouldn't, but wasn't it likely that no matter how far she was willing to go to meet him, Shea would still lock her out?

She shrugged as she fastened the gate and climbed into the saddle. At least she was going to tell him to deliver his own gifts or she wouldn't keep them.

If he were alone— Her blood raced. Arguments between them now could lead to only one thing. But did she want that if all he could ever feel for her was lust?

Pardo high-jumped out of the eagle pen, pant leg in tatters. "Man, that is one damn mean bird!" he panted. "The way she was taking pieces of that rabbit out of my hand, I though we were finally buddies!"

"I told you." Shea grinned. "That wire's up to protect us, not her."

Pardo stared at the eagle in reluctant admiration. She

was running around the pen, nabbing bits of the rabbit Pardo had brought her. Fascinated with the big raptor, Pardo had almost taken over her feeding.

Though he continued to marvel that Shea could be a "farmer," Pardo had started coming by for a beer when he wasn't busy at Stronghold. He wanted to talk about the war. Shea didn't much, yet it was a relief to be with someone who knew how it had been.

"Think she'll fly again?" Pardo asked, peering at the eagle.

Sated, she had picked up a soft ball Geronimo had given her. She seemed to think it was an egg and perched on it by the hour or hopped around with it clutched in her formidable yellow claws.

Shea shook his head. "Too early to guess. She can flop around some but a lot of feathers have to grow back. Those damn cats!"

"Dead cats, you mean," chuckled Pardo. "What a scrapper!" He sobered, ran a hand through his sparse beard. "I know how she feels, man. Remember that time our 'copter was shot down? You and me got back to back. Figgered we'd rather die than get taken! And then that Huey picked us up just in time?"

"We were lucky."

"Yeah." Pardo opened a beer. "The cats could never quite get your number, sarge. You were the best shot in the company. But you never fired at those gooks who came cruisin' out of the bush in their little black suits with their hands over their heads, even though they kept on running. Most of them had to be Viet Cong."

Shea didn't answer. During his last year, as well as being crew chief and door gunner, he'd been a platoon sergeant, assigning 'copter crews. He'd put a lot of energy into teaming gunners who shot at everything that moved, with careful pilots who'd keep them out of temptation, and he'd paired scrupulous gunners with killer pilots. But sometimes he couldn't juggle it out like that.

There had been one pilot who loved to kill. Shea

finally went to the chaplain. The chaplain reported Shea to the commander, who gave him a sharp little lecture on hurting "fighting morale." But Shea and a couple of friends had gone to see the pilot. They told him he'd better flunk his next flight physical or he wouldn't live to kill anyone else.

He had flunked the physical and been assigned to maintenance.

Yet in a way Shea had envied him. It was easier to be all-out than try to fight and be humane, easier to kill everyone than show mercy that could cost your life or prolong the hell. There were times that if he'd had the power to push a button and explode the whole world he would have done it out of despairing outrage.

Was there hope for a species so addicted to killing and war? To start with, wars had probably been kidnapping raids to get sacrificial victims to offer the gods. War was still human sacrifice. Thousands of Vietnamese had been immolated on the altar of a democracy they didn't understand, or that of a communism equally remote. It was rotten. But you lived or you died. Shea had decided to live.

"It's over," he said roughly.

"Don't shit me, man. It's still in both of us." Pardo crumpled the can, tossed it in the trash barrel. "Know what wakes me up in a sweat? I dream Jim Thomas—you remember that long lean kid with the big grin who was downed in Cambodia—I dream he's working under guard and locked up nights. I dream he asks why I don't help him."

It plagued Shea, too, with renewed bitterness after the big fuss over the Iranian hostages. A government that seemed ready to get tough over all manner of distant threats seemed to care very little about finding out what had happened to those thousands of men who were missing in action. The country might want to forget the lost war that had divided it, but it had no right to forsake the men sent out in its name.

Pardo's almond-shaped eyes riveted on Shea. "Why don't you and me go find us a good, honest little war?"

"There's no such animal. Anyhow, I thought you said you weren't fighting for any more flags."

"Not for flags, sarge. Money. By choice, gold."

"I've got a better idea. Come work here."

"Fixing fence? Planting grass? Thanks, but no thanks." Pardo shaded his eyes with his hand. "You've got company—and I do believe it's the chick Judd had at Stronghold the day you came steaming down about that deer." He chuckled. "I'll get along so's you can give her your undivided attention."

"No need," said Shea, but the tightness in his throat made his tone gruff.

Pardo only laughed and moved off at an angle that would avoid the golden mare and her rider. Jaime and Aniceto had gone to town for supplies. Geronimo was helping the Sanchezes with some work. Shea was alone as Tracy approached, sun gilding the dark honey hair, modeling the strong, piquant face with those imperiously arched eyebrows and rather broad mouth. Through the thin cotton of her shirt, he saw the sweetly firm curve of her breasts.

He didn't know whether to be glad she had come, or sorry. Sorry or glad, she was here. Before she left, he was going to have her.

Tracy reined in outside the ramada. Shea tossed a beer can aside and watched her with a challenging smile. "Light and have a beer? I guess you didn't meet any snakes or you wouldn't be so tidy."

"Güera shied at something in a bush," Tracy said, dismounting. She stared into those unreadable gray eyes. "Did you hope she'd throw me?"

He laughed. "Not at all. Since you're both fractious, I thought you'd get along real well."

This was not going the way Tracy had intended. "I came to thank you," she said, still trying to startle or elicit some betraying reaction. "And to ask why you can't deliver your presents?"

"Let's water this one," he suggested easily, taking the reins and starting for the tank shaded by the big black walnuts and mesquites. "Geronimo had to go help Chuey so it was simple for him to bring Güera."

"And Le Moyne?"

Stripping off the mare's saddle, he slung it over the corral, led her inside and slipped off the bridle. Coming back to Tracy, he stopped a few feet away. "Maybe I thought if I brought you presents, you might feel obligated."

"I don't believe that ever entered your head!"

He laughed coolly. "Then what's your explanation?"

"If you didn't bring the present," Tracy groped, "it's almost as if you didn't give it. You aren't taking any responsibility, damn you!"

"Now when did making gifts cause responsibility?" he mocked.

"You know it does. You sort of guarantee them and—and— If you give, it means you care—"

She faltered under that remote stare. Clenching her hands, she thrust up her chin. "Shea, if you don't care about me, I don't want presents!"

"Le Moyne and Güera aren't exactly presents," he countered. He took her wrists, holding them loosely. "Anyway, you've come. We both know why."

She didn't wrench free. Searching his face for some softening, she cried inwardly, *Love me! Oh love me, and say you do!* But he was silent, only smiled and drew her toward the house.

Blinded, she moved as if swept along by a fiery wind. As they stepped inside the adobe, a shadow struck. There was a sickening sound and Shea went down, bending slowly at the knees, trying to turn.

"Am I in luck!"

China-blue eyes gloated from a sunburned face surrounded by lank yellow hair. "Only thing better would be to get that Indian bitch, too!"

He had crashed the gun now pointed at Tracy into Shea's head. Blood trickled from the thick red-gold hair. Tracy started to drop to her knees by Shea, but the blond man snapped her wrist up painfully, keeping her on her feet.

"Maybe you've killed him!" she cried.

"Maybe I didn't. But unless you want me to make sure, sweetheart, you'll come along like a nice girl and do just what I say."

A frantic glance revealed no weapon in reach. The escapee tossed her a rope. "Tie him up—good, or I'll fix him so he won't need tying, ever."

Tracy complied. At least Shea was breathing. "I'd guess those keys by the door are to that old pickup," her captor went on. "Get 'em. We're going for a little ride."

"If you want money—"

He pulled Shea's wallet out of his hip pocket, tucked it into his own. "Thanks for reminding me." He gestured with the gun. "Now, baby, move!"

XIV

HE MADE HER DRIVE. HIS SWEATY ODOR WAS RANK WITH A hint of decaying fungus. He kept the gun pressed in her side. "Don't try anything cute. A gut wound hurts like hell. You'd take a long time to die."

Her hands were clammy. She had to swallow before she could speak, but her mind was icily clear. "Why make a lot of trouble for yourself? Let me out and keep going."

"I'll let you out when I'm ready."

"If you're heading for Mexico, you can't get me through the guards."

He rested his free hand on her knee. "Don't you worry about a thing."

That touch confirmed what she'd feared. He wasn't just going to leave her on foot a long way from help. Grimly, she resolved that if they sighted any vaqueros, she'd sound the horn and take her chances. If they got on the highway, she'd take the ditch where someone would see them.

They never reached the highway. "Take this set of tracks," he ordered, indicating a faint road turning off up a cãnon.

"It stops at an old corral."

He chuckled in a way that made her feel as if a centipede were crawling over her. "That's far enough, babe."

He meant to rape her, probably kill her, and make for the border in the pickup. Tracy's thoughts raced, seeking her best chance. She swung onto the tracks widely enough to, she hoped, make fresh prints on the slim chance someone might follow.

Should she hope for a second when they stopped and were getting out of the truck? Wait for an opportunity when lust might throw him off guard?

That might be smartest, but she thought of Houston. No, not that again. She'd ram the corral.

A useless windmill spun above an empty concrete tank inside the corral. This camp had been abandoned several years ago because the well was dry. Several of the big trees around it were dead, but half a dozen were showing new leaf.

"Shade and grass." The blond's voice rasped with excitement. "Now we'll just have us a good time— Hey! You crazy?"

Tracy caught a deep breath and jammed down on the accelerator. "Bitch!" He numbed Tracy's ankle with a kick, grabbed for the wheel and tried to get his foot on the brake.

The momentum of the pickup was too great. As they fought for the wheel, it smashed into the corral, scattering poles and posts, glanced into the cement tank and turned over.

Tracy came slowly, foggily out of flame-shot darkness. Crushing pain in her legs sent her briefly back into the haze. Then she remembered what had happened. She tried to move, found that her legs were pinned beneath the cab.

A slow obscene cursing came from a few feet away. Painfully turning her head, Tracy saw that her abductor was also trapped, only his head and shoulders clear of the wreckage. With the nearest arm, he groped for her.

"Going to choke you like I should have at the start,"

he gasped. "Feels like my ribs are all broke! When I get hold of you—"

His fingers brushed her arm. Desperately writhing as far as she could to the side, Tracy tried again to work her legs free. She gained an inch or two.

The dirty broken-nailed hand sought with a blind intelligence of its own. He had called her every filthy name she'd ever heard and was starting over.

"—split you wide open! Should of done it in front of your boyfriend, made you—"

Tracy's searching fingers closed on a rock. It took all her strength to grip it. Her legs screamed with strained agony as she turned, half-raised and brought the rock down as hard as she could on his hand.

He shrieked. Maddened into superhuman effort, he heaved till the pickup moved a fraction. The effort must have done something to him. He collapsed and was still. Frothy blood bubbled from his mouth.

Punctured lungs? Tracy felt not a twinge of concern or pity. That awful, crawling hand! Horrible to think of lying here by a dying man, but that was better than being trapped while he tried to reach her.

When would they be found? Sometime, Jaime and Geronimo would find Shea, unless Aniceto got there first. If Shea didn't have a concussion from that blow on the head, he could explain what had happened. Some of it would be clear, anyway.

If they'd just notice the tire tracks where she'd swung wide to follow the old tracks— Surely, she wouldn't have to lie here and die of thirst.

The sun beat brightly, cruelly down. The ankle her captor had kicked throbbed dully. Were her legs broken?

There was a sort of choking sound from the blond man. His hands flailed. Then he was so quiet that she was sure he was dead. She couldn't be sorry, though she wondered if anyone had loved him and what kind of a family he'd come from.

If they weren't found soon— She had seen decaying,

bloated animals, knew the sweet putrid smell. That would send her crazy if she didn't die first.

Oh Shea, Shea!

She prayed that he wasn't much hurt, then pushed herself up on her palms to see if there was anything she could do. A glance at the man showed his eyes staring at the sun while his stubbly jaws gaped in a snarl.

Shuddering, she confronted the top of the cab. Was there any way to lever it up enough to let her wriggle free? Looking around, she dragged together all the rocks she could reach, including the one she'd hit the dead man with.

None was big enough to wedge the cab up enough to get her loose, but they could at least take some of the weight off her. She worked them beneath the truck, pushing small ones as far back as she could, increasing the size near the top.

The earth wasn't as hard as usual here. If she couldn't lever up the truck, maybe she could dig out. No useful sticks were available, but she wrenched off a windshield wiper and began to dig with the metal end.

She couldn't reach far enough to get beyond her knees. Bitterly disappointed, she still scraped away as much dirt as she could. It was something to do. She thought of the women of her family, especially of Socorro, who might have died in the desert if she hadn't refused to give up.

That helped. As she labored, Tracy suddenly wondered if she couldn't burrow out enough space beneath the cab to bend her upper body under and eventually dig her lower legs loose.

"You've got nothing but time," she said aloud.

Inspired by the possibility that she *could* escape, she looked about for a better tool. Where was the gun? Distasteful as it was to touch the corpse, she felt around the arms, sighed with relief as she found the pistol.

The gunbarrel was a better tool than the wiper. Rearranging the rocks, she dug out a space beside her and tediously lengthened it. Her throat was parched and she no longer had enough saliva to moisten her tongue.

Blisters began. She worked off her shirt and padded the gun with it, but the blisters grew and broke. Now and then she put the gun aside to clean out her diggings.

It seemed that she'd never done anything but scrape with the heavy pistol against the hard earth. She could get her arm back almost to her feet, though. Just a little farther!

Face pressed into the ground, bent forward and reaching down through the hollow she had tunneled, Tracy was at last working near her feet. After what seemed forever, she could scrape painfully alongside her one foot and beneath it till it could move.

Dizzy with exertion, she rested, then cleared enough room to work at the other foot and leg. At last, she could move that foot, too, but it brought such a white-hot searing in her ankle that she almost fainted.

When the wave of nauseating agony passed, she clamped her teeth together and maneuvered herself out of her prison. Her left leg was cramped and sore, but her right ankle was the problem. Pulling down the sock, she groaned as she saw how puffy and swollen it was.

After all that, not to be able to walk!

She could crawl and drag herself around, though. There should be water in the pickup; it was foolhardy to drive without it in this country. Hitching herself over the cab top, she looked in the window. There were several plastic jugs of water behind the seat.

Nothing had ever tasted so good. She drank deeply, washed her blistered hands, and drank again.

Feeling better, she sat on the hood and considered. At the latest, Shea would be found that evening. Even if—her heart shriveled at the thought—he couldn't speak, the presence of Güera would show she'd been there, and the missing pickup would tell its story. The vaqueros would search and there was the plane.

She'd be found. Certainly by next day. There was

plenty of water to last till then. Rather than crawl and get her hands in worse shape, she'd better stay close to the wreck, which could easily be spotted. Her stomach knotted at the thought of spending the night near the dead man, but she was in no condition to be squeamish. About the best she could sensibly do would be to get over to the other side of the tank.

The pickup yielded a pack of Geronimo's cigarettes, book matches, first-aid kit, flashlight, tools and an old jacket. There were also a few grungy Life Savers.

"Supper," she told herself wryly.

She was dousing her blisters with Merthiolate, swearing and wincing, when she heard a humming sound overhead. Wings flashed in the sun. She scrambled to turn the outside mirror over to catch the sun.

The plane flew over. Hadn't the pilot seen? She breathed again as it swept in a wide turn. At that moment, she heard another motor. The plane started to descend. The area beyond the trees near the tank was level for at least a half-mile, trampled almost to barrenness by cattle.

It was Judd's plane. As it touched down, Geronimo's old truck came in sight. Tracy peered to see who was driving. It was Geronimo, but Shea was beside him!

Overjoyed, she sprang up, forgetting her ankle. Pain scalded like a fountain and she fell.

She knew that Shea's arms were cradling her even before she opened her eyes. It was so sweet to be held like that, hear him calling her name, that she was tempted to keep still, but his tone was frightened, and besides, she wanted to know if he was all right.

Looking up into his worried face as he knelt beside her, she managed a smile. "You—you must have a headache."

"He's got one thick skull," Geronimo said. "Jaime and I came in early and found him trying to get on a horse in spite of being so groggy he couldn't get his foot through the stirrup."

Tracy sat up. Dried blood crusted the side of Shea's head. "You need to see a doctor," she said.

"So do you," he retorted grimly.

Judd suddenly scooped Tracy up in his arms. "We can be at an emergency room in Tucson in half an hour," he said.

Tracy caught Shea's arm. "You come, too! You may have a concussion or something."

"I'm fine and there are things to see to here."

The dead man, the sheriff. Shea disengaged himself. "I'll get over this evening to see how you are. If you can't stand on that ankle, you'd better stay at the big house for a while."

"But Le Moyne—"

"I'll get him, *chica*," Geronimo promised. "Don't worry about this *bobo*. If he starts acting crazier than usual, I'll get him to a doctor in Nogales."

Bruised and sore as she was, it was foolish to argue against going to the hospital, but she was glad when Judd put her in the seat of the plane and she was no longer in his possessive grasp.

It was sunset when he carried her upstairs to see Patrick. They had agreed not to tell him about the thug, but just say that her vehicle had flipped and she'd be staying at the house till she could get around.

"They X-ray you?" Patrick rumbled. "Sure you don't have cracked ribs or such?"

Tracy laughed, though it hurt her chest. She hurt all over. "They gave me a good going-over, Patrick. I'll be black and blue awhile but not even this dumb ankle is broken."

"You were lucky."

She shivered, kissing him. "Yes, I was."

Judd helped her to a chair, and Mary brought food. Her eyes questioned Tracy, who smiled and merely made an "okay" sign, for Geronimo had brought Le Moyne over and he would tell Mary the whole story.

Presumably, Shea was all right, but Tracy took her first really deep breath since the whole thing began when steps sounded on the stairs and he strode into the room. Tracy touched her lips with a finger as his gaze swept over her.

He nodded and greeted his father, shaking his hand, before he sat down where he could study her.

Quickly, Tracy let him know she had no serious hurts. He had washed the blood off his head, and though there must have been a scalp wound, thick red-gold hair concealed it.

Once assured her injuries were slight, he seemed to forget about her. "Sure wish you could see the love grass coming up," he told his father. "You always said a good spread of grass was prettier to you than a field of flowers."

"Should be to everyone," Patrick said belligerently. "When you get right down to it, plants are the only things that can change air, soil and water into food. We step on 'em and never think, but our life depends on them."

"Fat lot of good Shea's grass will do anyone," Judd snapped.

"There you're wrong," Shea said easily.

Judd frowned. "What do you mean?"

"When the range is ready, I'll run some cows. What it'll carry. No more than that, and not till then."

"Hell's bells!" Judd choked. "It's already better than any graze on the ranch!" He flushed to the roots of his tawny hair as he realized how that sounded. "For God's sake! This isn't Kentucky bluegrass country!"

"No, so we can't act like it is."

Patrick sighed, rubbing his eyes. "I sure wish I could have a ride around and see," he muttered.

Judd said impatiently, "Dad, the only way to keep up our operation the way you've known it is to grow more feed. Sell off the land that's really gone and irrigate alfalfa."

"We're not selling the old house and land around it, even if we go broke." Patrick's tone was final. "And what happens when the wells run dry?"

"That won't be in our lifetime," Judd shrugged.

Patrick's sightless eyes glared at his oldest son. "What the hell difference does that make? There are people coming after us! You want to be the last generation that lives on this ranch?"

"You want me to manage the ranch but you tie my hands!" Judd accused.

Patrick's paralyzed side seemed to drag him down. "I'm goddam tired of this wrangling between you boys." His voice frayed. "Can't ride out or see for myself or judge who has the right of it. I feel like a log the two of you keep stubbing into. If that aggravates you, it does the same to me. Hurts, too."

It was the closest Patrick had ever come to self-pity.

Both sons looked startled. "Sorry, Dad." Shea got to his feet and squeezed his father's arm. "If you ever believed anything I said, believe this: That new grass is as pretty as any you've ever seen. There can be people at El Charco just as long as they remember this is desert and act accordingly. See you later."

He gave Tracy a nod and left.

"Make me a drink, Judd," sighed Patrick. "Join us, ladies?"

"I'd like to stretch out," Tracy said. "Mary, will you give me a hand?"

"Judd, you do that," urged Patrick. "Then come back."

"With pleasure."

Judd grinned at Tracy as he picked her up. "We'd have better balance, honey, if you put your arms around my neck."

She compromised by clasping his shoulder. He'd been kind and helpful at the hospital and hadn't taken advantage of her condition. She felt more friendly toward him than she had since his deceit with the cattle and was ready to make a truce as long as he didn't pursue her.

Mary had followed them down. There was nothing Judd could do but deposit Tracy on her bed, drop a kiss on her cheek, and say he'd see her in the morning.

"Now," said Mary, helping Tracy undress. "Tell me all! The sheriff rousted me out to identify that bastard. I'm sorry he picked on you instead of me, but at least we won't have to go in for his trial."

XV

BEFORE MARY LEFT, SHE BROUGHT IN LE MOYNE. HE whimpered his joy and resoundingly licked Tracy's hands before he could be persuaded to lie down on the bedside rug.

Tracy was glad of him. In spite of the pineapple juice heavily laced with rum that Mary had made, she kept reliving the terror of that day, especially those horrible moments when she'd been trapped beneath the pickup with the man reaching for her, and then when he was dead.

At least, she thought with grim amusement as she reached down for a reassuring caress of Le Moyne's head, this experience would effectively blot out her memories of that attack in Houston. A change of nightmares.

And for it to happen like that, when Shea was about to make love to her! Unhappy puzzlement made her turn restlessly, though her body ached at the motion. He'd come as he'd promised, but had practically ignored her and hadn't waited so they could talk.

How did he feel about her, anyway? She had intended to find out that day, but now she was more baffled than before.

The sheriff came for her details next day, and Vashti was avid for the whole story. "He didn't—uh—?"

"He didn't rape me," Tracy answered shortly.

"But to drive into that concrete tank! When he had a gun!"

"I hoped he'd be too busy with the truck to kill me."

Vashti shook her head. "I couldn't have done it." Her tongue touched her upper lip. "Judd says he was young. Was he good-looking?"

Tracy gave Patrick's wife a stare of surprise. "He might have been, cleaned up."

"Don't look so prim," Vashti giggled. Tracy realized that the older woman had been drinking, though it was only ten in the morning. "If you must be abducted, dear, better it be by a handsome brute than an ugly one!"

"At times like that, you don't care what anyone looks like," Tracy said. She pulled up, awkwardly manipulating the crutches that had been unearthed for her.

With the help of the handrail, she was halfway up the stairs before Mary ran down to help. "If you can stand some raunchy stories, Patrick's telling some good ones!" Mary laughed.

"That's just what I need," grinned Tracy, and thrust Vashti almost forcibly from her mind. Why was Patrick stuck with a woman like that instead of one who could have brightened his darkness?

A few days later, Judd flew to New York for the talk show and some business. Though he hadn't crowded her, Tracy was more comfortable without him around. She hoped she could move back to Last Spring before he returned.

"You really like that little place, don't you?" Patrick asked when she was describing the ringtail, the owls, the blue-bellied lizard who did push-ups to dazzle his lady love.

"I love it." She pondered a moment and thought aloud, in surprised realization, "I guess it's the first place I really felt at home." She added hastily, "I loved the old ranch house, Patrick, and you were all tremendously good. But I missed my mother and—well, it was home to all of you, but I was just sort of tucked in."

Patrick chuckled, not in the least offended. "Some places belong to some people and some people belong to some places. Maybe you've found yours."

"It's been wonderful but I can't stay there forever."

"Why not?"

She laughed. "You know how that is, Patrick. I have to go out in the wide world and seek my fortune."

"What if your fortune's here?"

Her heart turned over as she thought of Shea. "I doubt I'll be that lucky," she said wistfully, then laughed to cover it. "I come from the roving-stranger side of the family, Patrick. We never have stayed put."

"It's about time you did," he said crossly. "And it's time those boys of mine, both of them, got married. It would tickle me pink if you decided to have one of them."

"I don't think they're the marrying kind," Tracy countered lightly. "And I don't think I am, either." *Not unless it's Shea.* She changed the subject to Mary's mechanics course, much safer ground.

Shea came one evening and played Christina's piano. It sounded beautiful to Tracy. Mary sat in rapt delight, and Patrick smiled dreamily.

"You've got a gift," he said, when Shea paused. "I swear, listening like that, I'd think you were my mother playing, except your touch is stronger and you've got more flair."

Shea forced a grin. "You're an encouraging audience, but hell, I sound so bad to myself I almost hate to play."

"You don't do it often enough," Patrick argued.

Shea stared at his scarred hands. "That's not it, Dad."

Patrick was silent a moment. "Yeah. But practice would help, wouldn't it?"

"Sure. If I practiced up to the best of what I can do

now, I might be good enough for a roadhouse or a country church."

"You're good enough for me," Patrick insisted.

"Me, too," said Mary.

Tracy just looked at Shea, aching to make up to him the pain he'd had.

"Play some more," said Patrick. Shea did, and they listened in the twilight that was soft and enfolding as a mother's arms.

Hal Fricks was back with a higher offer from Vistas Unlimited, but though Patrick refused it, Fricks stayed on as Vashti's guest, swimming with her, playing tennis, mixing her drinks. His sandy hair and moustache were streaked yellow from the sun and, bronzed and fit, he could have posed for bathing-suit ads.

He clucked over Tracy's ankle and obviously set himself to be charming, but she avoided him all she could. Vashti was furious at Patrick's refusal of the developer's offer, but Frick's attentions diverted her to the point of leaving Patrick alone.

Four days after his arrival, the developer intercepted Tracy as she came down from lunching with Patrick and Mary. "Too bad about your ankle, but it's clear that your foster-father's glad to have you back. He worships you."

"He always wanted a daughter," Tracy said, and started past, but Hal Fricks caught her arm. "We never have a chance to talk. Let me get you a glass of wine and let's visit a few minutes."

"I'm rather tired and—"

Taking her crutch, he almost forced her to sit on the long couch. "I won't beat around the bush, Tracy. You have influence with your uncle, probably more than anyone. If you can get him to sell Last Spring and the land near the highway, you get not only a free luxury condo, but a percentage of the profits on the subdivision."

Astonished that he'd approach her again, she stared

at him. "Big bucks, Tracy!" he smiled, caressing her arm.

Dry, harsh anger rose in her. "No."

She reached for her crutch but he put it beyond her. "Come on!" His tone was incredulous. "I know you've got a trust fund, but it's not enough to turn up your nose at a condo worth a couple of hundred thousand and a lot more cash!"

"I wonder how you draw up contracts for bribes." She raised her voice. "Le Moyne!"

The big dog trotted out of her room, looked inquiringly at Fricks, who reddened and got to his feet. "Craziness runs in the family," he snorted and stalked off.

With difficulty, Tracy retrieved the crutch, patted Le Moyne and was starting for her room when Vashti came running from the pool, a lavender towel clutched over her bikini.

"You little bitch!" she choked breathlessly. "I wish you'd never come back! Cosying up to Judd, bringing in that Indian slut, and when you could be a little help, oh no, you're too good to want money!" She shook her fist. "Well, let me tell you, Miss Priss, the only reason you're so high and mighty about money is because you've always had it. I wasn't so lucky."

"You're drunk, Vashti."

"And you're not, you damned goody-goody!" Full breasts heaving, eyes blazing almost black, Vashti hurled her words. "This damned ranch is losing money, not making it! Offers like Hal's don't come along every day—"

She collapsed on the couch and began to cry. Physically nauseated by the woman, Tracy went down the hall to her room, called in Le Moyne and locked the door.

"My friend," she told him, rubbing the broad head between the pricked-up ears, "we'll stay till that charm-boy landshark leaves, but then we're heading for home!

Otherwise, I may wrap this crutch around that female's conniving head!"

He made a soft sound of approval, but Tracy felt so dirty and disgusted that she took a shower.

To her relief, Fricks said good-bye next day at breakfast. Vashti was flying him to town and would stay in to shop and see friends for a few days. The house was much more relaxed without them. There was singing from the kitchen and giggling among the young women who did the housework.

Tracy didn't want to make it clear to Patrick that she was avoiding Vashti, so she announced that day that her ankle was much better and she needed to get back to her photography. A good publisher was interested in her idea, but wanted to see some pictures and text.

Patrick squeezed her hand. "I won't interfere with your rise to fame," he said. "But I still expect to see you every day. One of the Sanchez lads can chauffeur you till you can drive yourself."

Tivi took her and Le Moyne home, helped her across the creek, and promised to come for her about nine next day. He also pumped several buckets of water and fetched in cookwood.

Tracy thanked him. When he was gone, she looked around the little cabin with pleasure and a sense of peace. "Good to be back, isn't it, Le Moyne? But I hope you haven't gone off soyburgers while you were eating steak bones!"

Her ankle was well enough now that she could limp around the tiny cabin. She puttered for a bit and then settled in the rocker with her photographs and notebooks. What she really wanted to do was climb to the owl blind and see how the owlets were, but she was going to have to be cautious. Her picture-taking, for a while, would be limited to whatever came close to the house.

She sighed impatiently, but was soon absorbed in the

pictures. Out of hundreds of exposures, she had sifted
two dozen. These would have to be screened again by
the editors, for she simply couldn't, herself, reject any
of them. The owls were her favorites, except for the
doe and fawn touching noses, but the foxes were such
beautiful creatures, and the little ringtail—

Le Moyne got up and moved to the open door.
Alerted, she heard the sound of horses. When she
hopped to the door, her heart went into her throat.

Shea, on a big iron-gray, was leading golden Güera.
"Heard you were back in residence," he called, dismounting. "Since your left ankle's okay for mounting,
maybe you can ride easier than you can drive a car."

"It'll save my life." Tracy's voice was so fervent that
she blushed. "It's really kind of you to bring Güera."

He grinned. His gray eyes made her tremble inwardly. He had such a power with her, such a power, and he
didn't seem to care. "I thought I'd better bring her
myself," he said. "Seems she belongs to a very pernick-
ety lady who looks gift horses in the mouth."

Without waiting for her response, which was just as
well, because Tracy couldn't think of one, he led the
horses to the corral. Tracy's breath came fast. He was
unsaddling the gray, too!"

When he strode to the cabin, he took her in his arms.
She drew down his head, reaching up to press against
him, lose herself in the harsh sweetness of his kiss.

He was her man. When he came to her, she couldn't
ask questions or bargain or stand on her pride. Lifting
his head, he smiled into her eyes. "That day you rode
over, we were just starting something important when
we were rudely interrupted. Want to try again?"

A tremulous laugh was all the answer she could
make. That, and clasping her arms around him as he
gently picked her up.

He stayed for supper, making them an omelet and
salad from the food Concha and Henri had loaded her
with. Topped off with coffee and some of Concha's flan,

it was a feast. Anything would have been, shared with Shea, together in this little cabin that was more a home than any she had had.

"You're not afraid here?" he asked. "After that guy, I wouldn't blame you for being nervous."

"There's Le Moyne." She gave a little shrug. "Anyhow, I'm not going to let what's over keep me from enjoying what's now."

The words were out before she realized he might take them as a criticism, but his smile was approving. "That's the way to get the most out of catching butterflies."

She blinked. "Catching butterflies?"

"*Coger mariposas*. It's a phrase for what we just did." The edges of his eyes crinkled. "Nicer than the English slang?"

"By a long way." She laughed back at him, blissful.

This was the first time he hadn't left her immediately after making love, the first time they'd talked easily and joked. Was he starting to trust her? His gaze traveled slowly around the room.

"Pretty Spartan. Are you trying to be like Thoreau at Walden?"

"I'll confess I'm beginning to wish I had a refrigerator. But there's no use getting in electricity and plumbing unless I stay into the autumn."

"And that depends on?"

"Patrick. Mary's made a wonderful companion for him, but I'll stay as long as he seems to want me."

Bronze eyebrows lifted above his straight nose. "You're not just itching to get back to Houston?"

He didn't know what had happened to her there and she didn't want, not yet, to tell him. Repressing a shiver, she shook her head. "Whatever happens, I doubt I'll go back to Houston. Traffic's horrendous and that steam heat wilts me. Maybe I'll try San Francisco. That's an interesting place."

"Should be."

He got up and began doing the dishes, his usual

reserve settling around him like an invisible shell. Perching on a stool to wipe after he rinsed, Tracy tried to banter him into the relaxed mood that had just inexplicably ended.

"Speaking of Thoreau, you guys have a pretty basic setup there at El Charco. Do you sleep in the ramada?"

"Till it gets cold. Makes sense in this country to live outside in warm weather. You need a roof for shade, but walls only hamper the breeze. And the roof needs spaces for ventilation. We don't put a mattress over the springs of a cot. That keeps the air from reaching and cooling you, and there's no cloth to get fouled by mice or birds. When it gets really hot, a hundred or so, which seldom happens at this altitude, you can throw water under and around the cots for coolness and keeping down the dust. As long as there's plenty of water to drink and you get enough salt and minerals to replace your electrolytes, you can cool yourself by sweating."

"And siesta half the day?"

"Why not? We're working by five in the summer. We can knock off by nine or ten, cool it in the ramada till three or four, work till dark, and get in a full day's work."

"That doesn't sound much like Thoreau."

"It's not *Walden*. However, he had his cabin furnished so it could be swept out in two minutes. He didn't believe in letting things own you. If he'd lived down here, I bet he'd have had a ramada, a clay water *olla* and bare spring cot."

Tracy sniffed. "He lived at Walden only about two years. And he scarfed up a lot of Mama's cooking even then, carried home lots of her pies."

"Is nothing sacred?" Shea groaned.

"He doesn't need myths. But I'll bet you if he'd been less ascetic and had a wife, he wouldn't have died in his early forties."

"He might have died sooner."

"Married men live longer," said Tracy doggedly,

though she wished she hadn't tilted the conversation in this direction.

Shea nodded. "Maybe it just seems longer."

Tossing out the dishwater, he hung up the pan, neatly draped the dishcloth over it and turned. He saw the photos and notes, came to look down at the one of the ringtail. "May I look?"

"Of course."

Anxiously, she waited while he went through the pictures. He smiled a couple of times, but was frowning when he put them down. "I didn't know you were so good."

"It's more luck and patience." He was impressed, but the effect on him worried her. She laughed nervously. "I took hundreds of shots. These are the good ones."

He gave her a long slow look. "Don't apologize for what you are," he said. A kind of tightness seemed to dissolve in him. "You can ride, probably, but you're not up to saddling a horse. Shall I come back in a day or two and give Sangre a workout?"

"Sounds like fun."

He didn't kiss her, but at the door he stopped. "Maybe we could catch a few butterflies." He laughed and went out into the dusk.

XVI

HE WAS WAITING NEXT DAY WHEN TIVI BROUGHT HER back from visiting Patrick. Since it was close to noon, they made a quick lunch. Then he saddled the horses and, followed by Le Moyne, they rode up a trail that wound through the cañon and up a steep narrow way to a broad mountain meadow. He lifted her down and carried her to a pile of smooth rocks. After he had loosened the horses' cinches, he untied the blanket from behind his saddle and spread it on the grass.

They made love, bodies sensuously laved in sun and air. Afterward, they rested lazily, while happiness glowed warm as the sunlight inside Tracy.

He *must* care about her. In time, if she didn't crowd him, surely he'd admit it?

"A great place for butterflies," he said, stroking her from breast to flank. She leaned over and kissed him.

"I wonder if Socorro and her San Patricio ever made love up here?"

"Who knows? But I've thought it'd be interesting to go to the Pinacates, where they rescued each other, and try to retrace the journey. Maybe go around by Tinajas Altas, where Judah Frost and so many others died, and then head south."

"I'd love to do that!"

"Well, maybe we can. Before you go to San Francisco."

She wanted to say that she wouldn't go anywhere if he wanted her to stay, but that might jar his escape mechanisms. Maybe he'd become less wary since he thought she would be leaving and was no permanent threat to his Thoreau-ish desert-rat existence.

Sitting up, lips tightened, she began to dress.

When they rode up to the cabin, Judd was waiting. He stood proprietorially on the step, arms crossed, squarish gold-brown head atilt. Shea's face closed.

"You've got company."

Judd strode forward to lift her down. "You should have come to New York with me, doll! It was a blast. The calls and telegrams I've gotten! I'm going on a speaking tour and—"

"Shea, won't you stay for supper?" Tracy asked desperately.

"You and Judd have catching up to do." Shea's tone was brittle. He didn't look up from unsaddling Güera.

Tracy despaired. So quick to be suspicious! So ready to shut her out! Didn't their loving mean anything? Fighting tears of furious hurt, she said brightly, "Thanks for the ride—and the butterflies!"

Back stiffly erect, she slipped her arm through Judd's and let him help her to the house. Full of his talk-show triumph, he boasted about its results. Several prominent senators had invited him to Washington to testify at Congressional hearings and he was deluged with applications for Stronghold.

"That article of yours did it, Tracy." His big hand closed over hers. "How'd you like to be my public relations honcho?"

"Honcha? Honchess?" She forced Shea from her mind and tried to smile, though she was appalled at her article's apparently having had an effect exactly the reverse of what she'd intended. "Thanks, Judd, but I'm doing PR for some owls."

His yellow eyes lingered over her. "Maybe I can make you an offer you can't refuse."

Afraid of where that sort of talk might lead and

preferring to stay on cordial terms with him, for Patrick's sake, she got up and hopped over to the stove.

"Will you stay for supper?"

"Sure, but I'll help."

He built the fire and made salad while she put together enchiladas. They had a pleasant meal, but she was glad when he left early, saying he had to make a number of phone calls.

When he kissed her, she turned her face so his lips brushed her cheek. He laughed, apparently too exuberant to be put off, and went away whistling. Tracy sat down, propped up her ankle and patted Le Moyne, who came to lie beside her.

"Dog," she said, "your former master is one hardheaded man!" Just when Shea'd seemed to be thawing, he'd frozen up again. She was damned tired of it.

All the same, when she lay down that night, she remembered the sun and air of the mountain meadow and used the memory of their loving as a shield against those nightmares that waited to engulf her in the darkness.

When Tivi drove her to the big house next morning, Tracy saw with a sinking heart that the plane was back so Vashti must be. The best to hope for was that she'd stay booze-numbed enough not to harass Patrick.

That expectation died as Tracy limped through the door. Vashti's strident voice reached all the way downstairs, though Tracy couldn't distinguish words till she started up the steps.

". . . fantastic offer for that worn-out land and isolated spring! This is our last chance. Hal's given us till Sunday. If you don't see sense by then, he's offering for another property."

"He can offer right damn now!" came Patrick's weak growl.

There was a hiss of rage. "You blind old fool! You miserable cripple!"

"Patrick!" Tracy called, gripping the handrail and taking the stairs as fast as she could. "Patrick!"

That should quieten Vashti. Mary must not be in the room. She ran down the hall, though, as Tracy neared the top of the flight, and when Tracy entered her uncle's room, Mary was standing by Patrick, arm protectively around him.

"Quit shouting, Mrs. Scott. You're upsetting your husband."

Vashti was past restraint. "Husband!" she sneered. "Might as well be a fallen log, rotting away in the middle of the road, blocking everyone who can move!"

Tracy caught her arm, smelled whiskey on her breath, and shoved her toward the door. "Go sober up!"

Vashti sprang for her, hands clawed. Tracy dodged awkwardly. Mary grabbed Vashti, pinned her arm behind her back. "If you were a man, I'd kick you in the balls!" she said between her teeth. "Get out of here, Mrs. Scott, or I'll kick your ass up between your shoulders!"

"You dirty Indian bitch! You think I haven't seen you rubbing yourself against that old wreck, letting him feel you up—?"

Mary slapped Vashti halfway across the room. In the same instant, there was a gasping, strangling sound from the bed.

Patrick's body arched, convulsed. Tracy made for the phone, sure he was having another stroke, but as she dialed the doctor, he choked, "My—my heart—"

Mary ran to him. He died in her arms.

Vashti, unsurprisingly, ordered Mary off the place at once. "You can stay at the cabin," Tracy told her. "I'm staying here till the doctor comes, and Judd and Shea."

Weeping over Patrick, Vashti lifted her shining head. "I suppose you'll tattletale! I loved Patrick! But he could be so goddam aggravating!"

"He won't aggravate you anymore," Tracy said. Her voice sounded as cold and disembodied as she felt. "Certainly I'm going to tell his sons what you said to him. You caused his death."

"I never touched him!"

"That was part of the trouble," Tracy said.

Brushing Vashti aside, she closed Patrick's eyes and sat down to wait.

Husbands and wives quarrel frequently. That Patrick had died during such a fight was, of course, no legal charge against Vashti. Judd shrugged helplessly when Tracy told him.

"Hell, baby, it's just lucky for me Dad didn't do this when he and I would be arguing about managing the ranch!"

"An argument's one thing," Tracy said. "Calling him the names she did, making those filthy accusations—"

"She was drunk."

"That's an excuse?"

Judd stared as if amazed at Tracy's implacability. "What the hell can I do about it? You want me to try to get her cut out of his will?"

"No." Tracy drooped.

After all, realistically, what could be done? Vashti's behavior since Patrick's death had even convinced her that the woman had loved him, though she'd shrunk from his paralyzed body. "I guess I don't want her to pose as a heartbroken widow and expect a lot of deference."

"I expect she'll move to Tucson or Phoenix right away," Judd reasoned.

Tracy sighed. "I suppose so. It was just so cruel, what she said."

The scalding tears that she'd suppressed burst out. She leaned against the wall and sobbed, not just for Patrick, beloved as he had been, but for the manner of his death. If only he knew that Mary had held him against her warm young breast and deeply mourned him.

"Here, sweetheart." Judd took Tracy in his arms and let her cry till she could stop before he gave her his big handkerchief. "It helps to know that Patrick didn't want to live the way he was. He hoped for a while to get back some use of his left side, but when it got pretty clear he wouldn't, it was worse than jail for him."

"But he—he laughed. He joked and told stories."

"Yes," said Judd. "And at night, when everyone was gone, don't you reckon he cried?"

Tracy had no answer.

Tivi had gone to tell Shea before taking Mary to Last Spring. Shea, Geronimo and Don Aniceto came up almost as the doctor did. Vashti was in her room.

The look in Shea's eyes as he gazed down at his father made Tracy resolve not to add to his grief by telling him what his stepmother had done. Patrick was dead. There would be enough trouble over his holdings without embittering the struggle. Vashti knew her guilt. Let that punish her.

The doctor made his examination, asked questions, filled in the death certificate and left. Singly and in groups, the vaqueros came, hats in hand, brown faces sorrowful, to pay their respects. Patrick was godfather to many of the younger, the working companion of the older, and the friend of all of them.

Shea didn't stay long. After a few silent moments, he took his father's hands and pressed them to his face. Bending, he kissed the wrinkled cheek. Then he turned swiftly away, not looking at anyone. Geronimo followed, and Don Aniceto who was weeping unashamedly.

The hearse and funeral director arrived. Vashti had pulled herself together enough to make the arrangements, with Judd's help. Day after tomorrow, Patrick's body would be brought back to the ranch to be buried in the family graveyard as he'd desired.

Two of the Sanchezes carried Patrick to the hearse. Tracy watched the dark-gray vehicle out of sight. She could still not believe that the man who'd been like her father, who'd kept his zest in life even when blind and paralyzed, was really dead. She longed to be with Shea. But he'd left without a word.

"I want to go home," she said.

Judd helped her to his RV. "I'll take you."

When they parked by the stream, he caught her arm as she started to open the door. "Tracy. What do you plan to do now?"

She hadn't really thought, though staying at the ranch on Vashti's sufferance was unthinkable, even if the older woman had allowed it. "I don't know," Tracy said slowly. "I'd like to finish my book. Maybe I can rent something around Tubac and Patagonia."

"Why not stay here?"

Tracy gave a bitter laugh. "Vashti may leave the ranch as fast as she can, but she won't want me here."

"I do." As she stared at him, Judd took her face in his hands. The smoldering light in his eyes sent a tingling shock through her. "I never thought I'd get married, but you've changed my mind. Stay here, Tracy. Let's get married."

Taken completely by surprise, Tracy tried to draw away, but he laughed and found her lips. His mouth was hot, avid, seeking. Tracy didn't fight. She only was still.

After a moment, Judd lifted his head. "I guess it's the wrong time for kissing. But hell, I've got to keep you from running off someplace!"

"I can't marry you, Judd."

His eyes narrowed. "Why?"

"I told you before. I don't love you."

He snorted. "I suppose you still think you're in love with someone else?"

She thought of Shea as he'd been that day with

Patrick and sorrow for him tightened her throat. "I *am* in love, Judd."

"So when's the wedding?"

"There may not be one. All the same—"

He got out and came around to help her out. "We'll talk about it later. This isn't a good time."

"It won't make any difference."

He grinned at her cockily. "We'll see."

He steadied her across the foot-log and walked her to the cabin. "Take it easy," he told her. "And don't do anything sudden. You can stay at the ranch even if you don't marry me."

Dropping a kiss on her forehead, he moved away, while Tracy went inside and into Mary's arms.

Tracy had known that Mary liked Patrick, but she hadn't known how deep the affection went. "There's no one left like him," Mary sobbed. "Him or Grandpa. That bitchy wife of his!"

"She loved him," Tracy said. "But she couldn't handle what happened to him."

"She's still a bitch."

"Why, yes, I think she is," Tracy agreed. "Let's not worry about her. What do you want to do now?"

"I've saved most of my wages. Enough to finish up my mechanics' course if I can find a job in Nogales that'll pay room and board."

"Poor Geronimo!"

Mary sniffed. "Maybe when I'm certified, he'll believe I'm good, and we might work something out. But I'm going to be a mechanic and I won't put up with a macho dude who wants to keep me barefoot, pregnant and in the kitchen!"

"I can see it now," teased Tracy. "When you have a little girl, you'll give her a tool set instead of a doll."

"It'd do her a lot more good!"

Comforted by each other, they got supper and did the dishes. Mary got out her texts and studied while

Tracy worked on her notes. The busy, companionable silence gave Tracy an idea. She'd already been trying to figure some way to advance Mary the money to finish her training without offending her. What might be more acceptable would be to rent a house they could share till they were both through with their projects. Tracy could plead her ankle as a reason for needing someone to help cook and keep house.

Le Moyne came to put his big head on Tracy's lap. Unless Shea really wanted him back, she would keep the dog. He'd need a big yard, which would complicate things, but she'd become too fond of him to give him up unless she had to.

And Güera? A pang shot through Tracy but she hardened herself. She could board Güera at a stable, but the mare would be far happier and healthier running free. Shea would have to take her and Sangre.

Mary yawned for the third time in five minutes. Tracy put down her pencil. "Do you kick?" she asked.

"My sister always said so." Mary grinned.

Tracy shrugged. "I moan and groan. We ought to do just fine."

XVII

AT SHEA'S INSISTENCE, THE FUNERAL WAS HELD IN THE *sala* of the old ranch house. It had been Patrick's home, and the vaquero families felt welcome there. Patrick had belonged officially to the Episcopal church in Nogales, whose priest read the service. Then Judd, Shea, Geronimo and Chuey Sanchez carried the coffin up the slope to the little iron-fenced cemetery.

Patrick was buried between his second wife, Judd's mother, and his own mother, Christina. His father, Sant, was beside Christina, and a little distance from them was Johnny Chance, Christina's lover and the father of Tracy's offbeat side of the family. Caterina and James had markers, as did Shea, the San Patricio. Strange. A little turquoise bird, discolored by time, was nestled by the earlier Shea's cross. Here was the legendary Talitha beside her patient Marc, and there was the first grave of all, that of Socorro, the Spanish girl who'd become the ranch's patroness.

Tracy felt an overwhelming surge of kinship with these people of her blood whose stories she'd grown up with. How good that Patrick would rest with them! She wept as the grave was filled, not only for Patrick, but because she must go away.

The lawyer had come down for the funeral and had asked if he could read the will that evening before going back to town. Tracy had told him she was a foster-child with her own inheritance, so there was no use in her waiting, but balding, rosy-cheeked Mr. Phelps asked her to stay, and Mary waited with her.

The will began with a surprise and kept on with them. Judd inherited the main part of the ranch, but Shea was left the old ranch house and several hundred acres along the highway. *"Maybe he can reclaim the land,"* Patrick's words ran. *"However that may be, I charge him to never sell the house but to pass it to his children."*

Judd recovered first. "I think you'll agree that land's past redemption," he said. "But it's worth plenty commercially. I'll bet Fricks—"

Mr. Phelps held up a hand for quiet. Vashti received property in Tucson and Phoenix and assorted investments along with life tenancy of the new house. If she ceded that right, Judd was to remunerate her.

There were small legacies for all the vaquero families and a provision that they should be employed for life.

"To Mary O'Rourke who has brightened my night, I leave $20,000 to complete her mechanic's training or buy a trousseau or for whatever she chooses. I also ask that she be allowed to work at the ranch if she desires."

Vashti, though she'd been left rich, glared at the amazed young Apache woman. Tracy laughed with delight and squeezed her friend's hand. Good for Patrick!

Then came the biggest surprise of all. *"Since my foster-daughter, Tracy Benoit, has found a home at Last Spring, I do give and bequeath to her the hundred acres comprising that part of the ranch. I remind her that she is the last woman of our blood on the ranch, and it has been our women who often have preserved it."*

Tracy's heart swelled. Knowing how fiercely protective Patrick was of the Socorro, she'd never dreamed he would leave her a portion. Tears blurred her eyes. She promised him silently that there was one part, at least, that would never go to the developers.

"But Last Spring's the core of Vistas Unlimited's

acquisition," Vashti cried. "The whole plan revolves around that hot spring as an attraction!"

Mr. Phelps spread his palms. "That's what wills are for, Mrs. Scott. A person is allowed to dispose of what he or she owns."

"But that land's vital!"

Phelps peered at Vashti over his spectacles. "I would suggest to you, Mrs. Scott, that your husband left you well enough off so that you scarcely need be concerned about maximum profits from what he chose to give his foster-daughter."

Vashti's mouth thinned. "I may challenge that will! Claim undue influence. She came back here, buttering him up, doing that homestead act he thought so spunky, visiting him every day! She—"

"She kept him company while you lounged around the pool or played tennis with your buddies," Mary cut in. She gave Vashti a look that made the other woman flinch. "Take it to court, Mrs. Scott. There are things a jury would certainly be interested in hearing about you."

Judd said smoothly, "Look, everybody's on edge. We can work out details later between ourselves. Mr. Phelps, how about a drink and dinner before you start back?"

"The drink would be welcome," Phelps said thankfully.

He sat down by Vashti. Judd moved toward the bar. "What would you like, Tracy?"

"Nothing, thanks." She paused near the door with Mary. "We're going home." It really was home now. Hard to realize, but wonderful.

"I'll be over soon," Judd promised. "Shea, is it still bourbon on the rocks?"

"I've got to go."

Judd frowned slightly. "Brother, we've got some talking to do."

"I don't know what about," Shea said. "But you know where to find me."

Outside, he slowed down long enough to give Mary a quick smile. "Thanks for all you did for Dad."

Tears sparkled in Mary's eyes. "I enjoyed being with him."

His face was unreadable as he looked down at Tracy. "I suppose you'll make a killing with Vistas Unlimited."

His assumption that she would rasped on her overstrained nerves like sandpaper on raw flesh. "It's my land," she flung at him. "I'll do what I judge best with it."

Now why, when he'd made such hasty conclusions, did he look as if she'd slapped *him?* She almost softened her words, but he turned his back abruptly and strode to his pickup.

"The hell with him!" she said under her breath, but she was fighting tears.

Mary shook her head. "How come you two can't just level about how you feel?"

"The way you and Geronimo do?" Tracy gibed.

"We know how the other one feels," Mary said grimly. "Maybe that's our trouble. And I'd guess this money will really get his macho up. But you and Shea are different. Say mean things and hold yourselves apart like you were scared to come close."

"I've gone as far toward him as I can till he shifts a little in my direction."

Mary grinned ruefully as they got in the Toyota. "Got your mule up? Patrick sort of hoped—"

"What?"

"That you'd—well, you know, marry one of the sons."

"I don't know if I'll marry anyone," said Tracy darkly. "But, bless Patrick, I do have a home!"

"You're really staying?"

"Maybe not all the time, but it'll be my base. I'll get some remodeling under way. And you can stay as long as you like."

"Best offer I've ever had," Mary said. "Though I'm not sure Judd'll offer me a job."

"You could keep pretty busy just on Shea's and Geronimo's pickups."

"I'll get certified first." Mary lapsed into silence, but when they parked at Last Spring, she looked soberly at Tracy. "If I ever have a boy, I'll call him Patrick."

"So will I," said Tracy.

In the days that followed, Tracy would find herself planning to tell Patrick something that would entertain him, then wince as she remembered. Apart from grieving for him, his death made her feel aimless, unnecessary. Sometimes it had been difficult to get over to see him, but she realized now that it had been good to feel that someone needed her.

When Tracy thought of Vashti's last cruel words to Patrick, she grew so angry and depressed that two days after the funeral, even though her ankle was still weak, she began forcing herself to stay in her blind and wait for pictures. Just being outside helped, but she missed Patrick more than she could have imagined.

Mary had enrolled in classes in Nogales and would be gone three days a week, starting that day. For the first time at Last Spring, Tracy felt lonesome.

Thoughts of Shea plagued her, too. Maybe she should have told him she had no intention of ever selling Patrick's amazing and wonderful gift, but why should she explain when he was so ready to think the worst?

She loved him, there wasn't much she could do about that, but she wasn't about to be his doormat. If there was any hope for them, he had to show a little faith and trust.

One night she was playing her guitar when Mary looked up from her books and squealed. Tracy looked, too.

A pale small heart-shaped face peered in at them,

large round eyes staring. The head bobbed back and forth. "Why, it's one of the barn owls!" Tracy said. "But he's surely too young to scavenge on his own. I'll bet he fell out of the nest."

"Think we could raise him?" Mary asked.

"His parents could do it better." Even if it hadn't been true, Tracy shrank from catching the mice and boned hairy things the owlets needed to cast properly. Tracy stood up a bit reluctantly. "I'll get the ladder and put him back in the nest."

She wasn't enthusiastic about risking the adults' ire if they caught her near the nest, but there was no telling how long the little guy had been without food so she didn't want to wait till morning.

"I'll bring the ladder and flashlight," Mary offered.

Tracy put on a jacket, a hat to shield her head, and got an old shirt to swaddle the waif. He made alarmed clicking sounds with his beak and tried to flop over, extending his claws, when she started to pick him up. She dropped the shirt on his talons, gave it an extra thickness, and picked him up.

Fortunately, there was full moonlight. "If we don't need the flash at the nest, don't turn it on," Tracy said. "No use bringing the parents down on us."

Though the tree was in shadow, they located the hollow. Mary braced the ladder and Tracy started up. There was a blood-curdling screech, a swift rush of wings, and claws swept the hat away. As she clung to the ladder, a second fury scudded above her, talons plowing through her hair.

Mary put the flash on full beam. In the second's respite, Tracy reached up to thrust the stray into the nest, shielded her head with her arm as the outraged adults dared the light to attack again.

She reached the foot of the ladder, grabbed it and ran. The owls, content at having driven off an invader, left off the chase.

"Did they scalp you?" asked Mary.

Gingerly fingering through her hair, Tracy felt a

slight moistness. "Just a scratch. That steamwhistle of theirs, though!"

"Next one falls out, we'll have owlet soup," said Mary. She stopped. "Do you hear a motor?"

In a minute Tracy did. Headlights showed spottily through the trees as a vehicle nosed up the cañon. Maybe it was Shea. *And maybe it isn't,* she warned her racing heart. It could be another hoodlum.

"Let's go in and lock up till we know who it is," she said.

"It's times like this I'd like to have a shotgun," Mary said.

"Hey, now, descendant of Nana! Where's your confidence?"

"About where yours is," Mary retorted.

They barred the door, pulled the curtains, got out their most formidable knife and a chunk of firewood that could make a club. "The hell with being a picturesque homesteader," said Mary. "When are they installing that phone?"

"Next week," said Tracy, laughing in spite of her nervousness. "We're acting silly! That's probably Geronimo, or at least someone friendly."

"Probably," granted Mary. "But I still get the creeps over our blond friend. Here, let me put something on that owl scratch."

She used peroxide followed by Merthiolate. The motor had cut off. The two women looked at each other, sighed with relief as blithe whistling approached. Tracy's worrying took a new track. Judd was the only one of the ranch men she'd heard whistle, and she didn't feel like an encounter with him.

While he was still a distance from the house, he called, "It's me, ladies. Put up the kettles of boiling oil and raise the portcullis."

Mary put up the breadknife and started to collect her books. "You stay right there!" Tracy hissed. "Don't leave me alone with him!"

Mary shrugged and sat down. Tracy opened the

door. Judd filled it. Smiling, he ducked to enter. He greeted Mary briefly, then took Tracy's hand. "There's a gorgeous moon. Why don't we drive down to Nogales for a drink?"

"Why don't I give you a cup of coffee here?" Tracy countered.

He gave her an unperturbed grin. "Somehow, it's not the same. But I'd settle for a walk in the moonlight."

"I've already had my evening's exercise."

His smile faded. "Damn it, Tracy, I want to talk to you alone!"

"We have nothing to discuss that's that private."

"We sure as hell do!" He swallowed, pleaded in his most cajoling tone. "Let's go sit by the spring a little while. Hear what I have to say, and I won't pester you again."

Tracy sighed. He had been helpful and kind. Besides, he clearly wasn't accepting her past answers. So all right, she'd give him a new, final one.

"Happy study hall," she said to Mary. "I'll be back soon."

Judd favored Mary with a smile. "I've convinced Vashti that you deserve every cent of that bequest," he assured her. "Do you want it paid into your checking or savings account?"

"Gosh! I don't have either one."

"Better open them next time you're in town," he advised genially, helping Tracy into her jacket. "And of course you've got a job at the ranch helping Tivi maintain our vehicles and machinery."

"Helping Tivi?" Mary's slim eyebrows rose. "When I finish this training, I ought to know some things he doesn't."

"But—well—I don't think he'll like working for a girl."

"I'm a woman," Mary said firmly. "Why don't Tivi and I just work *with* each other?"

"Someone has to be in charge."

"Why, if we're both responsible?"

Judd rubbed his jaw. Mary gave him a brilliant smile. After a moment he said magnanimously, "I'll talk to Tivi, see what I can do."

"Thanks," said Mary and turned to her books.

Judd took Tracy's arm as they stepped outside. To ease the tension building between them, she teased lightly, "Sometimes it's hard to be Lord Bountiful."

"That's one independent wench," he grunted.

"She's my best friend."

Judd's grasp tightened. "If you'd let me take care of you, Tracy, you wouldn't need a best friend."

"I certainly would!" Tracy stopped in her tracks, faced him in the silvery light that showed his features plainly but without color, as if he'd been drained of blood. "Judd, please! Let's not make a big, messy thing of this! Your interest in me is very flattering but it's quite useless."

"Your next line," he prompted savagely, "Is 'Can't we be friends?'"

"Can't we?"

He took her arm again, moving her through the trees and spangled light to the rocks around the whispering stream. Making her sit down, he held her wrists. "No, doll baby, we can't be friends. I want you more than I ever wanted anything."

"I'm sorry about that, but—"

"I always get what I want."

"Not this time." She was getting angry at the way he considered only how he felt. "Can't you get it through your head? I'm in love with someone else."

"Who?"

"That's none of your business."

He gave her a small shake. "It's Shea, isn't it?"

"What if it is?"

"You're wasting your time." Judd's laugh was ugly. "All Shea wants or needs is a Nogales whore once a month."

He might be right. That taunt flicked Tracy's hopes and fears on the raw. "However that may be, I don't want you!"

She started up, but he brought her against him, heavy arms clamping her. His mouth closed on hers, hard and assaulting. As she writhed her face away, he panted in her ear, "You don't know what you've been missing, but I'm going to show you!"

Panicked, she tried to rake his face but he pinioned her hands. With one leg over her thighs, he groped at her clothing, tore her shirt open. "Tracy, Tracy! Let me—you'll like it!"

She turned from his muffling arm and screamed. From this angle, she could see the immediate oblong of light as the cabin door opened. Le Moyne bursted out.

"I'm coming," Mary shouted.

Judd cursed, but he decided not to tangle with the big dog, strode hastily away.

"Le Moyne!" Tracy gasped, straightening her clothes. The Ridgeback checked his course toward Judd, ran to her, and gave a soft whine of inquiry. Mary ran up with her chunk of wood.

"Tracy! You all right?"

"Thanks to you." Tracy put her hand to her numbed face. "I'd rather battle the owls! But I think he finally got the message."

"The question is, did you?"

Tracy glanced at her friend in astonishment as they went inside and barred the door. "He lost control. But his pride's hurt. I don't think he'll ask to marry me again."

"He can do other things."

"He'll get on some other woman's track and convince himself he never wanted me."

"Maybe," said Mary, but she sounded unconvinced.

"That probably blows your job," Tracy frowned.

"I don't care," said Mary gamely. "One of my instructors has already offered me a spot at his garage when I finish training."

"Does Geronimo know that?"

Mary grinned, eyes devilish. "I can't wait to tell him!"

XVIII

APPARENTLY, THE DROP-OUT OWLET WAS COMPLETELY accepted by his parents, for when Tracy climbed into the blind next morning, there were two fluffy young. Relieved, she was starting back for the house when she heard a distressed clamor from another tree.

A curve-billed thrasher called and swooped around its nest in a walnut tree. Up the trunk crawled a big gopher snake. Tracy hesitated. The snake had to eat, too. But the cries of the parent bird were too pitiful. Picking up a long stick, Tracy thumped it against the tree.

The snake veered and tried to swerve to the other side, but when the stick blocked him he gave up and retreated.

"There you go upsetting the balance of nature," came Shea's voice behind her.

Tracy whirled. Her heart lilted at the sight of him, though she said defensively, "I'm part of nature, too. My instincts made me help the bird."

His eyes danced before he turned formal. "Has Fricks been to see you?"

"Not again."

"He will be. And since he's still set on acquiring Last Spring and the property along the road that Dad left me, I thought you and I should know what the other intends to do."

Her ankle was aching. Tracy sat down on a rock and said carefully, "It's pretty clear that Patrick hoped we'd hang on to what he gave us. He knew Vashti or Judd would sell in a flash."

Shea eased down on another stone. "So?"

"So I'm keeping Last Spring."

"You're sure?"

"I'm sure. What'll you do with the homeplace?"

"Sanchezes will stay at the house for now. It needs a family. But I'll start clearing mesquite and planting love grass."

A good name for the drouth-resistant plant that could cover such sins against the land. Running those scarred but well-shaped fingers through his hair, he stared into the distance. "If you marry, your husband will have a half-interest in all you own. He couldn't sell without your consent, but he could certainly bring pressure."

"I don't expect to marry anytime soon."

Gray eyes swung to her, probed. "I thought— Judd said—"

"I don't know what Judd said, but I'm not going to marry him."

Shea's breath went out in a sigh. "Then maybe you'd better marry me."

She couldn't believe her ears. No word of love or even lust, just a resigned statement. And she'd believed that if he ever said those words, she'd be overjoyed. Now, humiliated, she had to wait a moment before she could trust her voice.

"Why had I 'better' marry you?"

He made a toss-away gesture. "You should if you're serious about carrying out Patrick's trust. As long as you're single, Fricks or others like him will try to make you sell." He added grimly. "There are more ways than offering money."

She bit the inside of her lip and tasted salt. "You think I'll give in unless you're in a position to run off developers!"

"Tracy!"

He reached for her but she eluded him, getting to her feet. "I admire your self-sacrifice," she flung at him. "But it's not necessary! I have no more intention of caving in than you do!"

He watched her unhappily. "Tracy, I guess I went about this all wrong. It's not just the land." His eyes traced the curve of her throat, lingered on her mouth. "I—it's not just that."

"No, I'm probably as good in bed as one of your Nogales women, and a good deal safer," she blazed. "Thanks. That's still not good enough!"

Stiff-backed, she whirled and stalked toward the cabin. In spite of her anger and hurt, she hoped at some deeper, elemental level, that he'd catch up with her, say he loved her, carry her to the bed where they'd been happy.

He didn't. As she stood in the kitchen, fighting for control, she heard the pickup start.

Fricks was out that afternoon. He offered condolences over Patrick before he gave her his most charming smile. "You showed integrity in not wanting to persuade your uncle to sell, but now he's gone, you're free, in all good conscience, to consider your own interests."

"Yes," said Tracy agreeably. "I'm doing that."

"Good!" Fricks' light brown eyes widened for a split second. He relaxed and chuckled. "I'm glad you're not going to play coy and try driving the price up."

Tracy beamed at him. "Now how could I do that, Hal, when I'm not selling?"

They were standing in the yard. His quick step toward her brought Le Moyne to his feet. Fricks retreated. He was a monotone man, tanned to the color of his eyes and hair, only his rather pink lips and the whites of his eyes making a contrast. He spread his hands. "But you said—"

"I think my best interests lie in keeping Last Spring."

"One little shack up here when several hundred

people could have luxury villas!" He sounded outraged at what must seem to him a criminal waste. His eyes slitted. "I'll up your percentage and pay you an even million for the land on top of building you that condo. Tracy, I know you're not hurting for money, but this is an offer you can't turn down!"

She shrugged. "Would you like some coffee?"

"Hell, no, I don't want coffee!" Le Moyne rumbled at Fricks's tone. The developer moved back another step. "You're as crazy as your cousin! And though Judd would be glad to sell this piece or that worn-out range along the road, he won't part with the land he inherited."

Tracy smiled. "Seems Patrick figured it all out pretty well."

Fricks hesitated. "All right. Name your price."

"There isn't one," said Tracy in exasperation. "Quit wasting your time, Hal. Go look someplace else."

He stared at her. "Maybe I've rushed this. Take a week to think it over." She shook her head. "My offer's good for a month," he said, and turning on his heel, he left her.

Shaky with unused adrenaline, Tracy hugged Le Moyne. "I'm surprised he didn't propose to me, too!" she told him with a bitter laugh. "Nothing like being an heiress to increase the action."

It was the only reason Shea had proposed to her. That knowledge embittered her sense of joyous honor in being left the spring, but made her all the more resolved to keep it.

A few days later, Tracy was riding Güera up the trail she and Shea had taken to the mountain meadow when she found a fox dead in a trap. It had gnawed its foot halfway off but had perished before that desperate effort could succeed. It couldn't have been dead long for nothing had been at it but insects. Tracy's first shock yielded to anger.

Her land was posted against hunting and trapping.

Who was trespassing? She tumbled fox and trap into an old mine shaft, rode home and took the truck to the little crossroads settlement of Sonoita, where she could use the phone outside one of the restaurants.

The game warden was apologetic but not much help. He didn't know of anyone in her area who was trapping, but he had to patrol a ridiculously large amount of territory. He'd get over and have a look around as soon as he could, but Miss Benoit had to understand there was no way one man could enforce the law over the whole region.

Chagrined, Tracy had to leave it at that, but when she got home, she found the remains of a field-dressed doe hanging by its back legs from her clothesline pole. Vultures rose sluggishly from the offal. Flies buzzed at the big glazed eyes. Convulsed with horror, Tracy wondered if this was the doe that had touched noses so lovingly with her fawn.

This had to be a deliberate effort to frighten her. It was also a double offense. Deer were out of season, of course, and does always were. After a quick check for any evidence, Tracy drove back to a phone and called the warden again.

He sighed as if he thought she must be a little crazy but promised to be over as soon as he could get there. When he came, he studied tracks and searched around but found nothing to identify the doe's killer.

"Hunter who'll kill a doe this time of year wouldn't care about messing up your yard, ma'am," the harassed young man said. His blue eyes were troubled. "You haven't seen anybody?"

"The people I've seen wouldn't do this themselves, but they might hire it done," Tracy explained. The warden, who had introduced himself as Terry Marks, gave a slow whistle.

"If you'll excuse me, ma'am, you're jumping to conclusions. No one could have guessed you'd find that fox, and you'd be surprised at what some of these slob hunters do."

"Are you saying I'd just better forget about it?"

He ran his hand through short yellow hair. "Miss Benoit, there's nothing here I can go on. But I'll sure have a look around your property and see if I can pick up any clues."

"Have some lunch first," Tracy said. She felt discouraged. Terry Marks was a nice young man, but his job was undoable and he couldn't be blamed for thinking she was slightly paranoid.

When he returned two hours later, he didn't think that. He carried a dozen traps, all shiny new and unmarked. "A good trapper makes his rounds every day, not just to keep the animals from suffering but to keep scavengers from ruining pelts." He shook his head. "Eight of these had something in them. Only one coon was alive and he was so far gone I clubbed him. These were all close to trails or places you'd likely go. I didn't find any traps back in the sort of places a poaching trapper would normally choose."

Tracy didn't want to think about eight creatures dying slow agonizing deaths. "There's nothing you can do?"

"I'll take the traps in. We can check fingerprints but unless your poacher has a record, that won't do much good. I'll come around as much as I can but—"

"You have other problems. But if this is deliberate—"

"Why don't you phone the sheriff? If he's skeptical, tell him to check with me."

After downing a beer cooled in the water trough, Marks departed. Tracy made a third trip to Sonoita and told her story to the sheriff. He was busy with a murder but promised to send a deputy over. "It's natural you'd be a mite jumpy after that bum kidnapped you," he said soothingly. "Why don't you get one of your cousins to stay at your place awhile?"

"They're busy," Tracy said briefly, but after she'd hung up, she tracked the suggestion a moment.

How stupid she was being! She'd ask Chuey Sanchez

to locate a couple of reliable men to patrol her land. She wouldn't involve him or the ranch vaqueros, since that might bring Judd down on her, but she felt fairly certain of two things: Fricks had hired someone to harass her and that someone wouldn't keep up his little tricks if it was made difficult.

She turned off the highway and took the ranch road. Chuey was at the corral watching Roque halter-break a young gelding. When she told him her problem, the graying foreman frowned.

"*Doncellita,* this is a thing you should take to Don Shea."

"I can't, Don Jesús." She gave him the title of respect with his proper name.

He said stubbornly, "The men of your family should know this."

She smiled coaxingly. "I'd much rather handle it myself. I don't think there's real danger. A couple of men around should discourage our trapper-hunter."

"Tivi and Rogue will come tonight. If they can't persuade this *sangrón* to leave you in peace, I will send for a couple of my wife's cousins."

Roque whistled. "Ay, papá! Those are real tough dudes!"

"That," said Chuey, "is the idea." He entered the corral and took the gelding's halter, speaking softly to the skittish animal before he turned to his rail-thin son. "You go right now with Teresita. I'll send your brother over after supper."

Roque picked up his bedroll and told his wife and mother where he was going. He and Tracy reached Last Spring a few minutes ahead of Mary, who had used some of her inheritance to purchase a bright-red Datsun. The sheriff's deputy was right behind them, a tubby gap-toothed middle-aged man who made laborious notes of what Tracy said, scuffed around the clothesline, and said he'd sure tell the sheriff all about it. "Call us if you have any more trouble," he invited.

"Maybe you could stick around and see that we don't," Mary suggested. He looked pained.

"Ma'am, I got two more places to go tonight. No one's been hurt here, hasn't even been assault or robbery." Tipping his hat, he drifted off.

Mary swore with color and feeling. "It probably is that sneaky Fricks bastard. But you can bet he won't be traipsing around where he might get hurt."

"Tivi and I will camp by the crossing," Roque planned. "No fire or light. Then if a stranger comes across, we'll cream him."

"Try to get him to say who sent him," Tracy urged. She rummaged around till she found her battery-powered tape recorder. "Keep this handy and start it if he's talking."

"He'll talk," said Roque. Tracy decided from his expression that he could be as mean a dude as his cousins once-removed when events warranted it.

After supper he went down to stand guard and wait for his brother. Tracy commanded Le Moyne to go with him.

"Isn't this a note?" Mary shook her head as they barred the cabin door. "Here we are forted up like the good old days, except what the hell is an Apache doing on the inside?"

"Slow-ground justice." Tracy laughed. She thought of the cruelly killed animals and lost her grim amusement. "This really is a pretty clever ploy. They're not hurting or threatening us, not even breaking in. If the trapper gets caught, he'll probably get off with a fine for killing a doe out of season and another for trespass."

"And if he gets nailed, it sure won't be by the sheriff's department!" Mary pulled the curtains, though usually, with the cabin so secluded, they left them open at night. "No offense to Roque and Tivi, but I wish Geronimo and Shea were on lookout."

"Not Shea!" said Tracy. She hadn't told Mary about his proposal. It still hurt too much, was too shaming.

"He thinks I can't hang on to this place without his help. I'm going to show him!"

There was the sound of a motor, then a shutting door, and soon after, the faint sound of the Sanchez brothers calling to each other. "It's going to look like a parking lot across the stream," Mary pointed out. "If our poacher's smart, he'll take one look and forget it."

"Maybe for the night, but if Fricks would try such tactics, I doubt he'll fold up so easily."

By ten o'clock, when they went to bed, there had still been no commotion. Tracy was divided between hoping her tormentor would be caught and the fragile chance that perhaps he'd decide it was too risky and quit. That was no real answer. Fricks or whoever was behind the harassment would just find another ploy.

She was absolutely determined not to appeal to Shea.

Tivi and Roque came up for breakfast. They had taken turns on watch. About midnight, Tivi had heard a truck coming and seen its lights, but it had turned around and retreated.

"Can't have much guts," said Tivi, draining his third cup of black coffee. "Guess we won't have to call in Mama's mean cousins after all."

"Don't be too sure," cautioned Roque. "Sneaks are harder to handle than machos. Tracy, you want one of us to hang around today? Papa said it would be okay."

Tracy looked at Mary, who chuckled. "I'll be here, boys."

"Only at night," said Tracy quickly, "please arrange that someone comes—and I'll be perfectly happy to pay your mother's cousins."

"Don't worry about a thing," Tivi grinned expansively.

"Nice guys," said Mary as the women watched the brothers, one skinny, one plump, both bowlegged, head for their truck. "But I'd still rather have Geronimo."

"You just want an excuse to see him without his thinking you've weakened," Tracy accused.

Mary wrinkled her pretty brown nose. "It's a good excuse."

"Too good." Tracy shook her head apologetically. "I'm sorry, my friend, but there's no way to call in Geronimo without Shea's knowing."

"You've had a fight," Mary diagnosed.

"A doozey. You could put all the confidence that man has in women on the head of a pin and have room left over."

"Geronimo says his wife gave him a raw deal."

Tracy shrugged. "And his mother left him. But I happen to be neither of the above."

"Men are devils," Mary said with such a droll look of intrigued disgust that Tracy chortled.

"I think I'll go see if our feathered friend is still in his nest. One day soon those little rascals should start flopping out on branches and trying to fly."

"Should make good pictures," Mary nodded. "You deserve some exclusives after the way mom and pop almost scalped you."

Tracy climbed the stilted blind, grateful that though her ankle was still tender, it was reasonably trustworthy again. She squinted through the eyehole. No valentine faces peered out of the hollow, nor could she see either parent roosting close by.

From all she had read and heard, it wasn't possible for the babies to have learned to fly and desert the nest so quickly.

Worried, she hurried down, froze as she noticed two bundles of feathers beneath the tree. Going slowly over, she nudged one body gently with her foot. It turned over; a half-devoured mouse in its claws.

One of the adults. Dead, but she could see no cause. The mate was equally lifeless. Some disease? If both parents were dead, the owlets would need food, and quickly.

Tracy scooted the blind's ladder over to the tree and climbed up. No wonder she hadn't been able to see the fluffy owlets. They were huddled in the bottom of the nest. They hadn't died of starvation. Mice, shrew and rabbit parts lay about.

Dazed, Tracy scrambled down and sat on a rock with her head in her hands, ignoring Le Moyne's snuffles of sympathy. She hadn't exactly loved the family of owls, but she'd admired them. Hours of patient watching and the rescue of the lost one had made them familiar, individuals who mattered.

It *must* be disease. Yet *all* of them? In such a short span? She stiffened at a horrible thought. Birds died from eating insects dosed with pesticides. It figured they could die from poisoned mice.

She shook off her baffled mourning, started to the house for a sack. Diseased or poisoned, the owls mustn't be left to feed and kill other creatures. She'd take them to town and get a veterinarian to determine what had killed them.

If they'd been poisoned— She fought back furious tears. She could call Fricks and tell him his campaign wasn't working, that if she had to, she'd get the sort of guards who'd maul his hirelings till he couldn't get any more. But he wouldn't care how many men were beaten up so long as he could get more, and for money there'd always be some.

Damn it! He could sit in his Phoenix office and claim innocence no matter what happened down here. Unless one of the poachers could be made to implicate him. Cagey as Fricks was, he probably had two or three middlemen between him and the actual pawns.

For a second Tracy thought of appealing to Judd. This should be right up his alley. But she didn't want to get involved with him again, and it went against her grain to ask for the protection she'd repudiated before things got touchy.

Explaining to Mary all that had happened and that

she was taking the owls to town, Tracy asked if her friend wanted to go along.

"I'd better mind the store," Mary said. "Leave me Le Moyne and I fear no man." She added vehemently, "It's bad luck to kill owls and if someone did it, I hope they have all there is!"

Tracy got her purse and a bag. She was scooping the baby owls into it, grimaced as she realized she'd better take the dismembered mice, too, both for analysis and to keep them from being eaten. Holding her breath, she used a twig to roll the ugly bits into the sack. She was collecting the adults when Shea's pickup roared to a stop across the stream.

———————— XIX

HER RIDICULOUS HEART LIFTED BUT SHE QUELLED IT IM-mediately. Damn it all, had the Sanchezes told him what was going on? Caught literally holding the bag, there wasn't much she could do but face him as he took the foot-log in a couple of pantherish strides. His gray eyes blazed as he caught her by the shoulders.

"Why didn't you come to me?"

"I can handle it myself."

"Sure! You called in the game warden, the sheriff and the Sanchezes! Hell, if Inez hadn't had more sense than you or Chuey, I wouldn't know now!"

"Inez told you?"

"She sent Lupe over." He sniffed in distaste. "What have you got in that stinking sack?"

Tracy showed him. "I'm taking them to the vet to see if the mice they ate were poisoned."

He put the sack down. "I don't think you need to do that."

"But—"

He grinned savagely. "When Lupe told me Tivi and Roque would be here, I decided to put off giving you hell and go give it to Hal Fricks."

"You *what?*"

"Routed him out of bed. Told him I knew he wasn't setting the traps and shooting, but if any more of it

222

happened, he'd need plastic surgery, if not an under-taker."

"Shea! What if it's not him?"

He shrugged. "Well, that's the chance we take, but he let enough slip to convince me." Shea grinned down at her. "I scared him so bad that if there *are* any incidents, I'd hesitate to maul him without more proof. But I'm betting there'll be a swift end to trapping around these parts."

"I didn't ask you to help," Tracy muttered. "And we'd have handled it some way. So don't start thinking I can't manage without you!"

He shut off her words with his lips. Her indignant sputter faded into the sweet, aching delight of being in his arms, till she remembered his insulting proposal and tried to struggle free.

"*I* can't manage without you," he said against her throat. "Marry me, Tracy."

Her heart was pounding and her knees felt as if they had melted. "Because you want to be sure I don't sell out?"

"You've proved you won't." He touched her hair, caressed her cheek. His eyes seemed almost black. "No, I guess I gave myself that reason, but it wasn't true, even before. I want you to marry me, honey, because I'm sick of reaching out in the night and finding you're not there."

Almost unable to contain her joy, she answered with her kiss. "Oh, Shea!" Her voice was tremulous but now it didn't matter, she didn't have to pretend around him. "I thought you never would!"

"So did I," he said a bit ruefully. "But, damn it, I guess the only way to get you off my mind is to get you in my arms."

"Not a bad solution." She laughed.

He put the owls in the truck, saying he'd burn them, and they wandered up to the spring. Helping each other undress, they bathed and played in the big rock tub, dried in the sun, admiring each other though she ached at the scars on his torso, which she traced with her fingers and kissed.

"It's too late to kiss them and make them well," she whispered.

"Scars don't count, honey." He spread his clothes and drew her down, holding her tenderly. "Only new wounds do. Let's be kind to each other."

She nodded.

This time, there was not only the passionate rapture, but a sort of healing, a sense of being completed, no longer a lonely fragment of humanity but a part of wholeness. It was the most perfect peace and quiet joy she had ever known. It seemed impossible now that they had distrusted and misunderstood one another.

After a long time, they went to the house to tell the news to Mary and to have lunch, for they were both ravenous. Mary hugged them both, but held Shea off a minute to admonish him.

"This lady deserves some luck. Be sure you give it to her."

"I'll try." He grinned inquisitorially. "What about Geronimo's luck?"

"He can try it again when I'm certified," Mary said firmly. "Now when's the big day so I can get the *tiswin* brewing?"

"Let's stick to beer and bourbon," Shea pleaded.

"Sissy!" jeered Mary, then dimpled. "It *is* awful. And you have to drink gallons to get a buzz. Let's drink your Jack Daniel's."

Before Shea left, they agreed to be married in the *sala* of the old ranch house by the priest who'd buried Patrick. Sunday afternoon would be the best time, so all the vaqueros could come.

"This Sunday?" asked Shea.

"First, don't you think we'd better decide where we're going to live?"

He looked comically surprised. "Guess we can't sleep under the ramada with the guys," he admitted.

"I'd love to move into the old house before we have children," Tracy said. "Though it seems a shame to oust the Sanchezes."

"They won't have to move far," Shea reminded. "We can renovate the old compound and give Inez that shiny newfangled kitchen she wants. Tivi and Roque need houses of their own, too, so it can all be taken care of in one swoop."

"I hate to leave this place," Tracy murmured, glancing around the cabin.

"We'll keep it for a getaway," Shea promised. "And we can live here till the old house is ready."

"I can be out tonight," Mary offered.

"It'll take me a few days to get things straight at El Charco," Shea said. "When do you get certified, madam mechanic?"

"Two more weeks."

"Sanchezes would make room," Shea considered, "but how about spending the time at El Charco? We could slick the adobe up enough for it to serve till you're ready to listen to my buddy's honorable intentions."

Mary thought a minute, then nodded her smooth black head. "Sounds like a good idea. It'll give me a chance to check that man out."

"Just don't break his finger," Shea urged, eyes dancing. "We've got work to do."

He kissed Tracy and left. Only then did she realize that he hadn't said he loved her.

Nor did he during the next few hectic days as they got blood tests, a marriage license, and made arrangements. It was a tiny mar on the shining glory of Tracy's happiness, but she told herself he'd already risked beyond what she'd dreamed possible.

He *must* love her. Actions were more than words, weren't they? Yet she hungered for the words.

He slept at El Charco but stayed late every evening with her. The summer evenings were warm and pleasant, so it was no hardship to leave the cabin to Mary and walk in the moonlight or spread a blanket and sit and talk till the moment came when he drew her into his arms.

The first night, as they melted into each other with excruciating sweetness and then rested peacefully, blissfully in each other's arms, she murmured against his cheek, "I love you."

He smoothed her hair, traced her eyebrows and nose and mouth, before he raised on one elbow to caress her body. "You're beautiful," he said huskily. "Head to toe! And one helluva woman with it!"

In spite of his tenderness, she felt denied, longed for him to say he loved her. Another night they decided to soak in the hot spring.

What began as a frolic ended in wild urgency, climaxing in a strange sensation of weightless, almost bodiless union. When they had toweled each other off and lay in the tree-filtered light, he said slowly, "Tracy, life here is different from the city. Sure you won't get bored?"

She laughed at such absurdity. "With you? And I've got my work."

"That's just it." Rolling over, he held her chin and gazed down at her. "I can't believe anyone as pretty and smart and wonderful as you will find me a good long-term proposition."

"You're wonderful yourself," she laughed. "Anyway, I love you."

He kissed her. Soon, they wanted each other again. But at no time could she bring herself to ask, *"Do you love me?"*

If he said yes, she'd be ashamed at having had to extract what should have been a gift. Worse, she simply didn't know what she'd do if he admitted plain sexual desire had driven him.

What was so awful about that? she asked herself roughly. There could be passion without love, but she didn't believe, in a man-woman way, there could be love without passion. If he didn't love her now, that might come later. She had to face the fact that perhaps the desertions of his wife and mother had left him unable to love in the way she wished. But she could love him. She *would* love him.

Sunday afternoon, the *sala* was thronged with vaquero families, from grandparents to babies. Little brown-eyed girls looked like flowers in their ruffly pink, yellow, blue and white dresses, and there were flowers in vases, flowers lovingly tended by women who longed for color and softness in the harsh desert.

Mary and Geronimo stood up with Shea and Tracy, but as the priest spoke the beautiful timeless words, Tracy felt that unseen presences blessed them, too.

Patrick, who had raised them both, able to see now, and to walk. That first Patrick, the San Patricio, flaming-haired, with his arms around Socorro whose sweet smile was like that of the dark little Guadalupana in the niche above. Santiago of the golden eyes and panther grace. Steadfast Talitha; Caterina united in eternity with the man for whom she'd died; their grandson Sant, with Christina, grandmother to Shea, great-grandmother to Tracy.

And surely Johnny Chance was no outcast here when his blood ran in Tracy. Even the giant ghost of Mangus Coloradas might tower in the door a moment with the host of other spirits who had been part of the life of the ranch.

The only person whose presence seemed strange was Pardo. After the ceremony, he wished them well and drank to them, but he refused to stay for the early dinner which in fact was more like a feast.

"Think I make these good folks nervous," he said with a swaggering grin that faded to grimness as he stared at Tracy. "You're getting one good man, lady. Take care of him." He thumped Shea on the shoulder. "Happy days, sarge—lots of them!"

"Thanks. Let me know when you decide to make an honest man of yourself, and we'll sure come to see the ceremonies."

Pardo shook his Pharaoh-like head. "It's not for me. But I sure wish both of you all the luck."

He went out between the people, who hushed and drew together to let him pass. When he was gone, as if a shadow lifted, Inez and Concha led the women, who laughed and embraced and kissed the newlyweds. "This would please Don Patrick so," breathed Concha, blowing her nose loudly into a tiny lace handkerchief.

"Ay, it is good," agreed Inez. "Good to have a woman of the old blood back at the ranch."

"You have done wisely, *hijito*," said Don Aniceto gravely. "I pray to teach your sons to rope and ride and hope to see a daughter as lovely as your bride."

There were many such courtly but heartfelt wishes before the crowd moved into the big kitchen–dining room where every family had brought a huge dish to round out the stew kettles of barbecue. Tivi tended an improvised bar and Lupe presided at a crystal punch bowl, where she poured iced fruit punch for the children and the women who didn't want wine or something stronger.

The priest departed after the dinner, saying he'd never tasted such delicious tamales or enchiladas, chilis rellenos, or posole. After the food was cleared away, Chuey and several other vaqueros got out their guitars. Those who weren't too sated rolled up the rugs and danced, an overflow spilling out into the paved courtyard.

Shea had opened the dance with Tracy. Bowing his head to hers, he gave her ear a quick nibble. "Hey, this is fun! Haven't been such doings at the Socorro since—" His smile died.

Tracy's heart convulsed. Since he'd married Cele? His arm tightened about her as he went on, "It strikes me that this family hasn't given the people a lot to celebrate. When I got married before, it was by the J.P. in Nogales because Dad hadn't liked the idea, thought we were too young. No one felt like partying over his wedding to Vashti." He laughed and whirled her till she spun breathlessly back to him. "I reckon the last family fiesta was your fifteenth birthday party. Remember that?"

"I certainly do! I'm glad I have enough Mexican blood to have rated one of those!"

"It's a sign the ranch needs you to add some sparkle." The warmth in his eyes kindled to a blaze. She felt that delicious, helpless yielding that went through her at his slightest touch. "How long do we have to stay before I can decently carry you off?" he asked.

"It may not be decent, but I'm ready anytime."

"Good. Let's make our good-byes then."

A round of their well-wishers. More embraces, felicitations, admonitions. Out on the veranda, Mary and Geronimo broke off a heated exchange. Geronimo's round face was doleful as he wished them joy and added dourly, "I've tried to tell this *mujer mala* we might as well get married now as in two weeks but she's more stubborn than a blind burro!"

"My mechanic's certificate's going to hang on the wall right along with our marriage license," she said, flushed cheeks making her even prettier. "But it's silly for me to sleep in that adobe while this big jerk beds down in the ramada a hundred yards away."

"You want Don Aniceto and Jaime to think I'm marrying a loose woman?"

"They'd better believe I'm loose!" Mary flashed. "If you want to clamp leg-irons and handcuffs on me, fella, you just forget the whole thing!"

"*Caray!*" Geronimo groaned, grabbing his forehead. "It's a good thing my mother's dead! I could never let her meet you!"

"That proves it!" Mary thrust.

"Proves what?"

"That you're more Mexican than Apache! Worrying about what your mother would think!"

"My mother's dead." Geronimo's look and tone were thunderous. "She knew a woman belonged in the house, not flat on her back beneath a car!"

"That's better than being flat on my back in some other places," Mary retorted. Swinging away from him, she gave Tracy's hand a squeeze. "Don't mind us! You're beautiful together. Have a beautiful life!"

Geronimo punched Shea and hugged Tracy. "He gives you any trouble, *chica,* you just tell me."

"Big talk," scoffed Mary. "You guys would stick together and you know it!"

"Have a nice fight," laughed Shea, drawing Tracy along with him. "Try to get it out of your systems now or you'll never stop quarreling long enough to get married."

They made their way through the crowd and paused near the corrals. Shea nodded toward a pair of red-tailed hawks that circled a big sycamore down beside the creek.

"Looks like they've nested. And by now I bet they're wishing their kids would take off on their own."

"Do you think one's the female you patched up?"

"I'm pretty sure of it."

The area between the house and corrals was full of vehicles from the most ancient of trucks to a few glittering Harley-Davidsons. To Tracy's surprise, Judd's camouflaged RV was parked next to Shea's green pickup. Judd and Vashti hadn't been asked to the wedding, since it had seemed unlikely they'd care to attend and Tracy would have felt strange to have either of them there.

Judd lounged out of the shade of a mesquite, smiling unpleasantly as he shambled toward them. It scarcely took the sour whiskey smell to know he'd been drinking more than he could handle. He raised a bottle in an awkward toasting gesture.

"Had to come to my little brother's wedding even if I

wasn't asked," he slurred. "Well, here's to the happy couple! To the uptight monk and the violated virgin!"

Lips tightening, Shea tried to get Tracy past him. Judd patted her on the arm. "You kids have any trouble figuring out what goes where, just let me know. Be glad to help." He lowered his voice confidentially. "Maybe he'll do better than that impotent nut who tried to rape you. He know about that, baby?"

Shea grabbed Judd, dragged him toward the RV. Judd grunted and flailed out viciously. Shea drove a fist into the softening midriff. Judd doubled up. Shea opened the RV, boosted his half-brother into it. He got out the keys and went over to some vaqueros who were smoking by the corral, obviously asking one of them to drive Judd home.

Back with Tracy, Shea helped her into the pickup, carefully lifting the white cotton-eyelet dress's long skirt out of the way. A search of stored family wedding dresses had turned up this one, which fitted and had been Christina's.

What a start to their marriage! Tracy's mouth trembled as she stole a glance at Shea's grim face. After what seemed a long time, they turned off the highway and started up the cañon.

"Tracy, what the hell was Judd talking about? Who tried to rape you?"

In as few words as possible, she told him. His knuckles whitened on the wheel. "Why didn't you tell me?"

"I—I don't like to think about it."

"But Judd knew."

"He scared me one night. That was when he gave me a gun and took me to Stronghold."

Shea drove in silence for so long that Tracy put her hand on his arm. "Shea! It doesn't make a difference, does it?"

He stopped the engine. "You bet it makes a difference!" He pulled her into his arms, kissed her deeply, tenderly, possessively. "All the time I was acting like a horse's ass, worrying about getting involved with you, you kept this to yourself! Tracy Benoit Scott, you are one hell of a woman and I love you!"

Tears stung her eyes. She met his lips and murmured longingly, "Oh, please, love, hurry! Let's hurry home."

Thrilling to its precise deadly beauty, Judd caressed the Magnum. What a weapon! Enough to bag lion or bear. Lots more than a man needed but—

The door opened. Spinning, Judd aimed at the intruder. Vashti gasped. "Judd! Is that awful thing loaded?"

"My guns always are."

She shivered. "Well, now you see it's me, point it somewhere else."

He cradled it in his hand. "You ought not to bust into a man's room." His tongue moved thickly, though his brain was cleared of the jealous rage that had driven him into that stupid clash after the wedding.

Vashti's eyes widened with horror. "Judd! You—you haven't—"

He laughed, fondling the black steel. "Just went over to wish sweet little Tracy and my kid brother happy." When the woman still looked terrified, he said impatiently, "Hell, I'm not going to jail for stopping that crazy bastard. Simpler for him just to disappear."

"You wouldn't really kill him!"

Judd just smiled, savoring the exquisite delight of stalking Shea, tasting a dozen chances to take him before finally the right, the ultimate moment came. With luck, that could be special; a chance to make Shea know who was winning their lifelong battle. Vashti's incredulous voice roused him from these gratifying anticipations.

"You want that girl enough to kill your own brother?"

"He's pushing. I don't know about her, but he's got to go."

"You're drunk."

"Not much."

Gauzy robe falling open, she put her hand on his arm. He kept the gun between them. "I'm not drunk enough to bed you, you randy old bitch!"

Gripping her shoulder brutally, he shoved her out, gave her a push down the hall and slammed the door. If she didn't get out of his life damn soon, he'd throw her out.

Pouring a drink, he sipped it, enjoying the warmth, lay down. He stroked the gun, drawing sensuous pleasure from its power. Shea wouldn't be in his way long. And once Tracy had a real man—

XX

WE OUGHT TO MAKE A WEDDING TRIP," HE SAID A FEW mornings later. They were lying in bed, with early sunlight warm and golden on their flesh, languorous and peaceful from having just made love. "Would you like to go to Europe? Or maybe Greece?"

She turned to nestle against his shoulder, marveling at the sweetness of being with him like this. "Let's do both sometime. But our wedding trip ought to be special. Something to do with us."

"Well?" He frowned in mystification.

"Let's go down to where Socorro and Shea met. Try to find the rancho where they rescued Santiago and pass by Sonoita along the route they took past Tjúni's village and up the Santa Cruz Valley. Let's make that our trip, darling."

"You know it's going to be hot?"

She laughed. "I didn't mean we wouldn't use our air conditioning or carry ice chests! But let's look for a water hole that could be the one they stayed at and camp there a few days. And Socorro must have died a little north of Ímuris. We should pass through there."

"All right," Shea assented, "I especially want to follow the Devil's Road to Tinajas Altas where Judah Frost got his. Of all the villains in the ranch's history, he's the creepiest. I've been there with Dad and Judd, but you should see it, too."

After breakfast they got out maps and made a list. They'd begin at Bosque near Tumacacori where Santa Teresa de Cabora restored the child Christina's sight. At Tubac, they'd try to look past the art and craft galleries to the old presidio and Charles Poston's fabled Christmas parties. A little north of San Xavier del Bac, they'd pick up Ajo Road and at Gila Bend turn to drive through the awesome Cabeza Prieta where so many travelers taking this shortcut to California's Gold Rush had died of thirst or Arenero arrows.

"Then we'll loop back and cross the border at Sonoita," Shea planned. "Pick up the Devil's Road on the Mexican side and follow it to where we can veer off to Pinacate and put on our walking shoes. Those lava flows are tough going."

"Sounds wonderful," sighed Tracy.

He raised an eyebrow and shook his head. "I married a crazy woman," he said, leaning over to kiss her. "But I sure do like it!"

There had been no more trapped animals, poisoned birds or butchered carcasses. Renovation at the old ranch compound was under way, with Inez excited over her new kitchen and her daughters-in-law jubilant at the prospect of their own houses.

"And you won't be a faraway godmother, Teresita," laughed Carla, whose baby was due that month. "Just across the patio! Maybe our babies will play together."

"Give us a little time," grinned Shea, circling Tracy with his arm.

They had brought the horses and Le Moyne to be cared for by the Sanchezes while they were away. "With respect," said Chuey, shaking his gray-touched hair, "that is a strange wedding journey."

But the women all thought it was excitingly romantic, a kind of pilgrimage. They understood place and family, for all of them had relatives scattered through Sonora and were proud that their ancestors had come to the Socorro shortly after it was founded and stayed through Apache and bandit terrors, through good years and bad. The bonds between them and the Scotts were rooted deep.

Swinging around to El Charco, they found Geronimo and Mary working on his truck. She had spotted the problem in the wiring and he was doing as she told him.

Stopping for a beer, they all talked about the wedding trip. Geronimo looked out across the mountains and whistled. "Have a good time, kids! We're going to Mazatlán for our honeymoon. Stay at the Camino Real, eat fancy and swim."

Tracy raised an eyebrow at Mary for confirmation. Mary wiped a smudge off her nose and nodded, slipping her hand into Geronimo's. "If you'll be back by then, we'll get married the day after I get my certification."

"We'll be back!" Tracy promised.

"Invite everybody," Shea said. "We'll have a dance and barbecue."

"Maybe you'd better sign a peace treaty along with your marriage certificate," Tracy teased.

"She'll settle down," predicted Geronimo fondly.

"So will he," said Mary.

Shea threw his beer can into the barrel and strolled toward the eagle pen. "How's our wetback bird?"

"Meaner every day." Geronimo rolled his eyes. "She can flop up on that stump now. I'll be glad when she sails right over the fence and keeps going."

"So will she be," Mary pointed out.

Tracy and Shea were loading cots, summer sleeping bags, and other gear into the pickup that evening when Judd's RV squealed to a halt beside them. He greeted them as genially as if he hadn't attacked Shea at the wedding and looked curiously at their preparations.

"Going on safari?"

"Sort of." Shea faced his older brother without any softening in his expression and waited for him to speak.

Judd heaved a gusty sigh and hitched up one big shoulder. "Okay. I turned up skunk drunk on your big day and made a damn fool of myself. I'm sorry. But hell, little brother, you got the only girl I ever wanted enough to marry! Can't you be big about it?"

"Let's forget it," Shea said. He added wearily, "You didn't come over here just to say that."

Judd looked hurt, then shrugged and grinned. "It's Henri's day off and I hate my own cooking."

"We're having leftover beans and cornbread," Tracy said.

"Sounds great to me," he beamed.

While Tracy was whipping up the bread and the beans were heating, they had beer and nuts. Judd inquired about Mary. "Tell her she's got that job Dad promised her as soon as she's ready," he said largely.

Tracy frowned. It was hard to believe he'd forgotten that Mary had turned Le Moyne loose on him. He had to be after something, and Tracy didn't think it was brotherly love and harmony.

He pried the bare outline of their trip from Shea and said it was something he'd always wanted to do. Though neither of them had asked, he gave a report on Vashti. She was redecorating the town house and going to Europe for the summer.

"We had our problems," he said, "but I rattle around in that big house." He gave Tracy a look so frankly appraising that she blushed. "I won't find anyone like you, cousin, but I guess it's time I started looking for the next best thing."

"A description to thrill any bride-to-be," Tracy said drily.

Judd only laughed, and went on to say that his talk show appearance was still bringing in Stronghold enrollees, so many that he'd added another instructor. "It's good supplemental income," he said, "but I see it as a public service."

"Sure. An Armalite at every window." Shea put the blue kettle of beans on the table as Tracy cut the golden-brown crusted cornbread into squares. "Pull up your chair, Judd."

Judd declared the simple meal exactly what he'd been needing. It wasn't till afterward, when they were having coffee, that he settled back and looked at Shea. "We've got to come to an understanding. We'll both do better if we work things out sensibly."

"What's sensible?"

"It still hasn't rained."

Shea's eyes were unreadable. "I'd noticed that myself."

"Damn it, I'm hurting! And you've got 40,000 acres going to waste!"

"Not to waste," Shea corrected. "It's just about back to where it could carry a reasonable number of head, though since it's so dry I've decided to hold off another year to restock."

Judd's square jaw thrust forward. "Well, I can't hold off a year," he burst out. "I've got the damn cows right now!"

"I'll do what I said before," Shea said levelly. "Sell down to what the range will carry and I'll let you run a herd on the lease."

"Damned if I'll let you tell me how many cattle I can have!"

"I'm not telling you. If you don't trust my estimate, we can hire a range biologist to give the ranch a study. I'd go along with his recommendations if you would."

Grating back his chair, Judd got to his feet. It was twilight but his eyes burned yellow in the dimness. "He'd come up with the same nonsense you spout!"

"Then we don't have much to talk about," Shea said.

Judd stared at him, face hardening as if molten lava visibly cooled into a human visage. "It'll always be this way, won't it?" A strange note of regret colored his tone. "There's no way you and I can put the ranch back together the way it used to be—the way it ought to be."

The brothers watched each other a long moment. Shea's voice was soft and a little sad. "You won't believe it, Judd, but I'd like to help."

"Sure!" Judd flared. "Help me go broke on the cattle end of the operation! Some brother you are!"

Tiredly, Shea said, "I owe a duty to the land and the people who'll live here after all of us are dead."

Judd's furious gaze took in Tracy, swept back to Shea. "Your kids!" he jeered. "Sure, you'll have a parcel of brats and you're willing to have green pastures for them! Well, I don't have kids or an old woman and I care about right damn *now!*"

Stalking to the door, he spun around, teeth flashing in a malicious grin. "I don't have you by the balls like you've got me," he said. "Not yet. But I can sure start making you uncomfortable! Think I'll start by calling the Border Patrol on that wetback you got working. And that good buddy of yours, Geronimo! The Army still might like to know where a deserter is."

Shea's lips tightened. "The immigration folks would be a lot more interested in those mercenaries you're training. Pretty cute trick, having your recruiters smuggle illegals in. You've got them where you want them then. Teach them to shoot and hire them out wherever such fighters are wanted. Real profitable for you."

"You've been spying!"

"No. Jaime talked to some of them a week or so ago."

"They'll get their wages—more than they'd ever make at anything else."

"And a lot of them are going to get shot."

Judd shrugged. "That's war. Those damn Commies have got to be stopped. This is my way of helping. I just about break even."

"You probably think you deserve a medal," Shea said in disgust. "Stronghold's the pits but you're within the law there. This other deal, though—Close it out, Judd, or I'm going to turn you in."

Flaming brimstone described the color of Judd's eyes. "You're not even a half-brother of mine," he said thickly. "Some lousy bastard got to your whore of a mother and what they had was you!"

This time he wasn't drunk. Shea knocked him out into the yard. Judd felled him, kicked savagely at his head. Shea rolled out of the way, sprang up, and nearly lifted Judd off his feet with punches to the gut. Judd bellowed and closed his big arms around Shea, crushing him. Tracy snatched up a skillet and was going to bring it down on Judd's skull when Shea locked his leg against Judd's, threw him.

They struggled in light and darkness, broke free and dragged themselves up. Judd aimed a vicious kick at Shea's crotch. Shea grasped the booted foot and forced it up and over. Judd flipped like a roped steer. This time he didn't get up.

Tracy helped Shea carry Judd to his RV, followed with the pickup while Shea drove Judd to the Sanchezes. Judd was still groggy and Shea warned Chuey to watch for signs of concussion and call the doctor if Judd didn't come around fully in a short time. As Shea climbed into his pickup, Judd roused enough to mumble through split, swollen lips.

"You're a goddam bastard, not my brother. You've as good as stolen that land you're hogging."

Chuey said in bewilderment, "What is this, Don Shea?"

"Never mind, Chuey. Just call him a doctor if he needs one."

Shea leaned heavily back as Tracy drove them home. "I wish you'd just turned him into Immigration," Tracy said. "Now he's got two reasons to hate you."

"Make it three." Shea laid a hand on her thigh. Distraught though she was, a thrill hummed through her. "He wanted you."

Shea was battered and bruised but not seriously damaged. "Maybe we ought to let you rest up a couple of days," Tracy suggested. He shook his head.

"I'd just stew around. And it'd be better to fade away while Judd chews over the facts and phases out his war games. He knows now he's got to do it, but it'll save his pride a little to close down while I'm away."

Tracy sighed. "We'll certainly be uneasy neighbors after all this."

"I doubt we'll be neighbors."

With a rush of fear, Tracy caught Shea's hand. "What do you mean?"

"Nothing drastic," Shea grinned reassuringly. "Judd can't keep on raising cattle on the scale he wants to. It's costing money now and there's a limit to what he can pay for prestige, though he gets a nice income from other Scott-O'Shea-Revier interests."

"Then what—"

"My guess is that he'll make a deal with Fricks or someone like him. Sell his part of the ranch for development. With the bundle he'd get, he could start a new ranch someplace else where land's a lot cheaper."

The Socorro ranch cut in two, with acres of golf green, and mock Mediterranean villas around a country club? "But that'd be awful!"

"No more than what he sees as the waste of El Charco is to him," Shea reminded. "I wish I had the money to buy him out—have to use a front, of course. But I haven't been making anything off El Charco, just spending plenty to bring back the range."

"I don't have anything like a smell of what it would take," Tracy regretted. A possibility, repugnant, but still perhaps better than what Shea predicted, struck her. "Shea, supposing we sell Last Spring? Fricks would pay enough to maybe swing an offer to Judd, pooled with what we could borrow and scrape together from our incomes."

He didn't even hesitate. "No." Circling her waist with his arms, he leaned his marked face against her belly and his breath warmed her. "That's your dowry, honey. If we keep it and the land around the old ranch house, that'll do for sentiment and in time El Charco can be productive. We'll do our best." He chuckled.

"Patrick and all our ancestors couldn't ask more than that!" He drew her down and kissed her hard in spite of his bruised lips. "What they'd all be proudest of, though, is those good-looking, spunky, smart kids we're going to have!"

He carried her to the bedroom. Ecstatically pleasured, cherished in his arms, Tracy exhausted herself with giving, offering, taking. Judd's threatening face receded and she fell blissfully asleep, head cradled where she could hear the steady comforting beat of Shea's heart.

Stopping at Bosque and Tubac, they lunched in the shady patio of a restaurant on a back road near San Xavier and drove the long road through mountain-sur-rounded desert to Gila Bend. That improbable metallic oasis of trailers and fast-food places existing mostly as an escape from Luke Air Force Base soon faded like a mirage, as they threaded along a rutted dirt road twining into a wasteland of sand-covered lava flows, exposed mineral like large black pockmarks, dry wash-es fringed by persistent, hopeful trees, and mountains that looked pink or blue or golden or gray, depending on the light and their composition.

When they stopped at the ruins of what had been the Tecolote Mine, run by Marc Revier before he married Talitha, they remembered Lonnie, the young Texan who had died near here to save her. He was buried at the Socorro, but this secret region had many graves, topped with crosses formed by stones, crosses some-times the size of a man, sometimes as small as a child.

"And a lot that died away from the road must not have even had graves," Tracy said.

Shea nodded. "It would be kind of interesting to know what percentage of people who look for gold find death instead. One guess is four hundred died on the Devil's Road during the Gold Rush. You can still die in this country. It wasn't so far away that that group of Honduran refugees died of thirst a few years ago. If we had time, we'd go southwest of Yuma to look over what has to be one of the weirdest projects anyone ever dreamed up."

"What's that?"

"You know that besides watering California and Arizona, the poor puny Colorado has to deliver an allotment to Mexico, too."

Tracy nodded. "The Mexican government was complaining that the water's so salty from irrigation runoff that their farmers can't use it."

"Right. So our Interior Department's set up a $356 million plant to take out enough salt—just enough, mind you—to make Mexico's water usable. It sucks the water through its works, a hundred million gallons a day, then dumps it back in the river while a canal drains the brine into the Gulf of California."

"Whow!"

"And then some. Be a great place to grow halophytes."

"Come again?"

"Plants that can grow on salty water. The University of Arizona and the Mexican government are doing some joint research. Fascinating. Salt bush seems the best bet so far, though pickle weed is edible and Palmer's grass has a seed that's very tasty and eighty percent protein."

"Can they grow on pure sea water?"

"Not too well, but even slight desalinization helps. The big thing is that much of the world's water is too saline for regular crops but could grow halophytes."

They climbed back in the pickup. Stunted palo verde, meager saguaros and an occasional hundred-headed cactus gave way to creosote flats, endless expanses of widely spaced tiny-leaved bushes, some still brightened by small yellow flowers.

Only a particularly mean and tough species of cereus shared this isolation. The few rabbits and quails disappeared. Tracy gazed across this waste at the black peak for which the area was named, Cabeza Prieta. Far to the southeast Shea pointed out the purple shape of Pinacate and Carnegie Peaks.

"Map or no map," said Tracy with feeling, "I'm glad you've been here before!"

"Patrick took Judd and me a few times when we were kids." Shea's jaw hardened and Tracy ached for the bitter alienation between the brothers. They had grown apart as adults but there were years of shared memories as well as the blood bond. Judd couldn't really have believed his slur on Shea's parentage. Shea, when it came right down to it, looked a lot more like Patrick than Judd did. "I've been to Pinacate once since I came back to the ranch, but I've never made the whole grand tour at once, the way we're doing."

A range of fierce granite mountains rose above a wash that sustained a growth of trees, shrubs and vines, which seemed breathtakingly lush in this arid wilderness. Shea stopped at the bottom of a small elevation facing sheer gray stone walls. Cleft down the center, the rock let rain sluice down it to collect in a series of rock hollows reaching from near the top to a large pool at the base.

"Here it is," said Shea, grim wonderment in his voice. "The only sure water in the hundred miles between Quitobaquito and Yuma. Awful thing was when travelers made it this far but found the first tank, or *tinaja,* empty and couldn't crawl up to the second or third." He swept his arm around at the dozens of graves. "Most of these poor devils died that way and were buried by the next party—if they didn't die, too."

Tracy shuddered, shielding her eyes against the glare. "That's what happened to Frost. He died trying to get to the higher tanks."

"From all they say about him, it couldn't have happened to a nicer guy." They wandered through the thick bushes to explore around the cañon, and Tracy exclaimed over the countless holes in the flatter rocks where Arenero women had ground seeds and mesquite beans, gossiping and laughing in the shade while naked brown children played nearby.

Shea squinted at the westering sun. "Want to stay here tonight? I'd rather not try to find the way out in the dark." Tracy looked at the hill of graves and thought of Judah Frost. She didn't believe in ghosts but she thought it likely that extreme emotions might linger in a place, charge the atmosphere with despair or grief or joy.

"Could we camp down the wash a little way?"

Shea grinned as if he guessed her reason. "Sure. Would you like the tent?"

"No. Let's just put our cots close together, hold hands and look at the stars."

He kissed her. The wild sweet fire that could only be banked for a short time flamed up between them. He said huskily, "Do you think one cot can hold us both a little while?"

Drawing him closer, she whispered, "Let's find out!"

XXI

THEY PASSED MORE GRAVES NEXT MORNING ALONG THE faint tracks of the Old Yuma Trail, as the Devil's Road was also known, and took a short cut through Organ Pipe National Monument. As the black top of Cabeza Prieta and the lava and light-painted shapes of the other mountains receded, Shea asked Tracy if she'd ever heard of Pablo Valencia.

She frowned. "I don't think so."

"Back in August of 1906, he just about duplicated Patrick O'Shea's ordeal by thirst. Practically nothing was known about this area then, but W. F. McGee, an early geographer, was spending the summer researching at Tinajas Altas. It was at his camp that Pablo stopped to rest before he headed into the sand dunes searching for gold. Eight days later he dragged himself close to McGee's camp—on top of that hillock with all the graves—and gave a sort of hollow roar. He'd been six days without water!"

"In August? I can't believe it!"

"McGee was logging temperatures. Over a hundred in the day, though they dropped to the eighties at night. Ground temps probably ran as high as one-twenty or more when Pablo crawled or lay down. He should have died on his third day without water, but he set a world record for survival."

"He completely recovered?"

"Yes, but he wouldn't have without McGee's nursing. I've seen a picture of him, Tracy. He looked like a mummy with the wrappings off. Baked skin; mouth, eyes and nose peeled back. They soaked him in water as you might rawhide and he was so dehydrated that his cuts couldn't bleed."

"The stories say that's how the first Shea looked when Socorro found him." Tracy shivered. "We have plenty of water, haven't we?"

"Lots more than we'll need. Person ought to figure on two gallons a day if you're moving around much in the desert summer. And I always carry extra in case I meet someone who's run out." He grinned at her. "Don't worry, honey. When I go into country like this, you can bet I have extras of everything, including gas. It's a long way to help."

Crossing the border, they traveled down the highway that connected Mexico with California, turning off on a dirt road. They passed a ranch where dogs ran out barking and cattle drifted around the windmill-fed tank. Granite mountains resembling those in a child's play set rose from the flat plain to the northwest. Southeast stretched the Sierra Pinacate.

Beyond the ranch the road became tracks. Pinkish-gold shone in the distance, with what looked like the top of a small range rising above it. "The sand dunes and the Buried Range, or Sierra Enterrada," explained Shea. "The dunes run toward the gulf till the salt flats begin. There were three ways a Sand Papago or Arenero youth could become a full man. Capture an eagle, kill an enemy of the tribe, or walk to the gulf."

"They're all gone now, aren't they?"

"They have descendants in western Arizona and Sonora, but the main group disappeared from El Gran Desierto a hundred years ago. They'd been knocking off too many travelers so a posse from Sonoita went after them. One version is that nearly all of them were killed. Another is that a good many captives were taken to Caborca and settled there, but one Sand Papago named Juan Caravajales lived near where we'll stop, at Papago Tanks, first with a woman, then alone, and vanished about 1912."

"He liked his privacy," Tracy said.

She was used to desert, but this was moonscape country of cinder cones, lava flows, barren mountains and vast craters of ancient volcanoes. Their first crater was McDougal. Tracy wondered why Shea had parked at this rather unpromising location beneath a small slope, but got out and walked with him through bits of brown-red lava that shone as if they'd been waxed.

"Desert varnish," Shea told her. "And look, where small bits are pressed down in the earth like a mosaic, it's called desert paving."

She nodded, then gasped as they topped a small elevation. A vast hollow spread below, walled by spills of rock. Far below on the flat bottom was a small world of dry watercourses fringed with trees.

"We could go down," Shea said, enjoying her awe. "But let's save our energy for Sykes'. It's three miles around and 750 feet deep."

Tracy groaned. "That had better be a morning project!"

"First light, honey. We'll take a quick swing to the edge of the dunes and head back to camp at Sykes' tonight."

They stopped near Papago Tanks and trudged up the wash till they had to scramble up boulders to find the natural cisterns. It was an oasis of trees and grass, a prime watering place for birds and animals. "That Sand Papago hermit picked about the only place to be," Tracy decided as they munched trail mix and enjoyed chilled oranges and iced tea. She watched a humming-bird sip at a red chuperosa flower. "If Socorro and Shea had found a place like this, they might have just homesteaded rather than trying to walk out."

"Enjoy it," advised Shea. "This is the only Triple A on the tour."

Past the forbidding Sierra Estraña—"The Strange Range," Shea rhymed—the dunes appeared so close now that they dazzled, endless sweeps of that glowing rosy gold.

Moon Crater was almost silted to its rimmed circumference, but the reddish core in the center rose like a jagged crescent. There was breeze enough to inspire them to climb up the rugged sides to the top. From there they could see scattered ranges, isolated tracings of green growth along arroyos, and the sensuous tawny dunes to the south and east. White droppings showed that hawks and eagles had often perched here, too, surveying their vast and undisputed kingdom.

On the way back, they stopped for no reason that Tracy could discern. A bit grumpily, she followed Shea, who searched around a bit and then called triumphantly. "Papago Tanks is prettier but this place is air-conditioned!"

"So's the truck," muttered Tracy, but she clambered up a small slope and gazed down into a large opening in the rocks. Ten feet below was a dirt floor and on either side there seemed to be a cavern.

Shea, already on the bottom, offered a shoulder for her to step down on till she could reach a pile of rocks. It was a good twenty degrees cooler, but Tracy sniffed and wrinkled her nose. "What's that musty smell?"

"Caves smell musty," Shea teased, "But I suspect that aroma comes from bat guano!"

"Bat!"

"Well, sure," he said reasonably. "If you were a bat, wouldn't you like it here?"

Wings brushed her cheek just then. She squeaked and almost stepped on one of several small corpses that her accommodating vision could now detect on the ground.

"I want out of here!"

"But, dear! If you were a Sand Papago—"

"Well, I'm not and if you don't boost me out *muy pronto* I'll put cactus in your bed!"

"I'd hoped for something nicer," Shea sighed as he obediently stooped to hoist her out.

They camped among palo verde and ironwood trees in a broad wash beneath the rim of Sykes' Crater. Shea grilled steaks over ironwood coals, while Tracy put together a salad. With cold wine, nothing had ever tasted so delicious. After the few dishes were done and scraps thrown a good distance down the wash for some fortunate coyote, they sat in their camp chairs, holding hands and watching the stars as the embers blinked companionably.

"In spite of your bats, it's a lovely honeymoon," Tracy murmured.

"Yes," he said, and turned her face up for his kiss.

It was deliciously cool when, before dawn, they made a hearty breakfast and started up the side of the vast crater. It was hard going in the crumbly volcanic rubble. Tracy took off her light jacket and left it on a rock.

"Good idea," approved Shea. "You won't need it again today."

When they finally reached the 130-foot-high rim, the sun beamed its first light against the side of the immense crater, painted the reddish mountain to their left. Far below spread a small universe of arroyos, fallen boulders, grassy plains and trees.

"Can we get down there?" Tracy eyed the rugged rock walls with apprehension. "And if we do, can we get out?"

"I did it before," he assured her. "And this time I've got ropes for the worst parts."

"Water?"

He patted his daypack. "Two quarts." He chuckled. "I've even got trail mix and one of those light emergency blankets in case you decide we ought to stay all night."

She shuddered. "It looks a little too much like a penthouse of hell!" Lifting the brim of her hat, she turned to scan the region. Pinacate Peak lay below Papago Tanks and its lava flows spread across the lower country like a jaggedly cut mantle.

Dead volcanoes and cinder cones, eaten into strange silhouettes by wind, rain and time, showed black or red or blue-gray on the barren plain where the water courses marked the only bright threads of green. Up close, of course, the seemingly flat expanses were toothed with jagged lava and studded with limber bush, creosote and brittle bush, even white prickly poppies and orange globe mallow. But from here, Tracy gazed down at a relief map of some strange and awesome planet that seemed devoid of life. Beyond the Buried Range and the shining dunes sparkled the distant waters of the Gulf.

"Shall we?" Shea made a sweeping welcoming gesture as he got out his light nylon rope. "We don't really need this, but it'll make the first part of the going easier. These cinders at the top are darned slippery."

They certainly were, even with the help of the rope Shea tied to a palo verde and attached to another tree farther down. "We'll leave it there," he said. "We'll be mighty glad to have it on the way back."

Tracy believed him. The fine black cinders were shifty as sand and already absorbing solar heat. It was a relief to reach the rock ledges and firmer footing, though even this could give way. "If you must grab something," Shea warned, "try not to make it cholla."

Cholla's many spines made prickly pear seem like a velvet cushion. Tracy had once spent an agonizing hour picking cholla out of a dog's tongue so she didn't need Shea's warning to avoid it here. Where soil was stable enough for the scant foothold they needed, stunted trees and shrubs grew on the descent. Working through outcroppings and eroded lava, Shea produced a shorter rope, tied it to the best tree he could find, and lowered himself to the next rock level, helping Tracy down. "We'll leave that rope, too," he said.

They were about halfway down. Tracy shielded her eyes and looked up. It seemed an impossible climb. She looked down. It was a dizzying fall. She groaned a little.

"Drink up," Shea said, handing her a canteen. "It's easy going from here."

"You'd better not be lying!"

He wasn't. The angle became more gradual and there was real earth instead of cinders and rubble. The eastern rim shaded them now though it wouldn't be long till the sun reached the bottom of the crater.

They explored this little world, wandering through sizable boulders fallen from the sides, thickets of mesquite, following washes that ran only when the occasional rain filled them. A rabbit flashed through some yellow-flowered brittlebush. It was a strange thought, that it had been born here and would die here, knowing nothing of the region above.

Sun filled the central crater now. No breeze could stir the warming air and heat reflected from the sides would turn this into an oven. "We'll rest on the way up," Shea decided. "The sooner we're out of here, the better."

They rested in the shade of a small grotto near the ledge-climbing rope, sipped water and munched a mixture of chopped dried fruits, nuts and seeds.

"Why doesn't this crater have a Mexican name?" Tracy puzzled, sprinkled a few drops of water on the pulses of her wrists.

"Godfrey Sykes was an Englishman who came down here with William Hornaday in 1907 to explore and map the area," Shea explained. "He's also the one who named the boojum trees out of Lewis Carroll's *The Hunting of the Snark*, but you have to go farther down the coast or over to Baja California to see them.

They're like big upside-down carrots with a few roots waving in the air." He chuckled. "Godfrey Sykes' sons, Glenton and Gilbert, still live in Tucson. I got to know them some when I was at the university. Glenton told me that on one expedition down here, everyone wanted something different to drink at breakfast—tea, coffee, chocolate. The cook got mad about it and just mixed all the stuff together, put it to brew, and quit."

With a boost from Shea and the help of the rope, Tracy climbed to the upper ledge. That was where the sides got steeper and more treacherous with rubble. Though they stopped frequently, she was panting and had a stitch in her side by the time they reached the last rope.

It still seemed an impossible distance to the top. The cinders glittered like crumbled coal. Tracy looked down the dizzying way to the bottom and fought off a wave of vertigo.

"You go first," Shea said. "I'll untie this end of the rope when I'm climbing up."

She sank ankle-deep into the cinders but the rope let her stay upright rather than making her literally crawl up the shifting, unstable funnel. Catching her breath at the palo verde, she trudged on to the top and collapsed beneath the only tree big enough to offer any shade. In a moment Shea joined her. They emptied the canteens and polished off the trail mix.

"Only ten o'clock," Shea grinned, glancing at his watch. "Want to do Pinacate today?"

"Absolutely not!" winced Tracy. "The only sensible thing to do is go lie under that big ironwood till the sun goes down!"

She felt better, though, by the time they got back to camp. They made a big chef's salad with hard-boiled eggs and cheese and consumed it along with quantities of iced lemon tea.

"We can siesta if you like," Shea said. "But it'll be cooler in the truck with air conditioning on."

"I'm surprised you'd stoop to having anything so decadent!" she teased. "But I'm glad you do! Maybe we can find Socorro's *tinaja*."

"It was probably a seasonal hole," he said, "but we'll look."

They visited several of the other *tinajas* and found what Shea said was a sleeping circle, a wall of rocks piled about two feet high, just enough to break the wind. "People who lived here were ace survivalists," Shea mused. "But sometimes it's been too tough even for them. Julian Hayden, who lives in Tucson, knows this region better than anyone. From analyzing tools and desert varnishes, he feels sure people were here over twenty thousand years ago, vanished during a prolonged drouth of the kind that seems to be setting in now, and came back during a rainy period that lasted till about nine thousand years ago." Shea paused, his tone ironically dreamy. "Man disappeared again but when the rains came about five thousand years ago, the ancestors of the Pimas and Papagos moved in."

Tracy shook her head. "Padre Kino passed through here in the early 1700's, but those dates make him sound like a newcomer!"

Shea continued her thought. "So where does that leave us? Yet these volcanoes were old when the first humans drifted here."

"It's eternity made visible," she said slowly. "Imagine being here alone, on foot and without supplies, the way Socorro was."

Shea caressed her cheek, the curve of her throat. "The saying in this country is, 'It is not good to walk the Gran Desierto alone.' That goes for life, too. I'm glad you're with me."

Their eyes met. Aching with loving him and with her unbelievable good fortune, Tracy was glad that they had made their wedding trip to this strange country where most things became irrelevant; but water, shelter, a companion, assumed tremendous importance.

They were in a broad field at the edge of the dunes.

Shea located the track of an ancient river and followed it quite a distance into the dunes which rose above them in endless peaks or sensuous curves, shaded lavender and ruddy gold by the afternoon sun. Smoke trees grew thick in stretches of the wash. Many had died from lack of water but others were a glory of hazy purple bloom. The way was blocked at last by dunes that had moved across the archaic watercourse, closing off a sea of their own that undulated as far as the eye could reach to the south and east.

"The Deadly Desert," said Tracy, remembering her Oz books.

"You've got that right. Guess it's time to start out anyway if we want to do Pinacate in the morning." Shea turned the pickup and soon they were following the faint tracks that led out of this mysterious world.

From stories passed down in the family, they guessed that Socorro had been somewhere south of Pinacate, and they hunted for a time, taking game trails, following arroyos. They found several empty tanks, which had held water in some past seasons, but were now dry.

"Wherever she was, she brought her Irishman back to life and he walked her out of this," Shea said.

Tracy's flesh prickled. "Do you think they know we're here?"

"Some of them is here in us." Shea laughed and kissed her. "That's all I'm sure of, but that's enough."

XXII

IT WAS DARK BY THE TIME THEY REACHED THE HIGHWAY and Shea drove slowly to find the turnoff. They camped beneath some big trees at a ranch abandoned because of the drouth and went to bed right after supper. Tracy didn't stir consciously till close to dawn, when she smelled coffee.

Stealing a blissful glance at Shea, still almost unable to believe her good luck, she snuggled into her pillow for one last delicious moment in this cool part of the day, when the warmth of a sleeping bag felt wonderful.

"Wake up, sleepy head." Shea hunkered down by her, offering a big blue mug of steaming coffee ameliorated with creamer. "It won't be as hot on top of Pinacate as it was down in Sykes', but it'll be warm. We've got a lot of *mal pais* to cover before we even start up."

After breakfast they drove toward the mountains and parked in a wash beneath a rock ledge. Hunters and woodcutters had been there before them. Rusty beer cans and other civilized jetsam littered the area, and there were the remains of many campfires.

They found a way up the ledge, crossed a small field and came out on a brown-black lava flow that spilled in a broad skirt of varying lengths around the base of the peaks. This lava wasn't silted over or softened with

256

vegetation. It was hardened into sharp ferocity and, in the worst stretches, honeycombed with holes that seemed designed to entrap a foot.

"It looks like hell barely cooled," Tracy said. "I can see why they call it bad land, *mal pais,* but bad rock would be more fitting."

They picked their way across, aiming for where green had encroached to shorten the lava border. Once across this, the climb along the slope was easier, much of it over terraces of volcanic rock. Shea paused several times before he nodded and led the way to a big hole gaping in the stone. The bottom was perhaps fourteen feet below, but—as in the bat cave—boulders and rocks were piled up at one end for climbing in and out.

"This is one of Iitoi's dwellings," Shea said.

Tracy looked at him in surprise. "I thought Elder Brother lived at Baboquivari over in Arizona."

"Sometimes he did, but like the Papagos, Elder Brother moved around a lot. I think you'd have to call Pinacate the number-one hangout. It was here that he fetched up after a great flood."

"Like Noah on Ararat?"

"Just like."

Tracy gazed around, at the forbidding peaks with their sparse growth, then out at the sweep of desert broken only by barren mountains and a great hollow in the earth to the northeast. "It's hard to believe it ever rained here, much less flooded."

They drank from their canteens and Shea stashed one of the quart bottles he was carrying in a rock recess. "That leaves us a gallon," he said. "We'll drink this on the way back."

"That gallon weighs over eight pounds," Tracy said. "Do we need that much?"

"In the summer, a good rule is six quarts if you're not moving much, eight quarts if you're active." He waved a hand at the peaks, which seemed impossibly high, discouragingly barren of any restful shade. "We'll be active."

"I guess it's our expensive evaporative cooling system." Tracy sighed.

"Yep. When outside temps go higher than body, say about ninety-two, our couple of million sweat glands go to work cooling body heat that's transferred from the center. You can lose a quart of water an hour by walking at a hundred degrees—and it's going to be that very shortly." He patted her arm. "You *look* solid, honey, but you're really two-thirds water. Dehydrate five percent and you'd stop functioning normally. Twelve percent usually brings death."

"The first Shea must have been way past that."

"Yes. Pablo Valencia certainly was. Both of them claimed they had actually died and watched their naked bodies crawling from some point above them. But I'd rather not try my luck."

They started on, winding around the first mountain. "If it were cooler, we might go up Carnegie," Shea said. "But for now we'll be content with Pinacate."

A little gorge twisted between the mountains and smaller hills, one of them thickly studded with cholla. They followed it, found a little shade among some boulders at the base of the peak, drank deeply and snacked on trail mix.

Tracy's ankle was paining her a bit. She wished she had an elastic bandage to support it. If she mentioned her problem, Shea probably would insist they turn back. After coming all this way, she didn't want to do that.

The climb, fortunately, was never very steep, and the footing was reasonably good. Even so, she was gasping when they reached the top. Her ankle shot messages of protest up her leg. Sinking down on a rock, she slowly looked around in all directions.

She could pick out the craters, the mountains, the comparatively lush green around the tanks, the luminous dunes, and beyond them and the creosote salt flats, the shining, distant Sea of Cortez that divided the mainland from Baja.

Awed, she looked northwest to the painted mountains of the Cabeza Prieta, then east to a distinctive rounded cone. She gave a cry. "Shea! That must be Baboquivari!"

"Iitoi's other place," he nodded, offering a canteen. "This is where Kino saw that California could be reached by land. Before that, it had been considered an island."

"He climbed up here?" Tracy asked incredulously.

Shea laughed. "Honey, he made four *entradas* through this area, and seems to have climbed this peak at least twice. As well as founding a string of missions throughout what he called Pimería Alta, that tireless Jesuit did a lot of exploring."

From a half-mile up, the region below looked ethereal and otherworldly, the landscape of some undiscovered planet. Tracy shaded her eyes and sighed in wonder. "From here, you can see forever."

Shea sat down by her and opened his pack. They savored the juicy sweetness of apples, chewed almonds and finished with halvah. The level top of the peak was small so it didn't take long to cover it, stopping frequently to gaze down and away.

Stiffened by even the brief rest, Tracy's ankle throbbed so insistently that she asked Shea if he had some bandage. "I never do this kind of walking without some," he said. "Your ankle? Lord, Tracy, why didn't you say so earlier?"

"I wanted to climb the peak."

"Well, you have," he said grimly, making her perch on a rock. "Next time, you holler the minute you start to hurt!" He eased off her hiking boot and wrapped the broad elastic bandage securely around her ankle and instep. "Stand up and see if it's too tight."

She obeyed, flexing her foot. "Feels fine."

His gray eyes were worried. "We can take as long as we need to get back," he said. "Tell me when you want to rest."

"I'm not that bad off," she protested.

He scowled at her. "Don't you pull a trick like this again! In this country, next to water, your feet are the most important things you've got."

"I believe it," she said humbly.

"You go in front and set the speed," he suggested, voice softening as he touched her cheek.

She did her best not to limp, but he called halts every twenty minutes or so. The bandage helped. Even so, as they rested at Iitoi's cave and drank their cached water, she dreaded the broad band of lava. She made her way across it with great care. Shea *could* carry her out from here if he had to, but her foolishness had already caused him enough trouble.

"We're almost home," he said cheeringly. "We'll soak that ankle and prop it up."

"But—"

"No buts. I'll get supper. All you have to do is sit back and look pretty." He glanced at the mid-afternoon sun and chuckled. "But first we'll have some nice frosty beer."

"You know how to urge a person on," Tracy laughed. She quickened her pace. He helped her down the rock ledge and they started along the wash.

Shea stopped abruptly. "The pickup's gone!"

Tracy stared in disbelief. Sure enough, there was the place they'd spent the night, just opposite that reddish butte. The pickup had been parked just under this overhanging tree. It was nowhere to be seen. Fear washed over her shock. She caught Shea's arm.

"What do you think?"

He shook his head. Examining tire tracks, his frown deepened. "If someone stranded on foot had walked up here and figured how to unlock the truck and start it with the wiring, I'd have some hope that they'd drive to where they could send someone back for us, even if they stole the truck and kept going. But another vehicle's been in here. Whoever swiped ours didn't need it."

"They might send help even if they're thieves," Tracy

suggested. Once he'd made her sit down on a half-burned log, Shea's dazed expression hardened to one of anger.

"I doubt that, my dear, if they'd take the pickup when they didn't need it, and even keep our water. Amelia Tanks happen to be close to us, but chances are they didn't know that—and it's damned lucky I do!"

"You—you mean they left us to die?" Tracy asked in horror.

"If they'd left water, I might have marked it down to boyish high spirits. But anyone who'd do that—" He shook his head. "They won't send help."

"Maybe they'll be caught," Tracy suggested hopefully.

"Why? The car permit's in the glove compartment in case they want to cross the border."

They were both silent a moment. "My darned ankle!" Tracy groaned.

Shea sat down and put his arm around her. "It could be a lot worse. We're close to water."

"But—"

"Honey, the best thing is for me to leave you at Emilia. I'll fill the canteens and get to the highway. Someone'll stop to give me a lift and I'll get them to drive back here."

Tracy clamped her teeth down on a wail that she was afraid to stay alone, but Shea guessed her feelings. "We could both stay at the tanks," he said. "Geronimo'll come looking for us if we're not back in two weeks, or someone else might possibly happen along. But our food supply is exactly a couple of handfuls of trail mix and a chunk of halvah." He managed a chuckle. "The *tunas* and mesquite beans Socorro lived on won't be ripe for a couple of months and I'd hate to see us live on what I could catch in snares or stun with rocks. I'd better walk out while I've got the energy."

He was right, of course. By the time her ankle was strong enough for her to go with him, they'd be weak from hunger. Or if they just waited, it could take

Geronimo and a search party weeks to cover their whole intended pilgrimage.

It still lacked a couple of hours till sunset. "You'll wait till morning, won't you?" Tracy asked.

Shea held her close. "Honey, I'd better start as soon as we get you to Emilia. If I can get to the abandoned ranch tonight, then I should make it to the highway tomorrow. With luck, I'll be back for you by tomorrow night."

Walking at night would certainly be less exhausting than making that long trek completely in the day. The only way she could help her love was to go along with what he said and not add to his worries.

"We'll get our desert survival merit badges for this," she said, rising, controlling a wince as weight came down on the abused ankle. "Where's the tank?"

Staying below the *mal pais*, crossing several small washes, they at last came to an arroyo that deepened as they followed it. In places, the earth had eroded to polished rock, and the course was littered with boulders. Though the going was fairly flat, it was rock and uneven. Tracy was grateful for the walking stick Shea had made for her from a dried yucca stalk.

The first stone basin was empty. The next harbored drying scum. Tracy's heart sank. Without water, their case would be much worse, though Shea should still be able to walk out. Clumps of brush and stunted trees concealed the next tank till they were almost above it. At the sight of the water, Tracy gave a soft cry of gratitude.

Since the last rain, it had sustained birds and animals from miles around. Dove feathers floated on it and dead insects were mired in scum at the edges, but it was still life. It looked wonderful.

There was a little water left in one of the canteens. They shared this as if it were wine, then Shea filled up the bottles. Through the semitransparent plastic, the water showed pale green.

"We don't have any iodine or purification tablets," Shea said. "But there aren't any cattle running in here and it looks pretty clean, considering." He opened his daypack. "You get to try out this handy-dandy moon blanket. Here are matches if you want a fire tonight to cheer you up. There's a flashlight and a first-aid kit. I'll leave you the food."

"You won't!" Tracy thrust the bag of trail mix at him and opened the halvah. "You eat up right now, before you start! You'll need energy for that walk."

"This water's full of nutrients," he laughed, slipping canteens into his pack.

"Shea Scott!" she threatened. "You eat this or I'll feed it to the beasts of the air and the birds of the field!"

"Aren't you a little mixed-up?" he teased.

"Eat, you stubborn redhead!"

"Who's stubborn?"

She made as if to scatter the nuts and dried fruit in her hand. He caught it. "All right! Let's gobble up our supplies. But you save the halvah for tomorrow. I'll be getting something to eat before you will."

"I should hope so, after a hike like that!" She broke the sesame-honey confection in half and made him take his. "Since I'm not as big as you, I'm still getting more than my share."

She made him keep the first-aid kit and flashlight, too. "I'm not going anywhere," she argued. "And there's not much way for me to get hurt."

Her heart shrank when he rose to go. She wanted to catch hold of him and beg him to stay. Instead, she got up and kissed him good-bye. "Be careful, darling."

"You, too, honey. I'll be back as quick as I can."

It was hard to withdraw from the comforting strength of his arms. Forcing herself away, Tracy produced the best smile she could. "Don't stop off at some bar and figure you can stroll in any time you're ready," she warned.

He kissed her again and left her.

It was a sort of self-torture, but Tracy couldn't keep herself from climbing out of the arroyo to watch him out of sight. After his light-blue shirt had apparently vanished for good in the direction of the red butte where they'd camped, she sat down on a boulder and let herself cry.

Of course, Shea was going to come back. Everything would be fine. This would make an exciting adventure to tell their children. But for now it was twilight, Shea was gone, and never mind facts, she felt abandoned in this ferocious country and she was scared.

It didn't help a lot to call herself names and remember that seventeen-year-old Socorro had been alone in this region with no hope of rescue, but it did brace her enough to make a prayer for Shea and to turn a practical eye to her own arrangements.

There was fine silt around the tank. Wrapped in the emergency blanket, she could burrow into that and be reasonably warm. She had no food to cook, but a fire would keep the night at bay.

There were no predators bigger than a coyote and she told herself that rattlers could detect body heat with pits located between their nostrils and eyes. It was handy for locating prey but it also warned when the snake was close to something too big for easy swallowing. As for scorpions—

The heck with it! Tracy thought. *I'm not half as scared of real things as of just the darkness, being out here alone. But I can make a fire.*

Wary of stinging things and snakes, she collected anything that would burn and scrambled down the rocks to the tank. She scooped out a fire hole, selected a place for her blanket and hobbled around the arroyo gathering fallen limbs and decaying stumps washed out by wind and downpours.

She had plenty of dry grass and small twigs to start the fire. It flared at the first match. She added larger sticks, and when those were blazing, edged in a fair-sized stump. It looked solid enough to hold fire through the night, be a reassuring glow in the loneliness.

Settling back on the folded blanket, she enjoyed the light and warmth. The sense of having done something to improve her situation made her feel less helpless and consequently less afraid.

She thought of Shea. He'd walk for hours yet. The road wasn't much, but it skirted a line of hills and it didn't seem likely he'd lose the way. Her stupid ankle! If only she were walking beside him! The sound of a far-off motor, which almost had to be an airplane, made her feel even more isolated.

It swept over Tracy in a rush, the malevolence of people who could leave others in this desert without water. What if someone just as evil came along and found her here?

Shivering, she realized that the fire that cheered her might be a beacon for prowlers like that blond thug who'd kidnapped her. Much as she hated to, she'd better deaden the flames. Easier to handle imaginary terrors than real ones.

Scooping up a double handful of sand, she was about to toss it in the fire when a voice said behind her, "Don't do that."

Spinning as she knelt, Tracy stared up at Judd. The fire cast a towering shadow behind him. Her first wild hope that he was a rescuer died at the triumph on his broad handsome face. His eyes glinted yellow in the light as he took her wrists and drew her up.

Trapped in those cruel hands, Tracy felt like dead weight, a heavy molten image stripped of spirit. It took the pitiless searing of his lips on hers to shock her into resistance. Trying to writhe away, she brought her heel down on his instep as hard as she could. He swore and swept her off her feet. "It's time you learned to behave, baby doll. I'm going to teach you right damn now!"

Tearing at her clothes, he sank down with her on the blanket. Panic flared blindingly in her. She tried to escape. Time and place dissolved in terror, she was back in the thick Houston night while a man battered at her; only this one was not impotent. She screamed in pain and outrage.

There was no one to hear.

XXIII

SHE ROUSED FROM THE NEAR STUPOR INTO WHICH SHE HAD retreated, as he carried her up the side of the arroyo and across the scrub-grown plain to where his RV was parked in a shallow wash. Dully, she realized it must have been the motor she'd heard. As Judd opened the back and dumped her on the thickly carpeted floor, she scrambled to a sitting position.

"You stole the pickup!" she accused.

"Sure did," he answered jauntily. "Wish I could have seen my baby brother's face when he saw it was gone."

Fresh dread gripped her. "Is he all right? You haven't—"

"He's just fine, though doubtless a bit footsore. No use interrupting such a nice healthful hike." Judd chuckled. "We'll all sleep tonight, sweetheart. Time enough tomorrow to head Shea off at the pass."

Terror blocked her throat like jagged ice. She had to swallow and clench her hands tight before she could speak. "Shea—what do you mean to do about him?"

In the darkness she shrank as Judd's hand slid over her breasts. "Don't you wonder what I'm going to do with you?" he asked softly.

Suffocated with fear, she fought to keep her voice steady. "I suppose you'll have to kill me. But Shea—

you could let him go. Let him walk out. He'd never have to know what happened to me."

Judd laughed.

Tracy caught his hands. "Please! Your father loved you both. For his sake, don't hurt Shea."

"My father didn't sire that crazy bastard," Judd growled. "He's got no claim on the land he's ruining and I'm not letting him ruin me! Some of his bones may be found sometime, but what Mexican cop's going to care about a gringo who probably got shot in some drug ripoff?"

The nightmare shame and hurt of Judd's brutalization had crushed Tracy's will to live, but at the threat to Shea a cold determination strengthened her. If Judd didn't kill her at once, she'd find some way to destroy or disable him.

One hand lightly on her throat but spread in a way that suggested strangling, Judd's voice dropped to a whisper. "How about you, cousin?"

"How about me?"

"If you're nice to me, I can let you live. I'd even marry you when the sad news of your widowhood came out."

"You must be out of your mind!" That wasn't smart. She should have played along till she had her chance.

The hand tightened ever so slightly, but even with her own and Shea's life in the balance, she couldn't bring herself to make such a promise. Judd's amused tone was edged with admiration. "You've got guts, cousin, for all your sweet look. That must be why you're the only woman who's ever mattered to me."

He gave a soft reminiscent laugh. "I thought Cele might be a winner, but once I got her she turned weepy and all full of guilt over Shea. I was damned glad when she took off. And Vashti—hell! She's hotter than a cheap pistol but she got the notion she owned me. Would you believe the stupid female thought I'd marry her after Dad died?"

Dazed, Tracy shook her head. "Your brother's and father's wives—"

"They weren't worth the hassle." His voice sank to a husky murmur. "But you are. Did you really think I'd kill you?"

Involuntary relief washed through her followed by bewilderment. "You mean to kill Shea. You can't think I'd keep quiet about that!"

"No one listens to a crazy woman."

"What?"

He caressed her shoulder, testing her flesh with the balls of his fingers as if she were a ripening fruit. "When my younger brother and his bride don't return from their honeymoon, naturally I go looking for them. I find my brother, killed by who knows who, and finally track down his wife who's half-dead of dehydration. Of course, the poor girl has delusions about what happened. Of course, she says wild things. And I'm thought to be a wonderfully kind man to take care of her at home rather than put her in an institution."

It could work.

Stunned disbelief gave way to icy conviction that he could bring it off. He was her nearest living relative. No one would question him except—Mary would! And Geronimo might not swallow that story. As that hope flowered, Judd trampled it.

"With you deranged, I'm sure to be named to handle Shea's affairs. I'll fire those Apache friends of yours while you're locked up for treatment at a private hospital I know of. When I bring you home, the amount of freedom you have depends on you." His voice deepened. "If you ever got back your sanity, I could marry you."

She didn't answer. There was the sure consolation that he couldn't, for long, keep her alive. If escape proved absolutely hopeless, she believed she'd rather be dead than doomed to be his plunder. But the important thing now was to keep him from killing Shea.

She shuddered as Judd climbed up beside her. This time, through all he did, she absented herself from her body and held the image of Shea in her mind, repeating his name like a silent prayer. She had to endure. She had to find a way to save him.

Judd had tied her feet and hands. Everything came back in a rush as she stirred against her bonds in the gray dawning. Along with that consciousness, a strange dream faded, one so real that she would have sworn a beautiful dark-haired young woman in a torn old-fashioned dress had been smoothing her hair and talking to her.

I was ravished and lost in this desert, the girl had said in a gentle voice. But I lived, and found my love. So will you, Teresita.

The infinitely tender smile lingered, a comforting presence in the back of Tracy's mind as, tensing, she felt Judd stir. He embraced her, tossing back the blankets to watch and touch her body, but to her great relief, he glanced at his watch and sat up, hauling on his clothes.

"Time to meet Pardo."

"Pardo?"

He had come to the wedding. She knew he was a sort of friend of Shea's and felt a slight rise of hope.

"Yeah. He's stashing the pickup after keeping an eye on Shea to be sure some unexpected woodcutter or wandering archaeologist doesn't happen along to give him a lift."

"What if one does?"

Judd shrugged. "Pardo has orders to shoot if it looks like Shea might be crawling out of it."

Tracy's brief that Pardo might help them faded. He must have come on the expedition knowing its aim. He was a man who killed for money. There would be money in this kill.

Judd untied Tracy so she could dress. He let her go into the bushes, tied her hands again before he boiled

water for instant coffee and peeled an orange for her.
Tracy awkwardly ate it and a breakfast roll. She'd need
her strength today.

"Why didn't you just kill Shea last night?" she asked.

Pouring them both more coffee, Judd grinned.
"Wouldn't be much sport in that."

"Sport!"

"Sure." Judd's eyes glittered. "This is going to be the
most exciting hunt I ever had. I've never stalked a man
before."

"He doesn't have a gun!"

"That's his problem. When we catch up with him, I'll
explain the ground rules and give him a head start."
Judd patted her hand. "I'll leave you with Pardo and
the RV. Cheer up, doll. Maybe Shea'll kill me with a
rock."

"You'll never let him get that close."

"Not if I know it. But that's what makes it interesting."

"To make it really interesting, why don't you give
him a gun?"

"It's more poetic this way. Man as pure quarry with
only his brain for help."

"It's not your brain that'll kill Shea. It's your gun."

He laughed. "Well, that's what happens when people
think they don't need a weapon." Making her get into
the RV, he tied her ankles securely. "Just so you won't
kick." His hand lingered along her thigh. He lowered
his head and nipped her through her trousers, letting
his warm breath heat her flesh. "What is it about you,
cousin? I already want you again. But it'll have to
wait."

As they jolted back to the road, Tracy felt physically
sick, not only at the horror of his plan, but from the
merciless way he'd used her. Aching and nauseated,
she leaned forward and vomited.

Swearing, Judd braked to a halt. Roughly, he
scrubbed her face, but he untied her to make her clean
up the mess on the floor. This made her sick again.

"If this is your way of buying time for that bastard, forget it," Judd grated. "Pardo's to follow and kill him if we don't meet him at the old ranch by eight." He handed her a canteen. "Rinse your mouth and let's go."

Back on the road with its broad strip of weeds grown up between the tracks except where they passed over rock or gravel, they drove across the rolling expanse toward the mountains that marked the ranch and the way in. The moment the sun came over the mountains, it was instantly hot. Judd had on the air conditioner. Tracy thought of Shea, who had probably been walking for several hours by now.

When he saw them coming, he'd think it meant rescue. Tracy groaned silently before she said bitterly to Judd, "Shea's been walking while you've been riding. He hasn't had any real food since yesterday. Apart from guns, you're a long way from starting even."

Judd only chuckled. "When I'm after a deer, babe, I don't know—or care—when it drank or had its belly full."

Tracy's mind doubled back and forth, desperately searching some way to thwart the man beside her. Hurl herself against him? Even if she caused a wreck that disabled him, Pardo had orders to kill Shea.

A sudden thought sent a thrill of hope through her. If Pardo would kill for money, why wouldn't he spare a life for it? Though his training might allow him to murder Shea, he must have some liking for him.

I'll offer him double whatever Judd has, Tracy thought. *Why shouldn't he take it?*

It was possible, of course, that some perverted mercenary's honor would keep him bought once he'd made a bargain. Still, it was the only hope Tracy could see. In spite of the oppressive throbbing in her head, the bruised aching between her legs, she felt better than she had since the ordeal started.

Trees and brush grew thick around the deserted

ranch. Tracy relaxed slightly when she saw the pickup waiting in the sandy wash below the corrals. Pardo was there, not trailing Shea.

Dressed in camouflage, holster at his hip, the tall wiry black came out of the trees as Judd stopped the RV. "See you found your brother's wife," Pardo greeted, flipping his hand upward at Tracy.

Judd scowled at the words but asked impatiently, "How far ahead is he?"

"Seven miles, maybe eight. He only slept a couple of hours."

With a nod of satisfaction, Judd moved to the back of the car. "You drive, Pardo. Give me the Magnum."

Pardo handed over the lethal black gun. "Want I should drive right up to your brother?"

"He's not my brother, he's a bastard!"

"Ain't we all?" Pardo grinned. He slid under the wheel.

"Drive up beside him," Judd ordered. "I'll tell him how it's going to be and give him a start."

Pardo's ironic grin twisted his sparse beard sideways. "It'd be a lot more interesting if you didn't have a gun either."

"I'm not doing this to entertain you," Judd said curtly. "All you have to do is wait with the girl."

"Yassuh, boss," gibed Pardo.

They could go only about twenty miles an hour. Time crawled as they jounced along. Muscles tense, stomach feeling as if it had shriveled to a tight ball, Tracy caught in her breath when she saw, at last, the light blue of Shea's shirt showing around his darker blue daypack. His canvas hat and khaki trousers blended with the road and the barren land till they were a good deal closer.

At the sound of a motor, he'd glanced back and shielded his eyes. They he turned and came to meet them. When he saw Tracy, he broke into a trot, smiling with relief.

If there were only a way to warn him, at least prepare

him for the treachery! All Tracy could do was shake her head and bring up her bound hands.

Shea halted, smile dying. Judd climbed out of the back. The Magnum was in his holster. He had a rifle in his hands.

"I'm giving you a start," he said.

Shea's incredulous look hardened into a grim one. "You do like your little games."

"Especially this one."

Disgust, not fear, was in Shea's eyes. His gaze flicked to Pardo before he shrugged. "Even with that artillery, you may not come back, Judd. If we both kill each other, what happens to Tracy?"

"Don't worry," Pardo said. "I'll take her home before I split."

"Thanks," Shea nodded.

Incredibly, he grinned at Tracy. "Hang in there, honey. I may be back. And if I'm not—I'll always love you."

"I'll always love you," she promised, through what felt like blood clotting her throat.

Shea drank from his canteen, dropped his pack and started walking.

"Class," said Pardo. "That's class."

Judd grunted. "Want a beer?"

"Why not?"

Tracy declined. Shea had vanished around a bend in the road curving past a hill. Probably now he'd leave the road and hunt for a weapon of some kind. This wasn't good ambush country. There were few hiding places. But if Shea could find cover and Judd came close, he might be able to stun him with a rock or hurled stick.

He might— The overwhelming chances were that Judd would spot him from a distance and drop him with the rifle. Tracy wished mightily that Judd would leave the RV so she could bargain with Pardo. Of course, now that Pardo had handed the Magnum over to

Judd, he didn't have a weapon. Still, if the price was enough, he might think of some way to rescue Shea.

"Twenty minutes." Judd mashed the beer can together, tossed it away. "I don't expect this to take long," he said. "Just hang around here till I come back."

Pardo said slowly, "You're really going to do it."

"Damn right."

Judd started down the road.

"Pardo—" Tracy began.

He sighed. "You got a good man. Take care of him."

He started the engine. Judd whirled. "Stay there, you dumb black bastard!" he shouted, jumping to the side.

Pardo cut sharp. He headed straight for Judd. Judd brought up the rifle and fired in the moment the RV ran him down. Glass shattered. Pardo slumped forward, blood pouring from his face. His hands loosened, fell slack.

Tracy could do nothing with her hands but she pitched forward in the wildly lurching vehicle and got a foot on the brake. Then she was able, using both hands clumsily, to switch off the engine.

From the bloody mass that was Pardo's face, a drowning voice said, "Tell sarge—" The words choked off. Pardo convulsed, arched upward. Then he collapsed on the wheel.

Tracy looked back. The crushed body beside the rifle wasn't moving. She struggled out of the RV and was hunting for a rock sharp enough to cut her ropes when she heard a shout. Shea was coming from around the hill.

He passed Judd and looked in at Pardo before he came to drop beside her and work at the knots. "I couldn't believe Pardo sold me out. And he didn't. Are you all right?"

"Now that you're here."

They held each other a long time before they got up

and went about the things they had to do. As Shea composed Pardo's body, he bowed his head. "He wouldn't die for a flag. But he would for a friend. We'll bury him with the family."

A week later, there was another wedding in the *sala*. The service was followed by the christening of Tivi and Carla's baby girl, with Tracy and Shea standing up as godparents, a joyful and sobering experience. Socorro was their responsibility, and the land which was the future of those born upon it. But for now there was joy and celebration.

Two pickups full of Mary's relations came down from San Carlos. They were going to stay for several days, quartering in the new ranch house where Geronimo and Mary would live, sharing it with several bachelor vaqueros.

"Lots of things have happened in this courtyard," Tracy laughed to Shea. "But I think it's the first time Apaches have danced with ranch families."

"It won't be the last." Shea danced her into the shadows and kissed her tenderly but with purpose. "Geronimo's bet me they'll have a baby before we do."

"Oh?" returned Tracy. "Mary's assured me there won't be any baby till Geronimo's promised to split the diapering and getting up at night."

"Maybe he's already promised," Shea twinkled.

"Then maybe there'll be two Patricks running around here at the same time," Tracy smiled.

"Dad would have liked that. But he would have been just as happy with a couple of little Marys or Teresitas."

"There's time for both," she said.

This time, when he kissed her, they didn't go back to the dancing.